BUSHWHACKED!

Into the loneliness, into the quiet, came a sharp hit on his shoulder, followed by the sound of a shot. Kyle recovered his balance and twisted his head to look at where the jacket was torn. Red blood was soaking the ragged edges of the denim. He thought the shot had come from behind him and from down close to the ground, and he leaned low and kicked the horse into a run, waiting for a second shot to come whistling after him.

He pounded the horse on another hundred yards and turned. There was nothing back there that he could see, not a horse, not a man, just a wide park of grass. Kyle swung to the ground, wincing at the pain that was starting to set in. He took out his bandanna, wiped his eye patch with it, then folded it and stuffed it between the wound and his jacket, buttoning the jacket up tight to hold it there. His arm was tingling. Or going numb.

The rifle boomed out again. . . .

Other *Leisure* books by James C. Work:

RIDE SOUTH TO PURGATORY

RIDE WEST TO DAWN

James C. Work

LEISURE BOOKS NEW YORK CITY

A LEISURE BOOK®

September 2003

Published by special arrangement with Golden West Literary
Agency.

Dorchester Publishing Co., Inc.
200 Madison Avenue
New York, NY 10016

ISBN 0-8439-5249-0

Epigraph

. . . But go, and if you listen she will call.
Go to the western gate, Luke Havergal. . . .

No, there is not a dawn in eastern skies
To rift the fiery night that's in your eyes;
But there, where western glooms are gathering,
The dark will end the dark, if anything:
God slays Himself with every leaf that flies,
And hell is more than half of paradise.
No, there is not a dawn in eastern skies—
In eastern skies.

Edward Arlington Robinson
"Luke Havergal" (1897)

Foreword

Early Arthurian legends tell of a quest by a young warrior named Owain. He entered a castle in a mountainous, unknown region; there, beautiful women entertained him and told him where to find his goal, the source of the Fountain of Life. A dark, one-eyed, man-like creature told Owain to strike a stone at the source, whereupon a deluge came and spread death. The guardian of the fountain arrived and challenged Owain to combat, but Owain killed him. By doing so, Owain himself became the next guardian. His memories of his king and warrior companions faded and finally flickered out in his mind.

> **"Having penetrated to the ultimate source and fountain—Owain had forsaken the length and breadth of the stream of existence."**
> Heinrich Zimmer
> THE KING AND THE CORPSE (1948)

The first mountain irrigation ditch I ever saw was in the Rockies of northern Colorado. Flat enough and wide enough at the bottom for a wagon and team, it was as deep as the backs of the horses. The road running alongside, also wide enough for a team and wagon, was built upon the dike of broken rock, gravel, sand, and dirt dug from the ditch by sweating manpower. It went for miles, vanishing around bends of the mountains, dipping back into valleys, interrupting the flow of a dozen small rivers and carrying their water eastward to a different sea than nature and gravity had intended.

Farther north and yet farther north are more great ditches dug into the mountains at unbelievable cost in human toil. They are found in Wyoming, in the Never Summers and Wind Rivers, north of the Tetons, in Utah, in Idaho, in Montana. For the most part they take water from the western slopes of the ranges, where rainfall and snow pack are greatest, and carry it to the fertile but arid land east of the mountains. In such regions water becomes as sought-after as gold; the person who holds the water rights controls the farming and grazing, even the building of cities.

In a way, Senator Joseph M. Carey of Wyoming is responsible for our story. It was he who sponsored the Carey Desert Land Act in 1894, under which a person could claim proprietorship of thousands and thousands of acres of "non-usable" land along the high plains just east of the Rockies. A person could patent, develop, and sell all the land they could manage to irrigate.

Even before the Carey Act there were dreams of making deserts into gardens. In 1888, Pat Garrett and three wealthy businessmen launched the Pecos Irrigation and Investment Company to water the desert near Roswell, New Mexico.

Cities far out on the plains got water for their development by building ditches in the mountains, claiming the water, and using existing rivers to deliver it to them. Mormon colonies formed citizens' corporations to build mountain ditches. And everywhere the ditches went, three things happened. First, there were incredible feats of manual labor, often at altitudes of 10,000 and 12,000 feet, as the ditches were dug through solid rock with shovels, rock bars, and blasting powder. Second were the ingenious inventions created to lift the water, to lower it again, to measure its flow, to regulate and apportion its use. Third, because of the value of the precious water, there were jealousy, secrecy, treachery, violence, and death.

Sometimes the violence became the stuff of legends.

<u>Chapter One</u>

The Fight

The big man they had spoken of was suddenly blocking his way. At this distance, Will Jensen could see only that both the man and the horse were damned big for their breed. They stood there like grim predictions against the graying sky.

A hawk that had been wheeling in a rising spiral seemed to stand still in the sky; a ground squirrel that had started when Will's horse came breaking out of the trees remained rigid with its back humped and a leg cocked on tiptoe for the dash back to its hole. The trees loomed tall and dense, even though the meadow was near timberline. Right and left they walled in the meadow; at the high end a gap in the trees marked where the meadow shouldered itself over the pass.

That was where the horseman stationed himself against the gray overcast blocking Will's way. Somewhere a songbird twittered joylessly, and it was the only sound except for the sound of Will's breath and the labored breathing of the horse after shouldering its way up through the final thicket of trees alongside the dry creekbed.

Here, at the meadow, the bed where the creek once flowed was wider and more shallow. Meandering in the flat meadow, it had cut oxbows and horseshoe channels into the black peat; all that was left was a deep winding track of dry gray glacial sand with mica flecks glittering. Where the park grass should have been May-high and light green, it was still the color of old wheat with pitiful few sprouts of new blades. The high country flowers had not bloomed, and would not bloom now.

Tired from the long ride up here, Will had hobbled his animals and stretched out on the ground to ease his back. The grass was so dry it crackled. The high mountain air had a warm smell of pine in it, and the sun was good on tired muscles. He drifted off to sleep.

Something awakened him some time later, and he sat up and saw the big rider on the big horse, motionless, watching.

Will didn't want a confrontation with the other rider, although back on his own range, on the Keystone Ranch, he was known as a fighting man who never backed down and who nearly never lost. Kyle Owens had once beaten him in a friendly slugging fest, and once Link had outwrestled him. But with those two, there was no shame in being beaten.

Here, Will didn't know who the man was. It might even be the person he had come to help. Or it could be a range rider, guarding the pass against trespassers. Will didn't even know for certain that he needed to ride that direction, over the swayback, treeless pass and down the other side. He only knew he didn't want to go back the way he'd come.

Will swung his arm in a friendly recognition of the other man's presence. He got up, stretched, and got his horses unhobbled. When he was in the saddle, he turned his horse toward the trees and waved again—the kind of gesture a man might make if he saw a neighbor at a distance and was waving to say: "Hi! I'm glad to see you! But I won't stop to chat because I have something to do right now." That kind of wave. He rode off to his right, sticking close to the line of lodgepole pines, watching for some kind of trail or opening that might lead to a way around the fellow guarding the pass.

He might be able to go north over the ridge, riding through

the trees until he got to timberline. It didn't look as vertical as the south wall of the park. He soon found a way to go, and, while it wasn't a trail, it did seem to be a natural corridor through the trees. He could see a hundred yards ahead, or so. Low branches made him duck and dodge to keep from getting slapped, but it wasn't bad.

Coming to a slight turning of the corridor, Will looked down at his horse's hoofs. The animal was picking her way over a fallen log. He looked up again. The big dark rider was ahead of him, far away through the pines, a shady silhouette barring his way again. How the rider had gotten there that quickly, Will couldn't figure. But there he was. Again Will stopped, and again the only sounds in the forest were the chirp of a songbird and the snorting of his horse and the sound of his own breathing.

He still didn't want to start a fight or push the issue. So he grinned and shrugged his shoulders in an apologetic way, as if he had just caught himself doing something stupid, as if he had strayed from the trail. He waved his hand again as if to thank the man for redirecting him, and turned his horse around to return to the meadow the way he had come.

When he reëmerged from the trees and rode out onto the open park, there was the big rider again, back in the center of the pass. Were there two of them? It didn't seem like it, but the man sure did move through the trees fast. And on a big horse, too.

His next idea was to ride right on up to the stranger, real slow-like, and talk. But before he had advanced fifty yards, the giant rider slid a rifle from his saddle scabbard and leveled it in Will's direction. It was a clear message: there would be no talk.

The southern range that walled in the park looked much less promising, but Will turned and rode that way anyway, making his movements look as casual as he could. The trees were fir and spruce, growing close together with branches that swept the ground. Dark faces of granite soared upward from the flatness of the park, broken here and there by ledges to which twisted, stunted trees clung like stubborn weeds growing out of a wall. It was just a vertical jumble of tough trees and unforgiving granite—no way a man could get up there, let alone a horse.

He rode into the spruce trees anyway, and did find a place where it looked as though he could ride up along a steeply sloping ledge and come to a place where it made a switchback to another ledge. As his horse carefully picked her way along, Will looked down through occasional gaps in the forest and saw the dark rider still sitting there in the pass below, watching.

A cliff stopped Will. No way down. But he could see down over the other side, where the valley opened out into a park of willows and aspen and grass. It, too, looked dead, and so extensive that he couldn't see the end of it downstream. It had been at least two seasons since there was a stream in the dry bed that curved and twisted in and out of the dried-up beaver ponds.

Off to his left, just below the ledge that turned into a cliff, he saw an irrigation ditch traversing the slope of the mountain. It looked to be about three feet wide. To the right, on the slope of the opposite mountain, a ditch twice that width went crawling along, following the contours of the mountain. That could explain the dried-up park below—these two ditches were intercepting the streams that had formerly flowed down from timberline to feed the river.

The black rider sat his horse about fifty yards from where the smaller ditch discharged into the larger one.

Will turned his horse, and they picked their way back

down. The only thing he could think to do now, since the day was growing late, was to go back to where he had ridden up out of the forest and make camp there. Maybe by acting unconcerned and friendly, he could just wait until the rider either came to him to talk or went away. The one thing he wasn't going to do was ride up to that pass and tell the guy to get out of the way. Homesteaders down in the foothills had told him rumors about a rider living up here, as well as stories of strangers who had disappeared in that lonely valley at the headwaters of two rivers.

He'd camp and see how things went. In the morning, maybe the rider would be gone. If so, he could go on into the pass and look down the other side, and he might see a trail or buildings or something connected with the diversion ditches. With plenty of supplies and little to do, he could stick around for several days.

Will built a fire and set some water on to boil, laid out his bedroll next to a couple of trees, picketed the horse to graze in the dry grass of last summer, and fixed himself some supper. Afterward, he cleaned the pot and skillet and put them next to the fire circle. He got a morning fire ready by piling dry sticks in a teepee around a wad of shavings and dry grass and then covering it with a scrap of canvas so that even if he woke to rain, there would be a fire ready to go. Just before letting sleep overtake him, Will turned his face toward the pass for one more look. He caught a glimpse of a fire glowing in the pass and a straight thin line of smoke rising against the dark sky haze.

The first shot came just after first light. Will was awake, trying to stretch a kink out of his back without moving far enough to let cold air into the bedroll. He had been wondering how soon the sun would get high enough to give some warmth, debating with himself whether to crawl out and light the fire or lie there and wait for the sun to warm things up first. The shot brought him up in a hurry, grabbing for the Winchester he'd kept under the tarp covering his bedroll. The shots that followed seemed measured to his movements.

Wham!

A slug whopped into a tree trunk nearby as he pulled on his boots.

Wham!

Another slammed into another tree trunk as he stood up.

Wham!

This one kicked dry duff near the foot of his bedroll as he grabbed the holster with the Colt in it and ran for the cover of the biggest tree he could see. The horse, out in the open, had her ears tipped toward the forest of fir trees on the south side of the park. When no more shots followed, she lowered her head and cautiously went back to pulling small mouthfuls of dead grass.

Will peered out around the tree and looked toward the firs. At first he saw nothing, then a slight movement and a puff of smoke.

Wham! Bark flew, just a foot above his head, followed immediately by the report of a rifle. OK, Will thought, now we know where we are. He dropped down to one knee, steadied the Winchester against the trunk of the tree, and felt the steel butt plate slam into his shoulder as he squeezed off a shot into the trees.

He ducked back, then looked again. Nothing moving out there. Another shot came at him, this time from a different position, nearly catching him as it ripped more bark from the trunk of the tree. Will dropped to his belly, sidled and slid and slithered away from the tree, toward a fallen log that would be better cover. The frost on the dry grass was cold on his hands.

He stuck the Winchester up over the log, stuck his head up after it, sighted along the barrel, swung it to and fro, looking for a target.

Blam! He didn't hear that one hit anything, just the report of the rifle. He saw the puff of smoke and aimed into it and pulled the trigger. His Winchester barked again, and again he cringed behind his log and waited what seemed an hour before looking up to see if he had hit anything.

The big man in the dark clothes was standing there at the edge of the woods, his rifle dangling from one hand, just standing there waiting for Will to try another shot. Well, Will would oblige him, by God! He got to his feet and, against all reason, stepped across the log and out into the open, aiming the Winchester as he walked toward the figure on the other side of the park, getting off two more shots.

But he was breathing hard and trying to get too close too fast, and the shots must have gone wild. The big figure just stood there, slowly raising his rifle to fire from the hip. When Will saw he was about to shoot, he threw the lever again and fired again, threw the lever and fired again.

The big man's bullet kicked dust and dirt at Will's feet in the same instant as he heard the *boom* of the rifle going off. More gunsmoke drifted out over the grass. Will levered another shell into the chamber and fired back. And with gunsmoke drifting on the breeze across the meadow, he realized he had done this all wrong. Deadly wrong. He had hurried, too sure of himself, and now was standing in the open with most of his shots used up. He tried to remember how many he had fired. Six? Eight? Were there two shells left in the magazine, or none?

He threw the lever. The empty cartridge ejected, spinning away, and a fresh round slid into place to be chambered. One more, then, at least. But he had let himself be drawn out into the open, with no cover, no shelter. If he turned and ran, the other man could get off two or three shots at his back before he reached the first tree. He could drop flat and shoot from a prone position, but he wouldn't get a chance to reload. That one cartridge might be the last one, and then it was down to the Colt and its five cartridges. The other man probably had a full magazine again, by this time.

It was all he could do. Will dropped to his stomach and quickly looked toward his target, but the dark giant was no longer there. Out of the corner of his eye, Will caught a movement of something light-colored, there in the trees off to the right, but, when he twisted around to take aim, he saw the big man down on one knee and waving a hand toward someone in the trees. What was . . . ?

Ziiippp! An arrow came down in an arc, narrowly missing him, and he saw a small white figure of a person at the wood's edge. *Blam!* He heard the rifle and saw the smoke, but the other man had thrown his shot toward the smaller person who was over there in the trees. Like a warning shot.

Will saw his advantage and took it, leaping to his feet and zigzagging to the shelter of the nearest tree. In the shelter of the trunk he sank down, his breath burning in his throat.

He took stock. One cartridge in the chamber of the Winchester. His extra cartridges were in the saddlebags, hundreds of yards away. He had put a few into the pocket of his chaps, a couple of days ago, but the chaps were hanging on a tree next to his bedroll. His mistake was becoming clearer every minute: he hadn't really been prepared for this. Dammit.

Five rounds in the .45 Colt. He felt around the belt at his waist. Twelve more. Two men out there now, one with a rifle who seemed to be playing with him, one with a bow and arrow who seemed to be interrupting the play. It didn't figure.

Will got down on his belly and slithered to another fallen tree, looked out around the shattered butt of it. There he was again, that big bastard, just standing in the open meadow with his rifle under his arm.

Will slid the Winchester out real easy-like. The man didn't seem to see him. He took careful aim, although his hands were still shaking, but just as he squeezed the trigger, the other man's rifle came up to hip level and boomed and a blast of pine needles and dirt flew into Will's face, and his shot went whanging off into the distant horizon.

Damn it to hell. Will had had enough of this game. He wiped the tears and dirt away from his eyes until his vision cleared, hauling out the Colt at the same time and getting up and stepping around the log's end and moving out into the open, determined that he would keep blasting and keep walking toward that s.o.b. until one or the other of them got hit.

But he wasn't in sight. Will spun around, frantic to find his adversary. The meadow was silent. Over the frosted grass, gunsmoke drifted like tiny clouds over a miniature prairie. That arrow stuck up out of the ground fifty feet away. No birds sang. The horse was backed up as far as her picket rope would reach, and she had her ears straight up and her eyes wide open and wild.

Will heard only his own breathing. He walked forward, the empty rifle in his left hand and his Colt in his right, shivering in the morning chill with sweat cold upon his forehead and down his backbone, looking for the big man. But he saw nothing. He walked on, and on, and came to the other edge of trees, almost where the small white figure had been standing when the arrow came at him. Nothing.

Will was beginning to wonder if it had happened. He was beginning to feel like a fool. And he was. For when he looked back toward the far trees, he saw his enemy again. Only now the man was on his horse. Tied to the saddle horn was a lead rope, and at the end of the lead rope was Will's horse, her saddle in place, the pack in place behind the saddle, the saddlebags on.

How had this happened? However the s.o.b. had managed it, Will wasn't about to let it go on. He ran, boots sliding on the frost and slipping on the hummocks of meadow grass, the Colt waving in his hand, toward the rider who was taking his horse, and. . . .

His toe caught, on what he didn't know, and down he sprawled on his face in the frozen grass, splayed out like a winter-killed calf. Will shook his head, cleared it from the sudden vertigo that came with an unexpected fall, drew breath back into his chest which had had the air slammed out of it, remembered the Colt in his hand, and looked up.

He saw his own horse. The dark rider had ridden up to him and pulled up to position Will's horse between them, and rested his rifle across the mare's saddle so the muzzle was pointed straight at him.

The muzzle jerked in a silent command. Will dropped the Colt. But the rider gestured again—holster it. Will picked it up and shoved it into the holster. The rider gestured with the gun barrel again. Will unbuckled his gun belt, and hung it on the saddle horn. The rider gestured that he wanted Will to get the empty Winchester and slide it into the scabbard under the fender of the saddle.

The big rider looked down from his height atop his horse. No expression on his face, no word on his lips. He may have sneered a little and lifted his chin in a scornful sort of way, as he reined his horse around and rode off, leaving Will alone in the park, near timberline, where the sun was just beginning to lick the frost from the leaves of the scrub willows and the pines.

He vanished into the trees north of the pass, taking with him everything Will owned. Guns, horse, gear, everything. High in the thin air overhead, the hawk screamed and spiraled up until it was a tiny spot in the sky.

Mechanically, dazed, feeling humiliated and stupid, Will took a few halting steps after the rider, then turned back to the place where he had made camp the night before. Something caught his eye. There, where the horse had been tethered, on the ground, was the leather disk with the Keystone brand on it, the leather *concho* that all Keystone horses had on their halter stalls. Will picked it up. The big rider had not only sliced the leather *concho* from the headstall, he had dropped it on the ground and had his horse grind it with its hoof until it was torn and scarred.

Nothing remained of his camp except for the little pile of kindling with the scrap of canvas over it, and his chaps, hanging on the tree. He was afoot, a half mile from the backbone of the Rocky Mountain range and more than two hundred miles from the Keystone Ranch, with nothing but what he had on his back, a pocket knife, a few matches, a watch, four cartridges, and a pair of useless chaps.

A day earlier, he had been a Keystone rider, out to see what could be done to help some nervous homesteaders. Now he was on foot without even a coat, with no food, no better than any range bum riding the grub line. Except he wasn't riding, and he hadn't seen anywhere to beg for his grub. It was the emptiest country he'd ever been alone in.

Chapter Two

Towns of No Great Pity

Left on foot in the meadow by the pass, Will had three choices. He could follow the main ditch winding its way along the mountains, dipping out of sight in the valleys and emerging again on the slopes; a wide path ran beside it, wide enough for a team of horses. Or, he could follow the ditch on the other side of the valley, the narrower ditch vanishing into the trees. It had a narrower footpath, one made for wheelbarrows.

Will saw something smooth and white half buried in the sand at the edge of the smaller ditch. He dug it out and turned it over and over, feeling the cold smoothness of the porcelain and looking at its black symbols. It could explain who blasted and picked and shoveled these two ditches out of mountain rock, two miles or better above sea level, where days were short and cold and a few minutes' exertion left a man winded. Hard work at this altitude could cripple a man's lungs for life.

He'd seen rice bowls before, in a chop suey place. And he knew about the teams of Orientals who hired out to do the frontier's toughest kinds of construction labor. They were the ones who blasted the tunnels under the mountains, laid railroad track through the desert, dug ditches in swamps and places where even the Irish wouldn't work.

Will sent the bowl fragment spinning down the center of

the cañon beneath his feet, where his third option was. He had seen chimney smoke the day before, and now maybe the haze far away below him in the valley might be from a settlement. But it would be hell to get down there and find out. Still, it was better than staying with the ditch where that big s.o.b. who stole his outfit would find him again.

He'd try the cañon. It looked like there was some shelter down there in the rocks, and maybe some kind of wild game farther on where the cañon emptied out into a flat park. It was a long way for a man on foot, but it was there.

Will had seen badlands where rocks were shaped like toadstools and turnips and towers and such, but he had never seen anything like this cañon. Slipping and sliding, sometimes fighting to keep from plummeting down the slope, he came to where busted slabs of rock stood upright like stone walls. All through there, the footing was steep shale that gave way under his feet. Every few steps, the shale would start to slide until tons of it were moving under his feet. Then it would stop again.

The high tops of his boots saved his shins when these slides hit him and buried his feet, but riding boots weren't made for this kind of work. Once, when he slid on a mass of rock right down the hill and into the side of one of the standing walls, he looked up and it seemed like the whole fifty foot tower of crumbling stone was about to topple over on him.

Will made it past the shale slide, but after a few yards of fairly stable ground he came to a long, steep bank of yellow silt. The stuff was the color of sulphur, and each step went in up to the ankle, making it, too, slide under his weight. The cañon floor was a dizzy drop below, and the yellowish dried clay seemed ready to slide down with him, and bury him under it. Will fought with his feet, clawed with his hands to stay on top of it, only to feel it ripping out from under him, only to feel more of it coming down from up the slope. Sometimes, small shriveled trees came sliding down with the clay, old and gnarled and no bigger around than a wagon tongue. They slid slowly downward past him, dragging miniature landslides with them.

When he came at last to a rock outcrop in the slipping sea of yellow clay, Will dropped to his butt. Both legs were shaking and quivering. One boot was cracked right across the middle of the sole, and both were full of dirt. Somewhere he had torn the elbow out of his shirt, and his hands were streaked with sweat, blood, and dust. The chaps were hot and kept getting tangled around his ankles, so he took them off.

The bottom of this cañon had to be easier walking than this. Problem was getting there. One bad step, one place where the rock or the clay would let go under him, and the whole damned wall of the cañon would take him down with it. And bury him. But. . . .

Will began again, gingerly probing his way along, the chaps draped over one shoulder, his boots feeling for each step. He angled down the cañon as much as toward the bottom of it, leaving a strange trail behind him like the track of a snake going down yellow sand. He came to more rocks, except these were like fire ash that had gotten wet and been molded into free-standing walls. Round pebbles were imbedded in the ash, and, when he collided with a wall, these pebbles would fall out and the ash would rain down as if the whole structure were giving way on top of him.

He was about a hundred yards from the bottom, just thinking about whether to go ahead and slide the rest of the way, when the cañon wall made up his mind for him with a soft, sloughing sound above, like wheat being poured down a chute. Will looked up the slope to see the whole thing coming loose, all the crumbly clay and rock starting to slip, carrying trees with it as it came pouring down.

He began to run straight down the slope, the chaps slapping him, his feet flying forward out in front of him, comically, his arms flailing in all directions to keep his balance. But he made it. Will came crashing down off the slope to the narrow creekbed, leaped it, making it across the smooth, rounded rocks that made his boots slide like they were greased, made it to the other side, kept moving, hit the opposite slope of loose granite slabs, crawled up, clawed his way up on hands and knees, made it at last to a boulder deeply imbedded in the wall of the cañon.

Behind him, the yellow clay and loose rock slid on into the creekbed, casually and quietly filling it to a depth of twenty feet or more. When it stopped, the dust quickly settled and all sound stopped except for the warning whistle of some small animal in among the boulders, and the answering cry of a hawk up above.

Will braced his feet against the big rock, and put his head down on his raised knees, and relief and fatigue came over him in waves, leaving him shaking uncontrollably.

The rest of the passage to the valley floor was not any easier. Sometimes he had to follow the dried-up creekbed, where water-polished stones threatened to break his ankle at each step. Then he tried going up the slope of broken rock far enough to pick his way along. At one place, he thought he found a trail, but it must have been made by mountain goats. He had no chance of following it up the side of the gorge. As darkness came, he came to a patch of level ground that was real earth, real soil with dead grass on it. He lay down and draped the chaps over as much of his body as they would cover, and, in spite of his hunger and thirst, he slept like a dead man.

★ ★ ★ ★ ★

The first sunlight took Will by surprise, suddenly jumping the backbone ridge and pouring down into the dry cañon. He startled and jumped up from a troubled dream, looking wildly around him. But the cañon was as empty as a whore's hope of heaven, and quiet as a grave.

Water seeped under the edge of the grass patch, enough of a trickle that he could soak his bandanna and wring the moisture into his mouth. It helped. He stayed there a long time, sucking the wet cloth over and over, letting the warmth of the sun bake his back.

Then the trip down the cañon resumed. More of the polished creek-bottom rocks to slide around on, more of the loose, treacherous slab rock on the side slopes, more of the clay that powdered under his broken boots and made avalanches around his trembling legs. He came to a barricade of rock, weird and gray with all colors of small stones stuck in it like raisins in a pudding, and the creek, when there had been a creek, had worn only a narrow cut through it. He had to climb up, clawing at the puddingstone for footholds and fingerholds until at last he could drape himself, exhausted, over the top. And then he found he would have to claw and slip his way down the other side.

The sun rose high over his slow labors, then took its time dropping down the sky until it finally went behind a mountain. With the sun gone, the gorge became cold and dark. Will struggled on and on, as long as there was even the faintest light to see by, and, when the blackness finally won out, he was on a flat plain, standing in dry grass once again. He slumped to his knees, then rolled over onto his side, and slept.

He woke up shuddering and shivering with a spasm of

chills wracking his legs and spine. Something snorted, and hoofs pounded the ground; a swayback old horse that had been curious about the sleeping man went crow hopping in a panic away from him.

Will could smell wood smoke, and he could see low log cabins. Limping along with the chaps over his shoulder, he made his way to one of them, the nearest one that looked inhabited. All over the clearing were other cabins that were just stuck here and there with no order to them. Some were boarded up; others just stood with gaping doorways and windows staring like empty eye sockets. The near cabin had a platform of boards that passed for a porch, and on it sat a man in faded coveralls and undershirt. He was taking in the morning sunshine, smoking his pipe, watching Will's approach with slight interest.

"Water?" Will croaked, approaching the cabin porch.

The man didn't move except to lift his foot a few inches, indicating a dented bucket sitting next to the door. Will went to it and lifted it and drank. The water was cold enough to break the teeth, and there were tendrils of slimy moss waving in it, but he drank eagerly. The man studied him, then looked up in the direction of the pass, and studied him again. Far up toward the summit, Will could see the line of light-colored earth where the big ditch had been cut across the mountains.

"Lost my horse and gear up there," Will volunteered. The man merely nodded, as if he already knew. Will felt around in his jeans pocket and came up with a dollar.

"Anywhere around here for a man to buy some breakfast?"

The man smoked his pipe and looked off toward the pass, then let his eyes wander across the valley as if he had forgotten the question. He finally pointed the stem of the pipe at another cabin, from which came the sound of hammering.

"Grady's" was all he said.

Grady turned out to be a bulk of man who was busily hammering the boards off the side of a shed and salvaging the nails. He was throwing them onto a canvas pannier cover, half full of bolts, old hinges, latches, and assorted rusty hardware.

Will repeated his question, and found himself with a job, a breakfast of sorts, and a source of information.

"Keep your money," Grady said, "but you can sure help me split out these here boards and get the nails. And hardware. I was gonna burn 'er to get the metal parts back, but a fire like that'd set off this here whole park, dry as she is. Come to think on it, I ain't et this mornin', either. Come in."

He led Will into his cabin, a one-room affair with a dirt floor that looked as if it had been packed down with grease, and a roof that made both men stoop. It smelled like a badger's privy. Grady fed the stove a couple of pine chunks, slapped two fist-size lumps of venison directly onto the stove lids to fry next to a fire-blackened coffee pot.

"Ah, hell!" Grady said suddenly, dropping to his knees to probe around inside the firebox with a bent wagon rod. From the ashes and coals he dragged a black charred lump in the shape of a loaf of bread.

"Forgot I put 'er to bake in them coals last night," he said, breaking the bread open. Charred crust flew off in all directions, and inside was heavy dry stuff like the punky wood inside a rotten aspen. To Will, it was the best bread he had ever had. He ate the meat eagerly, too, using his pocket knife to saw bits from his lump. He couldn't get his mouth around the coffee, though, which reminded him of something a man might use to preserve fence posts in.

"Moving out?" he asked Grady.

"Hell, yes." Grady waved his piece of charbread at the tiny window opening near them. "Let them other pissants go on tryin' t' dig ore outta this hill. None of 'em workin'. Most of 'em just waitin' each other out, tryin' to be the last man to leave. They figure, see, that mebbe they'll be the last man left here when the water comes back. Then they'd get her all."

"Mining?" Will asked.

"Placer," Grady replied. "Only way to do this here fleck gold. I already tore my sluice down." He gestured with his tin cup, and the coffee was thick enough that it didn't slosh. "Back up th' valley there. Hell with it."

Later, out in the fresh air with a full stomach, Will felt saved. He pitched in with an old hammer, its cracked handle wound with wire, pulling nails and screws from the weathered boards. They had quite a pile of boards going when Grady suddenly stopped and dove into his badger hole of a cabin. He emerged with a can of tar and a flat stick. On one of the short boards he carefully lettered the words **FOR SALE** with tar, then nailed the sign to the stack of lumber.

Grady laughed and chuckled for the next hour. "Hell, that's funny!" he said. "Ain't a loose nickel in this here whole valley. Man leaves, like I'm fixin' to do, others just help themselves to whatever. Last man to stay gets it all. For sale. Hell, that's funny!"

Talking with Grady, Will learned that the giant guardian of the ditches and the pass was somebody the miners called The Foreman, and down in this deep boxed-in valley they feared him the way they would fear a ghost or a spook. Some men had gone up to the big ditch to see if they could break it and let some water down, and their mangled bodies were found where they had come rolling and bouncing down the slopes. Another miner had figured to strike a deal with whoever was diverting all the water, so he headed up out of the valley to find the reservoir or the ranch or whatever. Some thought they had heard a desperate scream in the dark, that night, and some said it was a wounded mountain lion, but no-body ever tried going that route again.

The safe route lay to the south, down what used to be the river, down to a larger settlement about twenty miles away. "Then that's where I need to go," Will said. "Any horses for sale around here?"

To Grady, the question was even funnier than his **FOR SALE** sign on the pile of soon-to-be-abandoned old lumber. While they worked on into the late afternoon, he would stop to repeat the question to himself and shake his big head at the joke. A dozen men half starved for meat and crazy with schemes to get out of this place, and this cowboy wants to buy a horse. Funny.

" 'Nough," he said abruptly, as the sun slipped down to touch the tip of a peak to the west. He dropped his hammer where he was and went inside to stir up the stove again. When Will followed, he had to duck under the pall of greasy smoke rising from the stove top.

"Elk, I guess," Grady said, pointing at the slabs of meat frying noisily on top of the stove lids. "Might be bighorn sheep. Been hangin' in the dugout so long I don't recall what it is. Like yours rare?"

Will took his charred on the outside, sort of gray inside. When he said no to the coffee, though, Grady went bur-rowing through his mounds of filthy bedding and came up with a jug. A large jug. "Beer," he explained, unearthing a rusty tin can and filling it for Will. "Fella left who made it, but it's good."

In spite of the mountain chill, Will took his can of "beer" and his slab of questionable venison outside to sit on a log and eat. Four, five sips, and the can was half empty. By the time the meat was gone, he had finished a second can, and the third one Grady brought him went the way of the first two.

Cradling the can like it was a family heirloom, Will accepted a fourth refill and sat with his legs spraddled in front of him. It puzzled him that they seemed to belong to somebody else. He stared out at the meadow where the broken-down nag was trying to find nourishment in the thin, dry grass. When he squinted, he could see two horses instead of one.

"Hey! Grady!" Will yelled into the open doorway, feeling that his head had mysteriously grown too large for him to enter the cabin without hurting himself. "Gotta rope, dammit?"

He wasn't sure if "dammit" was part of the question, but he let it slide. Grady, somewhere within the black hole, belched—"Rope?"—and Will burped back—"Yeah, rope." In the twilight, he realized that the old swayback mare wasn't all that far from the cabin. And in his mind, which the beer seemed to have miraculously transformed into a high-speed steam engine of logic and reasoning, he saw himself tossing a loop over her, saddling her, and riding off in style and dignity to the next settlement. If he could figure out where in hell it was.

Grady came out with a soft old rope, about thirty feet of dirty, frayed jerk line.

"Anybody own that fine mustang out there, hmm?" Will queried. "Either one of them?"

Grady stared and tried to focus his eyes toward the meadow. Alpine-glow lighting up the high slopes of the peaks above timberline gave the valley an eerie illumination.

"You see two?" Grady asked.

"At least two," Will burped. "Maybe a herd of 'em a while ago."

Grady put his big arm around Will's shoulders and patted him in that timeless brotherly way of two drunks pledging eternal loyalty and support to each other. "You jus' take any

31

of 'em you wanna," he breathed in Will's face. "That ol'
snake's too by hell tough t' eat and damn' no good for
nothin'. Me, I think th' one next t' her looks some better. I
think. But if you wan' her, you jus' go ahead an' drop a loop
on 'er. I need t' sit down here a while now."

Jug in hand, Grady sat down suddenly like a dropped sack
of flour. Will fumbled a loop eye into the rope and threaded
the other end through it. It took longer than usual, since he
wasn't sure which of the two loops he saw was the real one.
Finally, lariat in hand, the top cowboy began his stealthy ad-
vance on the spooky swayback. He whispered slurred sounds
to the horse, but it sounded like a snake hissing inside a half-
full chamber pot.

Will managed the trick, however, gradually slipping up toward the animal and standing still, moving again, and
standing still, finally getting close enough to flip the makeshift lariat over the tired-looking head. Now to jerry-rig some
kind of halter or bridle and reins and get on and break this
wild bronc'.

The rodeo began in the light of the Alpine-glow and continued until well after moonrise. Will spent some of that time
with his legs locked under the mare's belly. Then he got a
chance to stretch his muscles by riding hard for a mile or two
with his legs straight out and flying up and down. Most of the
dozen remaining residents of the tumble-down town had
come out to see the show, and they marveled at how the
cowboy could ride lying down on his belly, his arms wrapped
around the plunging neck. One of the sullen old miners even
went so far as to say he had never seen a man ride like that before. Right after that, another onlooker said the light was bad
but he'd swear that there cowboy launched himself clear
"off'n the swayback, puked in mid-flight, and landed still
hangin' onto the lead rope."

The last thing Will remembered, until the sun came at dawn to wake him, was somebody tying the horse to a nearby stump, then bringing a bucket of water from the seep hole down in the willows where the river used to run. They gave the water to the horse.

It took three more rodeos to determine who was the boss, and on the fourth morning it snowed. The clouds came down lower and lower until they seemed to be supported by the tops of the spruce trees. Peaks, pass, ditch—all had vanished. Snow lay wet and heavy on the grass and bent the willows into mounds reminding Will of creamy white helpings of mashed potatoes, back at the Keystone. The only dark objects in all that white valley were the pitiful low log cabins, still scattered across the clearing as if they didn't want to touch each other, even in the sharp cold.

Grady and Will stirred themselves later than usual, like a couple of hibernating badgers dimly sensing the coming of day. Grady burrowed out of his wadded-up tangle of filthy blankets and made a grunting noise with each movement it took to pull on his overalls. He stirred the stove, dumped the ash drawer into a rusty blasting powder can that stood in the corner, dropped in a couple of pine chunks, and took a look into the coffee pot as if he halfway expected to see something other than acrid sludge.

He shrugged, scratched himself under one armpit without much enthusiasm, and went on a search through his cupboards—a stack of packing crates and empty dynamite boxes leaning on the wall—for something to cook for breakfast, other than venison.

Will raked his dirty fingernails through the week's worth of stubble on his face and climbed out of the pile of blankets, followed by a rising wave of warm air and indescribable body odors. Week-old beard. Maybe more. Scruffy, wiry sort of beard, and he had the kind of whiskers that came clear up under his eyes. Wasn't much he could do about it. Most men didn't care to borrow razors, or lend them, and, besides that, he had watched Grady use his razor to trim a torn fingernail, scrape at a big sore bunion, and then cut sourdough into biscuit-size squares.

He'd rather wait. Nobody to see him out here, anyway. His hair was getting long enough to tangle, too. The three-day debate with that swayback snake over which was going to be the one on top had left his clothes worse for wear, too, with the result that Will Jensen, lately a top hand riding for the big Keystone Ranch, now looked like he really belonged with the rag-tag assortment of busted-down miners who had come here with nothing but faint hopes and a dull shovel and were always getting ready to take themselves on to the next bunch of nothing.

Will sat down and pulled on his boots, pausing to poke a finger into the hole that the rockslide had ripped. He tugged the cuffs of his jeans down over the boot tops; one leg was torn up the seam, and Will brought the two edges of fabric together, smoothing them down as if that would fix it, the way a man who has broken a cup handle will fit the pieces together as if he sort of expects that to make it whole again.

He pulled on his smelly shirt and opened the pine slab door. There was the mare, standing with her nose against the wood. She had a sweet maiden-aunt expression, as if she had come for a visit and was waiting to be asked in for tea.

"If you're looking for exercise, you jughead," Will said, "I can't oblige you. That stuff out there is snow, and I don't like getting thrown into it all that much, never have. And if you'll get the hell out of my way, I need to visit the bushes."

That done, Will went back in for his jacket and the water bucket and, as an afterthought, pulled on his chaps. They would be a little warmer and would be some protection from the slushy, freezing willow bushes that would slap his legs. He started for the sinkhole, his dragging boots making a double trench trail in the snow.

A sound behind him made him stop and turn to find the mare following him, trailing along just like an old dog. Her rope dragged along behind.

"What do you want?" Will asked.

The mare didn't answer.

Will walked past one of the other cabins and saw tracks in the snow where the owners had gone away, leading their two mules. One of the mules had been dragging a travois. The snow had pretty much stopped falling; the accumulation in the tracks showed they had gone at first light, or maybe in the dark. Maybe they owed somebody and didn't want to be seen leaving.

Will set down the bucket and went into the cabin. The hearth was nothing but a big flat rock in the corner with other rocks on it to keep the coals from rolling out. There was a battered tin hood and chimney. The coals were still warm. The floor, like Grady's, was dirt, pounded down hard from use and dark with grease, blood, and things a man didn't want to think too much about.

The tiny cabin had only three rafters, just skinny poles crossing the room to keep the walls from leaning in on each other. Above one of them, hanging by a cord from the center pole, was a rolled-up blanket. They must have stuck it up there to keep it away from the rats and mice, then forgotten it when they left.

Will reached up and got hold of one corner and pulled it down. "Well, it's mine now," he said.

The mare was standing in the doorway.

"Get the hell out of the light!" Will said. And he began hunting for other stuff the miners might have left. He dug into piles of old rags too shredded and rotten to be anything but mouse nests, pawed through the tin cans that had been thrown into the corner, ignoring the sickly sweet smells and fuzzy layers of mold. He ran his hand all along the surface of the top log where there was a ledge a man might hide something on. Choking dust and rat droppings, some rather recent, tumbled down inside his sleeve. "Got to be something else here," he said, "got to be something. Got to be. Got to be. Something I can use."

He found a big old can the size of a bucket and used his fingernails to claw the lid off, dumping the contents onto the floor. It was clear what the can had been used for, and it wasn't close to pretty, but Will kicked at the stuff anyway, thinking there might be something in there.

Still muttering, swearing at the horse when she blocked the light coming in the open door, Will probed into every filthy chink and cranny. Then he saw something. It was metal, half hidden by the ashes spilling over the hearth in the corner where the fire had been. Will made a pounce for it as if somebody else was trying to beat him to it, grabbed it, and held it up triumphantly for the mare to see.

"It's a broken knife!" he said. "Somebody must have forgotten it! A butcher knife, see? Only a couple of inches broken off the blade. I can fix this up! I can get a stone, I'll grind it down so's it has a point again!" Yes. It was good. This was good. He could . . . he could fix a point on it and it would be. . . .

Will slumped, all the muscle gone out of him, plopped down, sitting on the floor there. What had happened? What was wrong with him? He could only stare at the dull, rusted, broken remnant of a butcher knife he held so fiercely. A broken knife and a filthy blanket. Had someone come into the cabin a minute ago and tried to take them, he might have killed to keep them.

In the spring, when he had set out so proud to find the ranches being closed down by the mysterious water shortage, when Art Pendragon himself had personally seen him into the saddle and out the massive front gate of the Keystone Ranch to go help their unknown distant neighbors, he had been a top hand. Women had admired his ramrod-straight posture and strong square chin. Barbers had complimented him on the natural wave in his hair. Shopkeepers had thought so much of his good taste that they asked him for suggestions as to which patterns of shirts he thought they should keep in stock, and whether silk scarves or square bandannas looked better with a vest. He had gone out with two fine horses, riding tall and proud. Under his leg, a new Winchester. On his hip, a good Colt revolver. The pack horse had carried a trail tent, cooking pot and skillet, water bucket, tarp and quilt. And food enough for weeks.

Now he sat, ragged and torn and overgrown with matted hair and beard, slouched down in ashes and grease in a rank-smelling cave of a cabin, gripping the discarded knife and worthless blanket as if they were his great treasures, possessions worth fighting for. He had fought with The Foreman and had lost his other possessions. Now he had lost even himself.

He looked up at the mare standing in the doorway. She seemed to be sleeping. Her hoofs were split and sore; she had pus coming from wounds on her legs; her back swayed, and Will could count her ribs. Her head came up a little when he spoke.

"We gotta leave here," he said. "You don't look like much

of a horse any more, and I sure don't feel like much of a man. We gotta get out of here. I just hope we can make it."

Although the air would have seemed too cold to carry much scent, Will rode away with a stink about him that suggested a combination of sour buttermilk, mildewed pickles, raccoon musk, and horse piss. If he could have thought about it, he would have perhaps known that his mind, too, was changed from what it had been. He was submissive to his surroundings, accepting anything as being natural. He had gone back to Grady's and had eaten the soggy shapeless pancakes and had drunk the bitter, thick coffee. Then he had begged a length of cord and tied the stained blanket onto the horse for a riding pad.

He had muttered a sort of grudging thank you to Grady before setting off through the lifting weather, the toes of his ripped boots dragging little grooves in the snow on either side of the swayback mare.

The trip was long and the day was cold as hell. Will got off and walked to keep from freezing, then got on and rode again. He untied the dirty blanket and wrapped it around him. The road finally got better, and before nightfall he came to the town, a sort of junction on a wagon track that started out at Next to Nowhere and ran clear to Who Gives A Damn. Along the track there was a sagging saloon, a depleted general merchandise store, and something called a hotel which was more of a two-story cowboy barn that, even from a distance, looked like it would be infested with every variety of cootie and seam cricket known to man. He had no money for it anyway. He saw a few citizens, mostly looking rough and sullen, and a woman he took to be the town whore. He ignored her, like he did the hotel, and for the same reasons.

Then Will began to glower around him, under his hat

brim, his eyes glaring between his brows and his tangled beard. People were watching him, he thought. *Everybody's looking at me, thinking they'll get me.* He was wrong, of course. No one paid him the slightest attention. Just another bum moving along.

In his mind he was conspicuous. He slid off the mare and removed the blanket, folding it with exaggerated carefulness and draping it over his arm like the cape of a Mexican bull-fighter. He caught the rope up short and walked beside the mare's head, holding her close to him, walking with his chin pointing up and his chest out. Strutting, he thought.

One boot sole flapping, Will led the mare through the street to the far end, then turned with a flourish and strode back through town again. Had Frederic Remington been around, he might have made a romantic sketch of the swaggering tramp and the swayback. Had Art Pendragon of the Keystone been there to see it, Will would probably have found himself being dragged to the nearest river at the end of the longest rope available.

He had never begged before, and, although he had seen it done, he had not paid enough attention. Once more, turning at the end of the line of buildings, he retraced his steps, examining each building as if he intended to purchase the place. Several were boarded up. Several more had not even been given that gesture of protection, but sat with empty, unglazed windows opening into empty, unwanted interiors. The feed store was in business; a skinny dog sprawled on the welcome mat as if lying there trying to muster the strength to crawl off somewhere and die. There was a building Will took to be the stagecoach and Western Union office, only the sign was too shot full of holes to read.

Off of the street, a little behind the main line of buildings, there were some pens holding an assortment of range steers and a few goats and horses. There was a small one-story house with a lean-to next to the corral.

Well, Will thought, wasn't he supposed to be a horse wrangler, once upon a time? Might earn himself a meal, at least. He made a very careful knot as he tied the mare to the corral rail, and, sticking his chin in the air and looking all around as if about to do something proud and daring, he draped the rag of a blanket over the rail. Back of the house, he found a small barn; in it, a burly man was pitching dry hay into a cart. Flecks of hay dust filled the air and floated down on splinters of light coming between the boards.

"Yeah?" came the gruff voice.

"Name's Will Jensen." Then came a long silence, the man with the pitchfork still working and Will standing there looking off into the distance as if he had nothing important on his mind.

"Looking for work," he finally said, almost as if you'd say "nice day."

"Whatta you do?" the gruff voice asked.

"Wrangler. Cowhand. Some blacksmithing. I can break horses. Roustabout. Whatever you got to do. Got some carpenter experience lately." Will was referring to helping Grady pull rusty nails out of old boards.

The stableman knew how to test cowboys, knew how to see if they were honest-to-God range hands or not, and how hungry they were for work.

"Kin you fix a windmill?" he asked, coming toward Will.

"Hate the damn' things," Will replied. "Rather starve."

"You're hired, then." The man laughed. "Besides, we ain't got a windmill."

"Won't be staying long," Will said. "Just long enough to get together a stake and some supplies. I need to be heading east."

"That's what they all of 'em say," the stableman said. "And if y' look around, y' won't see none of 'em around here no more, neither. It's better, that way. All of 'em just bums, anyway."

Chapter Three

Back on the Keystone Range

A gunshot can travel for miles over frozen ground in the white winters on Wyoming's high eastward plain, where the crack of a rifle glances off hillocks of ice crust, skims between brittle spears of yucca, and echoes through motionless frigid air.

Two miles away, a lone rider heard it, even through the ragged upturned collar of his cast-off sheepskin and the filthy bandanna muffled around his ears. He was riding hunched over, chin slouched into the coat for warmth, eyes squinting against the painful glare of sun on snow crust. At the sound of the shot he straightened and looked ahead to see where his horse was heading. It was the first time that morning that the man showed any interest in where they were going; before dawn he had shivered out of the blanket and got up and wrapped it around his shoulders and stepped into the stirrup. The starved horse had been standing saddled all night. When the rider lowered his butt onto the saddle, the leather was so frigid that it didn't squeak.

His teeth chattered uncontrollably; he made a vague kicking movement with his heels, and the horse began to walk east again for another day. It didn't matter to Will Jensen if he was going northeast or southeast, so long as the faint line of mountains kept receding, however imperceptibly, behind him.

There was the one shot, and that was all. Where it came from he could not even guess, except that it seemed to be somewhere ahead. He was seeing more signs of cattle, which meant he was getting closer to where people lived. If someone were out for some shooting, they may eventually cut across his trail, or he may cut theirs. But he was out of strength, and the worn-down mare couldn't do more than plod on through the crusted grass and stumble over the ruts and hummocks. All he could do was drift east until some smoke or sign of shelter showed itself.

Shelter and food. Will thought of it and sneered, the lifting of his lip cracking the hoary frost caked onto his face hair. A winter and a summer and a spring earlier, he had set out going the other way across this high plains country, headed toward those mountains that were now shrinking to a purple wrinkle above the glaring, endless blankness. His pack horse had carried an elk-skin sleeping bag, coffee, flour, sugar, salt, bacon and jerky, cans of stewed tomatoes and cans of sliced peaches. Condensed milk for the coffee. There'd been a tent and tarpaulin, a good picket rope, cooking pot, coffee pot, frying pan. His saddlebags had held extra clothes, warm clothes. Soap and a razor.

Will had spent part of every day of the past two months thinking about the gear he had once owned. When he finished making lists in his head, he made himself remember every detail of what had happened. It kept him sane. He went over how he had ridden out, proud to work for Art Pendragon, glad to do this job for him. A cross-country job—he had carried pliers so he could cut fence and splice it behind himself, nails and nippers to fix a thrown horseshoe, an awl to mend busted harness. Now the old leather of a charity saddle chafed him through his threadbare old Levi's; now his food was a handful of parched corn in his sheepskin pocket.

He was returning across a range he did not recognize, stripped of everything but his shame and his sneer, returning to the Keystone only because he knew of nowhere else to go. His mind had gone dull, and he cared about nothing. He was like a fine tool used for the wrong job, like an good axe used to bust chunks of coal or chop sod—nicked and rusted, its keen edge destroyed, a pitiful thing.

One job had been night guard at a pigsty—his wages were the second-hand sheepskin coat that stunk of the pig manure, a cast-off shirt, and a much-mended halter for the mare. He had worked for an outfit slaughtering range steers, bringing the sledge hammer down on their skulls while another wrangler kept their heads to the ground by means of a neck rope run under a cottonwood log. His wages there had been the broken saddle, an old saddlebag, some food. At the last town, Will had become an unsanctioned deputy of an unelected town constable, where he earned himself a revolver with a loose cylinder and with most of the bluing worn off it.

He had left that town the morning after getting drunk on the cheap swill that passed for whisky. Somewhere in the brown blur he remembered pistol-whipping another drunk in the name of the law. But he didn't ride out of town because he was afraid of retribution. No. He left because there was still some scrap, some remnant of the Keystone rider still in him, a tiny grain of nagging decency and honor, and he could not remain where he'd whipped a man bloody and unconscious. After doing it, he dropped to his knees behind the saloon and puked into the pile of empty bottles and broken crockery before passing out.

Sometimes Will remembered the winter and summer and springtime earlier, when he had gone to Art Pendragon and volunteered to go north and look into the irrigation problem. Horse wranglers and cowpunchers alike had envied him when they heard that he was going to be the one to help the Keystone's visitor, the strange pale man with hair yellow like new wheat. His skin had looked like a bleached flour sack draped over bones.

He and some others had started in to settle a valley up north, the visitor had said, and then the streams had begun to dry up. One by one. There had been rain, and they could see snow in the faraway mountains, but one by one the rivers stopped flowing. And then there had been two huge floods that came down on their settlement, but there had been no storms. A few of the men had gone up into the cañons to see what was going on, and, when they had come stumbling back without their horses or their guns or anything but the clothes on their backs, they had told of a huge rider on a big horse who had surprised them and robbed them without saying a word. After that, no one would go into the mountains. But the settlers still had not wanted to leave, and so the pale old man had hitched his horse to his buggy and set out to find the Keystone Ranch.

Will shook his head to get that picture of the old man out of it. Had to think about himself and where he was now. He turned and looked back. The friends of the man he had beaten were nowhere in sight. He figured they had stopped chasing him days ago, probably. Since then he'd met the gold hunter who had given him a pocket of parched corn. Oh, yeah, and the crippled-up old elk. He'd killed him with the revolver before or after they stopped chasing him . . . he couldn't remember. Must have been after, because he had time to smoke-jerk some of the meat. A lot of days ago. And nights. Shivering nights with the high full moon looking so cold on the snow crust and losing a little of itself each night as if the freezing air were flaking parts of it away, and finally showing just a sliver of light hanging low near the horizon.

Will slouched down into the coat again, and the mare's plodding hoofs kept on taking them vaguely east.

At the sound of a second shot, Will pulled the horse to a stop and twisted one direction and then the other, scanning the terrain and listening. He dragged the bandanna down around his neck to uncover his ears. An animal was running, off to his right, coming over the low rises pretty fast. A coyote. Wolf, maybe. It didn't have that easy, swinging gait they use when they are just out to go somewhere; this one was running from something.

Probably what the shots were about. And if it was, they must have come from the slightly higher rise of ground he could see off ahead to the right. Maybe a half mile. Will rode that way, setting his course so that he could circle around the highest part, figuring he'd take a look at whoever was doing the shooting and how many there were of them.

When he got to a spot of cover, just an eroded draw with a couple of thick sagebrush growing on its rim, enough partly to hide the horse, Will tied her to a root and went on foot. At first he walked, limping painfully from the cold and the worn-out boots. Then he walked stooped over to stay out of sight, his back cramping and aching. He finally got down to belly along, snaking himself through the sage and yucca. He couldn't smell the sage he was crushing under him, but he could smell the dried puke and campfire smoke in his coat. When he pulled off his hat and raised his head for a look, he saw them. A couple of hundred yards away, two of them. One had field glasses. Both had rifles.

Will squinted hard. The two riders weren't very far from home; they wore sheepskins, but had no saddle rolls and no saddlebags. Whatever they were carrying in the way of food, they were carrying in their coat pockets. There may have been a canteen between them, but he couldn't be sure. Probably a couple of waddies out for an afternoon of shooting; wolf scalps were worth tobacco money, still, and an antelope always made a welcome addition to the stew or chili. Tobacco and hot food. The bundle of rags watching from the brush hadn't tasted either one in months.

The two riders were in no hurry as they ascended the slope in front of him. Will looked at the sun and figured there were only a couple of hours of daylight left. The riders would turn soon and start back to wherever they lived. He'd watch them, or keep track of where they went, and follow.

He huddled down in his ragged clothes and pulled the torn hat on again, yanking it clear down to his ears. He didn't want to be seen. All those weeks of terrible loneliness, weeks of riding without seeing a human or hearing a word, and now he didn't want anybody to see him the way he was.

He took the gun out and looked at it and thought about throwing it away, some idea that, if he didn't have it, he wouldn't run the risk of being shot. Then he put it away and burrowed down deeper into his old coat with a sly sneer twisting his lip.

He'd wait until dusk, that's what he'd do, then—this was the clever part—go out there where he'd seen them and find their trail, follow it. He'd find their place, all right. They'd never know he was there. Yeah. A trail. They couldn't hide their tracks from him. The tracks would take him straight to their place. Probably a ranch. Maybe even one of the Keystone ranches. This terrain looked like Keystone range.

And if it is, Will thought. . . . His sneer and narrow eyes gave way suddenly to wide eyes that looked as if they might produce tears. He sat up, wrapping his rags around him, rocking himself back and forth in the sand, back and forth. What if he came to the Keystone tonight, or tomorrow?

What of his story would he tell?

Everyone would remember the way he had ridden off all that time ago, all cleaned up and happy-go-lucky. He made people laugh at tragedy, made jokes out of the worst situations. He'd grin at misfortunes, and pretty soon everyone else would grin with him. Nobody could be unhappy around Will Jensen, not for long. He'd just tip the expensive Stetson back on his head, hang a thumb in his polished leather gun belt, and let go with a grin. And you'd grin along.

Thinking of that man he'd been made the man in the cold rags lonely and sad. One time he'd been taking the green off his remuda, and he'd straddled a sorrel snake that tossed him like a rag doll right into the only mud hole for miles around. Another time, a hammer-headed gelding took it into his pea-size brain to start crow hopping and sunfishing with Will aboard, until Will felt air between his Levi's and the leather, and looked down in time to see a mesquite limb headed for his crotch. To make it worse, a third bronc' had got him against a snubbing post and tried to erase him like a mistake on a spelling paper.

"Well," he had groaned that evening, as salve was being smeared into his punctures and bruises, "I guess I've had worse days." He had grinned. "And you boys know what I always say. . . ."

"Never had a bad day in your life," the others had chorused.

That was a different man. The Will Jensen, who crouched in the brush, stinking of puke and pig manure and his own filth, had had nothing but bad days. Failure and shame were his story now, and gave him more agony than anything any horse or any man could do to him. Will twisted suddenly and tore off the hat and flattened himself in the brush, peeking out to see where the riders were. He clawed for the pistol and thrust it forward, cramming the barrel with sand in the process. But whatever spooked him, it wasn't the two horsemen. They had turned their backs to him and were riding away, side by side. He trembled. When they were out of sight, he'd follow them.

It was the cook, going out early to get kindling, who found the crumple of cast-off clothes asleep against the back of the cook shack, his pitiful horse drooping nearby. Figuring him for a range bum riding the grub line, the cook went ahead and built his fire and got breakfast going. When the coffee had boiled, he took a cup outside and kicked the heap.

"Coffee," he said. "Wash up in the shed. Come get some grub."

The rags stirred, and a whiskered face stared up at the cook. "Grub?" he croaked. He took the coffee and warmed his hands with the cup, let the steam rise into his nostrils. "Obliged," he said. "Be glad o' a couple days' work, if y' got it. Headin' on east."

It was the litany of the range bum—never come out and ask for food, never accept it without offering to work, always make sure they don't think you're goin' to stick around. Oh, and give your name so they don't think you're on the dodge.

"Name's Will Jensen," he added.

"My God!"

The cook ran for the bunkhouse, gangly-legged with his apron flying, shouting: "Link! Link!"

Link was at the door, pulling on his coat.

"Link! It's Will Jensen! Over t' the cook shack! My God, you oughta see him. He looks terrible, just terrible."

It was the hands of friends that steadied Will as he lurched toward the cook shack and that helped him ease down into the chair beside the stove, the one where the cook sat to peel his spuds or take his naps. Gradually, with coffee and some food, Will got warm enough to get rid of the blanket and coat. Friends drifted in and out, looking at him, wanting to do something. Two men went to care for his horse. Another two hauled in firewood and water and went for the tin bathtub stashed behind the shack.

Link went to the main house to get Art. He talked with Gwen while Art got his clothes on, and her concern for Will Jensen was genuine; it put a furrow across her pretty forehead, a furrow that made Link like her all the more. Her eyes were large and deep and caring.

"Does he seem to be injured . . . or sick?" she asked gently.

"I don't think so," Link said. "But he's been through some kind of trouble, that's for sure."

Seeing that his rider was in no condition to describe where he had been and what he'd been doing the last eighteen months, Art was content to pat Will on the shoulder and tell him to take it easy. They would talk in a few days. Until then, he was in the care of the cook. The boys would fix up a bath for him—even though it was the middle of the week, he smiled—and he could just lie around and stay warm and rest.

"And the old man?" Art asked Will. "You were off for half a day huntin' some meat, and you never saw him again?"

"Hide nor hair. I prowled around like a coyote until it was gettin' late, then packed up my meat and went after the buggy. I tell you, Mister Pendragon, and this is the truth, I looked for that man for four solid days."

"Buggy tracks?" Art said.

"That's the thing. There was some, and they pointed off north and west a while, then they turned and went straight west. The grass was bent down, and then, when they was into the trees, you could see furrows in the pine needles and such. At one point I thought he was heading over the divide. 'Way, 'way off on the far skyline I got a look at a high pass between the mountains, above the trees. Snow on both sides of it, up there. But 'way to hell and gone . . . 'scuse me, ma'am."

Gwen Pendragon did not blush or smile, but lowered her eyes briefly to acknowledge the apology.

"So he went there?" Art asked.

"I don't know. You've heard of Bighorn Peak up there, 'way north?"

Art nodded.

"There's been a big flood there, bigger'n anything you've ever seen, not more than a year ago. The gravel and sand the whole width of the cañon there. Those buggy wheel tracks seemed to be headin' up it. It's not a road . . . really rough going after a while. Got so rough that I figured I was wrong about the tracks. Then it rained two nights and what-not, so I couldn't really backtrack very good."

Art Pendragon got up from the table and went to the big map on the wall of the dining room. He was always adding to it. Some areas were labeled with names of settlers who were living there, like **Riley's Place**. Others said **good cattle range** or **heavy timber** or were marked with streams. He located the triangle called Bighorn Peak. It stood in the middle of unmapped territory. West of it he had drawn some triangles where he figured the Rocky Mountain range went.

"Show me," he said.

Will pointed to the area southwest of the peak. "Lost him right in there somewhere," he said. "I rode in every direction, went up to the highest points I could find, looked for that buggy the better part of three weeks, I guess. Mister Pendragon, there ain't . . . 'scuse me, ma'am . . . isn't a sign of a ranch or building or anything for miles around that place. I rode back down out of the mountains and out onto the flats, two days' worth, and didn't find a road, trail, nothin'. Even found a real high place and sat there long after dark, in case I could see lights. You could see two hundred miles out over the flats from there, and there wasn't but one tiny light 'way out there, that I figured was Indians or some hide hunter's campfire. That's all."

"It sounds as though that old man deliberately wanted to vanish," Gwen Pendragon suggested. "You don't suppose he could have been sent to us to somehow lure one of your riders up into that empty country?"

"Why would anyone want to do that?" Art asked. "Go ahead, Will. What then?"

"Well, I coursed around up in there, like I said, until my supplies were runnin' low. If there was any houses in there, that flood must have buried them under gravel. One day, 'way back in a wide ol' beaver valley, I ran onto a trapper. Up there all alone. He thought he'd heard of some Mormons livin' farther on west, and he knew that there was some miners on the other side of that pass . . . the one I told you about . . . but he'd been shot at up there, and never went on over to the other side. So that's where I decided to go. Too far to come back here for more supplies, so I figured I might as well see what they're minin' over that pass. And I told you the rest, how I lost the horses and all."

The lantern oil burned low in the bunkhouse. Kyle was trying to keep Will interested in a two-handed card game at the table. Three of the cowboys were in their bunks and dead to the world. The Pinto Kid was sitting on his bunk with a broken-backed pulp novel flattened on the blankets, reading it while he plaited a horsehair halter.

Suddenly Will threw down his cards. "Y'know, I didn't tell Art everything."

"Yeah?"

"I think there might be some kinda place up there, somewhere around that pass. There's a half dozen places where a power of floodwater has come down, one time or another, and they don't exactly look natural. Truth is, I got scared to keep lookin', after I ran into that gunslinger up there. I tell you, Kyle, that guy, he left me feelin' lower than a skunk. If somebody down here done that to me, why, I'd've taken out after him stark naked, if need be, beaten the pulp outta him, and taken my stuff back. But that one. I don't know. Something wasn't natural about him, neither. Walked into bullets.

"Did y' ever need to start drinkin'? The kind where y' keep it up for a couple of days, till you get that kind of stupid dead feeling where nothin' around you seems to be anything to do with you? That's what it left me like. I might as well've been staggerin' around in some trail town somewhere. Finally I knew I had to find some people somewhere and get the hell outta there. As for that son-of-a-bitch, I didn't ever want to see him again. Didn't know what he might do to me next, and that's the scary part."

"Aw, he only could've killed you once," Kyle observed. He smiled his famous smile, the one that made any kind of trouble just seem unimportant.

"Not this bastard. He coulda killed me a lotta times. Sometimes I feel like he did just exactly that."

Kyle dealt out five hands of stud on the table, just to have something for his fingers to do, and curiously turned up each hand, one after the other. "A couple of us noticed you're some different than the Will we knew. You were cheerier when you rode away, if you know what I mean. Now you're

53

under the weather all the time, like you're feelin' puny every day."

"Not like you with that pie-eatin' smile you always wear, huh? Well you go up there and let that big *hombre* kick you around, see how you feel."

"So you figure there's people up there. Maybe this guy, you know, runs 'em. Kind of their leader, like."

"God, I hope that ain't true," Will said. "Pity 'em."

"There's a bunch of strange things in this world. Might be foreigners . . . is why he didn't talk at all. You recollect that crazy *hombre* that got loose among the Pawnee once, him that was half Indian, half French, half black?"

"He was three halves?" Will said, almost managing a grin.

"You know what I mean," Kyle said. "Got together a bunch of renegades from all over the Nations and they did whatever he told 'em to. Terrible."

There was a long silence. Kyle kept on dealing stud hands and flipping them over to see what they were. Will played with an empty sardine can used for an ashtray, pushing it here and there and lining the edges of it up with the squares on the checkered oilcloth.

"What're you thinking, Will?" Kyle asked.

"Thinkin' on that big ditch," he replied. "Thinkin' we go up there with five, six men. I figure I can find it again. Ain't gonna guarantee it, but maybe I can. We ride it out, find where it goes. That's where we're gonna find out some answers. It looks like it goes on for a lotta miles and cuts off the water to a lot of people."

"I don't know if Art's goin' to be too keen on sending an army up there to interfere with somebody's irrigation project. Might be legal, anyway."

"Legal?"

"That old man could've come from a bunch of squatters,

and they were the ones stealin' water. Besides, you said you couldn't find any places anywhere around there. I'm thinkin' maybe they just wanted the Keystone to get rid of the irrigation outfit for 'em, so they could go ahead and claim some land. When they seen it wasn't goin' to work, they hightailed it."

"But that's the whole thing, Kyle, that's the whole thing! If their water's gettin' stole, we need to know that. And if they figured on doin' the stealin', we need to know that, too."

"Yeah. Well. It's a damn' far ways from here. You want to play another hand of this, or not?"

"But here's another thing to think about," Will said. "That old guy, if he went back to his people, what did he tell 'em? That he had a Keystone rider with him to help 'em out? And lost him? Maybe they think . . . 'Hey, that Pendragon man just got bored and back trailed it outta there.' "

Kyle smiled at the idea, but knew that Will was right. Any man, anywhere, ought to finish what he starts. For a Keystone man, that went double in spades. Kyle thought of Will's description of a dark and silent gunman ripping the Keystone *concho* from the horse's halter and trampling it into the dirt. He thought of a little town of frightened people, people wondering if Pendragon's rider would ever come back—or if he had failed them.

Kyle pulled out his bandanna and wiped the inside of his eye patch with it. Maybe it was Will . . . maybe it just wasn't in the cards for him to be the one to do that job. He thought about it. Maybe he was supposed to do it himself. Maybe this unfinished problem was what that blacksmith had been talking about, the blacksmith with all the philosophy to share. Maybe this ditch and the gunfighter guarding it were the forge and anvil. And maybe he was the steel bar, about to be drawn out and shaped to fit a purpose.

Chapter Four

"It Could Happen To Any of You!"

"Will, let me have that bottle! I won't ask you again."

But Will only gripped it harder by the neck and swung with drunken ferocity. Link ducked away and planted a quick, precise punch on the cowboy's chin. Will staggered, straightened up, and stepped back, blinking. Any reasonable man would have quit; Link had trained for the boxing ring back East and was in top condition, heavy with muscle. Will, on the other hand, was still skin and bones, and his drinking binges had left his reflexes slow.

But this was no reasonable man. With alcohol raging in him, Will would fight it out to the end. He charged, swinging the whisky bottle. The weight carried his arm toward the floor as he rushed through the empty air where Link had been standing a second earlier. Link stuck out a foot and tripped him, tapping him behind the ear with another sharp punch as he went by on his way to the floor.

The bottle shattered. Will lay for a moment in the pool of whisky before lurching to his feet again, the jagged neck of the bottle still in his hand. He went at Link off balance, and again found himself slashing at empty air. Link merely twisted out of his way. As Will went past him this time, he coupled his fists together and gave him a blow between the shoulder blades that drove the air out of his lungs.

"Now I'm mad, Will," Link said calmly. "That bottle wasn't the cheap coffin varnish you've become accustomed to. You stole my best Kentucky bourbon. I'm damned tired of these drunks of yours."

"Ahghh," Will groaned, trying to suck air into his chest as he sat up with his head between his knees. "You shouldn't leave a bottle lyin' around f' a man t' trip over."

"Trip over, hell," Link spat. "You had to rummage to the bottom of my war bag for it. I don't like to see men drunk. And I hate a drunk who steals liquor. And," he said, looking around the bunkhouse at the other men who had frozen in various postures as this fight took place, "while I can't speak for any of these men, I wish you'd crawl off somewhere and sober up. Crawl away, or stand up to me again. Stand up, and I'll beat the very bejesus out of you."

Will chose the latter option. Again he swayed to his feet and took an exaggerated fighting pose, throwing a punch at Link's face. Link stood immobile, letting the punch glance off his chin with little effect. Will drove his other fist to the stomach, and Link took it with no more than a slight grunt. He glanced around at the other faces as if making certain they would agree that he had no choice, then he doubled Will over with a bread basket pile driver, caught his descending chin with an uppercut, and finally administered his best Sunday jab to the mouth, sending Will flying backward out the doorway to sprawl in the dust.

Link was just bending over the prostrate Will when Kyle came around the corner.

"What the . . . ? Link! What's goin' on here? Did you beat him up like that? Get away from him! Couple of you fellas give me a hand here!"

"No need," Link said. "It's over. Your friend here was in desperate need of a drink and helped himself to a bottle of good bourbon I was keeping for a special occasion."

"I imagine he'll make it right with you, when he sobers up."

"It's not the money," Link said, "it's the principle. Stealing from his own outfit."

"Yeah, we all know about your principles. Help me get him on his feet, will you?"

The two men supported Will between them and walked him around until he could navigate on his own. He was still weaving and trying not to step on his own toes as he set a course for his bunk to sleep it off.

Early the next morning, before the sun had poked over the rim of the horizon and while the night fogs along the creek were still tangled in the willows, Kyle, Link, and Jess were at the barn getting three Keystone horses ready to go. Jess swung up into the saddle and sat there blowing into his cupped hands to warm them as he waited for Kyle and Link to find some tools. They were headed up the valley to a line camp to make a few repairs and check some drift fence.

Will came toward them, or toward the barn, his eyes bloodshot and his face bruised. He had his torn old sheepskin pulled up around his neck against the morning chill and walked like a man in pain.

"Hey ya, Will," Jess said cheerfully. "Looks like a nice day comin'."

"Oh, Will!" said Kyle, coming out of the barn with Link. "Good to see you up and around." He smiled the magic Kyle smile to show things were OK.

"Sorry about that punch," Link added. "No bad feelings?"

"Aw, to hell with all of you," Will growled. "T' hell with you. I'm gettin' out of here. Gets to where a man can't borrow a drink and get himself drunk without everybody gettin' down on him . . . to hell with it. I'm off this damn' place! Not a rider any more anyway, doin' nothin' but fix chicken coops and haul wood in. Just so's they can keep an eye on me, ol' drunk I am. I'm saddlin' a horse and packin' my gear, by God, and then I'm gonna go to Art for my wages. Go to Texas, maybe. I don't know. Seen the last of me around here."

Will Jensen rode away from the Keystone that morning, following the long dusty wagon road alongside the willow-framed creek, through the low flat bluffs, and out across the sagebrush cattle range. Later on, there would be reports from neighbors far to the east who had seen him pass. Cowboys traveling in from the railroad town spoke of seeing him, too. He was obviously on his way, as he said he would be, to Texas. Away from the mountains.

The three Keystone men rode up the valley, trying to sort out what had happened to their friend. He was not a bad man. He had always been a pretty cheerful one to have around, making jokes about the tough moments they ran into, figuring out ways to fix problems, standing by his outfit no matter what. That he drank, of that there was no doubt; in fact, if any man on the ranch was liable to break Art Pendragon's rule against using alcohol during the work week, it would be Will. On their infrequent trips to town, Will would be the one who had a couple of drinks too many and needed to be helped out of the saloon. But this was something new. The Will they knew, before he had gone on that journey to the north mountains, had been sweet as a new calf.

"What do you suppose happened up there, really?" Link said as they rode.

"I don't know," Kyle replied, "but he sure is one different man now."

"Where do you suppose he'll go?" Jess said.

"Hard to say," Kyle said. "Probably south and east, like he said, toward Texas. East somewhere."

"Yes," Link said. "I don't picture him going west, at all. Not back toward the mountains."

For several minutes they rode without speaking. Then Link suddenly began again. "Kyle, doesn't it make you wonder?"

"What?"

"Will's story. That giant rider in black. The one-sided gunfight. I mean, a man like *Will*, not even wounding the other man in a shoot-up such as that? Have you ever seen him miss what he aimed at? Ever see him so rattled that he couldn't shoot? And then to give up and come crawling back to the Keystone like a castrated dog. No, I just can't add it up. Don't understand it."

"Yeah," Kyle said, "I've been thinking about it. Been through some hard times with Will. Never seen him back down. Or not get back up. Something happened up there that he don't talk about. Dunno if he even knows what it was."

"I was thinking," Link said, "that maybe it would help if someone were to go up there and get his outfit back."

"Yeah?"

"You said it yourself. He doesn't know what happened. And it'll be a stone in his craw all his life, unless he finds out. Seems to me that one of us ought to ride up there, confront this shootist, or foreman, or guardian, or whatever he is, and see what the game is."

"Judgin' from what Will said, I guess you'd have to kill this s.o.b. to get the stuff back."

"If so, so be it."

"Worth thinkin' about," Kyle said. " 'Cept that we're short-handed. Art won't be real eager to send any more men up there."

"What if the same thing happened again, if only one man went?"

"A man would have to take that chance, I guess." There was that smile again, like taking chances were the furthest thing from Kyle's mind.

"I think I'd rather be shot than end up like Will did."

"Guess I agree," Kyle said. "C'mon, we'd better make a little better time if we're goin' to get there by noon."

Kyle lost sleep that night. He woke once in the dark, sweating from a nightmare of a giant man with a grinning skull for a face. He slept again, and again came awake sweating. The dream ran through his head even though his eyes were open and staring widely into the gloom. In the nightmare he saw the giant with a long string of horses tied head-to-tail behind his own mount, and each horse carried the Keystone brand, and the giant and his stolen string were moving at half gallop down out of the foothills out onto the high ranges, straight toward the Keystone headquarters.

Kyle wiped the sweat and lay back in his bedroll, his good eye glazed and looking up at nothingness. He could feel Will's fear; it brought a strange sensation of worthlessness, powerlessness. The dry mouth and the clenched jaw. Fear of the guardian could spread like smallpox to men who had never even seen him.

Nice weather returned to the range, and Art put Link and Kyle to work on the irrigation ditches. Every spring, somebody got the job of clearing out the débris and making sure the water would run.

"Hold 'em up there, Link!"

Link hauled back on the lines and brought the team of heavy horses to a standstill. Standing between the wood handles of the slip, Kyle stretched his arms straight out and then forced them backward, the agony of cramped muscles showing in his face. He twisted back and forth to ease the shoulder cramps. He took off the thick leather gloves and wiped the sweat from his forehead, then pulled his bandanna and wiped out the inside of his eye patch.

"Man," he smiled, "those boys are really pulling hard today. Like to jerked my arms out of the sockets."

"Want me to take the bails a while?"

"Nah. There's not that much of this ditch to finish up. Then we'll pretty much be done with the slip. Don't you think? This afternoon you might take the ditcher and clean out that small ditch over by the draw. Might wanna bring up old Pete and make a three horse hitch with these here two."

"Probably have to. I saw a lot of brush in that one. Didn't use it last year, I guess, did we?"

They waved at a couple of other Keystone men in a wagon going past, headed out to build some fence. It was good to be outside again after a long winter of indoor busy work. Outdoor work was what they lived for.

The slip scraper was heavy and clumsy when it came to cleaning silt and trash out of smaller ditches, but they figured it was better than doing it by hand with shovels. The heavy team pulled the slip along until it was full, then Link swung the team and Kyle twisted the loaded slip up the side of the ditch to dump it. Over and over, all day long. A short run to fill the scoop, then up and out of the ditch with it. Strenuous work, but at least it was outdoor work.

Working on the ditches made Kyle think of Will's story of finding miles of ditch up at timberline far to the north.

"What do you suppose that was all about, Link?" Kyle leaned on one handle of the slip and rolled himself a smoke.

"Don't know," Link said. "I was in town a few weeks ago, and some of the locals had heard about it. Their theory is that it's a gang living up there, like the Hole-in-the-Wall gang."

"Aw, that's just a legend. Nobody ever found any bandits up at Hole-in-the-Wall."

"Maybe not. But this place up north might be takin' in outlaws of some kind. Who else would have somethin' to hide like that?"

"Could be somethin' else. Maybe a gold mine. Will said he'd run into some miners near there. A company trying to hide a rich strike would put up guards. A mine needs a power of water, too."

"But what would they mine up there?" Link asked. "No gold to speak of, or silver. There's a little copper been found up around Encampment Valley, but that's a long way from where Will was."

Kyle smoked his cigarette. Link stood idly, pulling the leather lines through his fingers and looking off toward the mountains. The spring day lay all around like a sun-filled caress, the rising warmth from the ground carrying the smell of earth and sprouting grass.

"I was thinkin'," Kyle said. "Might be some colored. Like that town down south on the Platte. Could be a whole colony of coloreds startin' up there, diggin' themselves a water supply and keepin' people out."

"Maybe Mormons."

"Yeah, maybe Mormons. They're a clannish bunch. And they do big water projects. I heard about wooden troughs hung on the cliffs. And ditches four times as wide as this here one, straight as a string for miles. They say they got a waterwheel fifty feet tall, just to lift water from a creek up to the top of a cliff. And down south . . . I hear there's a place where they drove posts into a cliff and built a road right down the face of it. Right down the face!"

"Aw, come on, Kyle."

"No, this fella told me he saw it. Post holes drilled right into the cliff, and a road for wagons laid on the posts stickin' out."

"Well, maybe it was Mormons that dug the ditches Will saw."

Kyle flipped his smoke away and took a shovel to free the slip from the mud. "Ditch won't clear itself, I guess."

Link clucked to the team and slapped the lines, and they were off again, scraping up another load of silt and manhandling it up out of the ditch.

"Back 'em!" Kyle shouted. Link backed the team two steps to make a little slack in the chains. Kyle threw his weight against one of the bails to turn the scraper so they could pull it out of the ditch. But his mind wasn't on the job, he was thinking of Will, real hard. Not that they were particular friends or anything. It was just that Will was OK, and it was hard to see him go away like that. Part of Kyle wanted to go up into the mountains and find out what was up there. Ever since he was a little boy, he had an itch to look at things, see how things work. And this was the biggest curiosity itch he'd ever had. Any time a bunch of secretive people had taken up residence in your territory, whether a band of renegade Indians or a bunch of colored farmers or Mormons, it made you want to know what was going on.

There was the Keystone reputation, too. At the outset, when Art Pendragon started the Keystone with little more than a horse and a rope, he had been the man people turned to. He might be short-handed at times, but never so much so that he couldn't send somebody to help a neighbor. Keystone riders took care of problems; they were known for it. Sometimes, one of the territory's little ten-shack towns would have a problem with a range bully throwing his weight around. Then, some early morning, a rider would leave town and head for the Keystone, and one of Pendragon's men would be sent to reëstablish the peace. The kind of justice they dispensed in the area was quick and sometimes sort of fatal.

"Aw, hell!" Kyle yelled. The handle caught him and flipped him bodily over the scraper and into the muddy ditchbank. The scraper kept moving and tipped over on top of him.

Link hauled the team to a stop.

"What the hell you doin'?" he said. Kyle was lying with the half-full scraper across one leg, mud all over him, holding his head with one hand and his ribs with the other.

"Dammit! Hit that root there and the handle came across my blind side. It got me a good lick. Wow, that hurts! Damn! That thing sure did kick me!"

"Anything busted?"

"Maybe a rib. I sure took a shot in the side. Wasn't paying attention to what I was doin'. Feels OK, I guess." He probed at his rib cage, relieved to find the bones pretty much in the right places. A rueful grin came back to him in a little bit. "C'mere and help get this thing off me. Probably have to shovel the dirt out of it."

Link shoveled out the dirt and pulled the slip away so Kyle could stand. Kyle noticed how Link worked with choppy, almost nervous strokes. He had been working that way all day, like he was in a hurry to get the job over with and get on to the next one. Springtime could do that to a man. In fact, spring did it to most men who worked with livestock and crops. The thaw would come to the ground, the little green beginnings of grass would show up, a calf or two would drop, and a man would start thinking of getting himself a new horse, or a new rifle, or going out to look at a site where he might build a cabin. He'd get nervous and jumpy. He'd ride a hundred miles to swap a horse or a mule. "Guess I'll go look at the country," he might say, and ride off. If that wasn't possible, he would work on his saddle and gear and talk about other jobs, other places. "Thinkin' of gettin' myself a little place," one would say. Or: "I wonder what Kansas would be like. This cold north country is gettin' to me."

Link was one such man, and had another springtime trait, besides. When the days began to come with long languorous evenings, when the nights breathed warmly through the open bunkroom windows, his thoughts would turn to the ladies. He might work harder than he had to, or suddenly snap at somebody for no reason. He might stand a long time without doing anything except drawing a bit of rope or leather strap through his fingers. He would wash all his shirts at one time, and start to grow a mustache. Or shave it off. Spring would find a man like that polishing his boots more often, and combing his hair two or three times a day.

Spring must be comin' early, Kyle was thinking while he walked the ditch with his shovel, throwing out clods and rocks the slip had missed. Link pulled the scraper out of the ditch and flipped its scoop bucket over so the team could drag it back to the barn. He showed off by riding on the upturned scoop, balancing on the sand-polished bottom while holding back the lines of a heavy team headed for their supper.

Will climbed out and followed the two tracks left by the upside-down slip. It felt good to be getting ditches ready for water. It was good to see the first water turned into the system, running along like it was eager to get the ditch filled, pushing sand and mud ahead of it.

This water business up north, Kyle mused. *This stuff about a ditch in the high mountains. A rifleman guarding it. Leaving a man without shelter or food or weapons. Will could've died up there, easy.* Kyle batted a rock with his shovel, and it almost struck a rabbit that had been crouching motionless under a bush. *Sure like to see what the deal is,* he thought. *Sure would.* But was he really interested in clearing up Will's story, or was it just springtime making him that way? Maybe it was his old Scotch-Irish blood, feeling that same end-of-winter restlessness, that eagerness for physical action that once made his ancestors paint their faces blue in the springtime and set out to aggravate the English. Not because they needed to, but because they wanted to.

Kyle decided he wanted to. He wanted to see what was going on with that ditch, and he wanted to see this guardian rider. For himself. It was a gamble, he knew, but to men such as Kyle every breath of life from birth had been a victory over the odds. Risk wasn't a way of life for them; it *was* life.

The next day being Sunday, the Keystone men cleaned themselves up and shaved and put on their best shirts and neckerchiefs and trooped over to the main house like a string of schoolboys being herded to an ice cream social. They took their seats on chairs set in rows in the dining room, the big table having been pushed against the wall, sitting stiff-backed and respectful, like roustabouts all dressed up for a formal funeral.

Art Pendragon read to them from the Bible, and they listened attentively. They listened even more attentively when Mrs. Pendragon read them an inspirational story from a little book she had. Her face was that of an angel, her figure was every man's idea of perfection, and her prayer-meeting dress made a sculpture of her waist and bust before cascading into layers of bustle behind. Any man would pay attention to her, unless he was dead.

After the meeting, as was the Keystone custom, the men were free to read their own Bibles or write letters or take solitary rides, but all labor was forbidden. Some played cards, which to some amounted to a form of professional endeavor.

They could be seen lounging on benches and stumps in the sunshine side of the bunkhouse, dealing hand after hand, gambling money they didn't have, and winning fortunes they would never collect.

Kyle had asked Art if he could talk to him, but he had to wait. The Pendragons always had a big Sunday meal at noon, and Art would take a nap afterward—his own private form of honoring the Sabbath. And so it was late afternoon before Kyle found him on the porch of the main house. Mrs. Pendragon was sitting in a bent willow rocker, doing her needlework. Art was smoking his pipe and whittling on a pine stick.

"So what's on your mind, Kyle?" Art said.

"It's this business of Will," he said. With Mrs. Pendragon there, he wasn't sure whether to call his employer Art or sir or what, so he didn't do either. Kyle also smiled real easy, sometimes at nothin', and that also made him feel self-conscious around her. He glanced at the lovely lady in the rocker, then his gaze was attracted by a movement behind her at the edge of the yard, near the chicken coop. Link and the Pinto Kid were playing horseshoes down there, and, while the Kid took his turn, Link stared at Mrs. Pendragon.

She was something to stare at. Her hair glistened in the sun in long, graceful curling cascades past her shoulders. A man could span her waist with two hands, and that snug bodice of her dress accented the rise of her breasts. The Wyoming blue sky seemed to be reflected in her eyes, or the transparent blue of those tiny forget-me-nots found in the mountains. A man found it hard not to stare at her perfectly shaped lips, usually parted just slightly in a little smile she wore everywhere. Even now, concentrating on her needlework, she had that tiny suggestion of a smile.

Seeing Link there bothered Kyle somehow. It was natural that he'd be looking in their direction, but somehow he seemed to know what Link was thinking about, and it made him uncomfortable, uneasy. Made him feel guilty of the same thoughts himself.

"So what's the problem?" Art said. "You want to go after Will, find him, bring him back to the Keystone? That the deal?"

"No. No, that's not it," Kyle answered. "He went his own way, and I guess he has to keep going until he finds what he likes. Or what he can live with."

"I heard from the mud wagon driver that Will had been seen heading into Crawford," Art said, whittling on his stick.

"Is that right? That's some place a cowboy shouldn't end up, that's for sure. It's called the Nebraska Sinkhole for a good reason, I hear. Several good reasons. All those soldiers and women and such. But no, I was thinking of back trailin' him up into that north country, see what's happening up there."

"Oh, you were," Art said. He took a draw on his pipe and let the light breeze lead the fragrant smoke along the covered porch. "Figure to be gone two years as well?"

"No, sir. I think I could probably get up there and back before roundup."

"Sounds optimistic. What do you think you'll find up there, besides a gunfight?"

"Link and I were talkin' about that. That big ditch project and all. We kinda had an inkling it might be Mormons."

"Mormons?"

"Well, they've gone through here. Gone over South Pass before. That ditch . . . that seems like an awful big project just to divert some water. Who'd do that, all that work, way up there? And then set a guard on it, like they expected somebody to come along and break it open or smash the gates or something."

"What about that old man who came to ask for help?" Art asked. "He didn't say anything about Mormons, just that their water was being dried up."

"Yeah, and he didn't tell us everythin' about that big gunman up there, either. But I'm surprised he ain't been back."

"Could be it discouraged them, Will not showing up. Could be they just saw that as an omen and packed up and moved out. Still, I'd like to know who they are, and what's going on up there. That's the thing. Don't like not knowing. This wouldn't just be you wanting to go up there and pick a fight with that big guy, would it?"

Kyle looked at Mrs. Pendragon and felt a warmth rise into his face. She had lectured him once about putting a curb on his zest for fighting. But instead of looking at him, she was concentrating on her pattern as if she wasn't hearing the conversation, at all. When she looked up, it was in the direction of the horseshoe pits.

"What happened to Will up there could happen to any one of us," Kyle replied. "I don't think it's right for a man to beat up on another man like that, then leave him with nothing, 'way up in God knows where. Not right. Doesn't make us look any good, either."

Both men were quiet for a while, watching the Kid and Link throw the horseshoes back and forth. Art scraped his pipe and stepped off the porch to knock the bowl on his boot heel. Kyle followed, the bright sun making him squint.

"I guess we need to find out what's going on," Art said finally. "I'd better send somebody."

"You lookin' at Link?" Kyle said. Mrs. Pendragon made a startled movement beside them, as if she had almost dropped her needlework.

"Link, or the Kid."

Kyle scowled and studied the toes of his boots. This wasn't what he had in mind.

"Or you, if you could keep your gun in its holster," Art said.

Kyle smiled. "Yeah, I guess I could." He grinned warmly. "So, it's OK with you if I go?"

"It's OK with me," Art said. "But I want you back here by roundup. You hear me?"

"I hear you. No reason at all I can't be back here in plenty of time." Kyle laughed, looking back over his shoulder as he started away. He had turned his bad eye toward Art, the one covered with the leather patch. "I'll see what I can do," he joked, winking with his one good eye.

Chapter Five

Over the Divide

Kyle rode eight days north by west. During the first four days he found settlers who knew the Keystone brand. Boys ran to care for his saddle horse and pack horse while men clapped him on the shoulder and led him to the house, or soddie, or dugout, for something to eat. Unmarried girls, shy in their shapeless dresses of homespun and conscious of their heavy work shoes, kept against the walls, openly gazing at the slim and handsome stranger with his leather eye patch and long body. When he cocked his head and smiled at them, they blushed.

Wives, also, wanted that smile. They served him supper on their best plates and watched him as he ate, asking about the Keystone and the doings of people who lived in the towns to the south.

After supper, there was time to talk to the men. Had they ever heard of these ditches, or a colony in the far mountains? Ever see an old man in a buggy? If the men seemed of the right sort to take it seriously, he would ask if anyone in the area carried a bow and arrow. A small man, maybe even a boy.

Kyle listened to rumors and guesses and studied the crude maps they drew in the dirt. And he rode farther and came to people who did not know the Keystone brand. He rode into the great sage fringes of the mountains where there were no people at all. After two more days, even from the highest hills, he saw no sign of houses or roads whatever.

Crossing one hill, riding south, and thinking about an open valley he had passed earlier, Kyle's bad eye was toward the mountains when his good eye caught the white flash. He swiveled his long torso around—it was an antelope making a dash into a narrow cañon.

Food had been rabbit, leftover dry meat, and hard bread from meager pantries of wives in remote dugouts and log houses. He also carried flour for biscuit makin's, coffee beans, dried red beans, and cans of boiled tomatoes in the pack. The antelope was fresh meat and too good to pass up. Kyle pulled out his bandanna and wiped the inside of his eye patch, then drew out the rifle, and urged his horse forward into the cañon.

They struck a sort of trail, and, coming around a bend, he caught the sound of tumbling rocks and swiveled sideways to see the antelope scrambling up the loose slope. Kyle's shot took the animal at the base of the neck, and it came tumbling down off the slope, dead, finally coming to rest on a trail, which was not a trail. It was a ditch. It was dry, but it was a ditch.

Two antelope steaks popped and sizzled in the pan over the small fire. Kyle kneaded flour and water into biscuits and dropped them into the pan beside the steaks, contemplating the ditch. It looked like it had been built about four, five years ago. He could still see where rocks had been marked by an iron pry bar. The bottom was smooth and even from being dragged with a scraper of some sort. For a short distance, near the flat place where he had decided to make night camp, a dike of quarried rocks had been built.

After supper, Kyle took sand and cleaned his pan and tin

plate. He took a little can of dressing from his saddlebag and rubbed down his saddle and his boots, carefully, where the day's riding had left scratches. He laid out his bedroll and put his guns on the saddle blanket beside it, doubling it over them against the night dew. He picketed the horses, telling them he would find water for them in the morning. When all was neatly arranged, he tugged off his boots and slid into the bedroll and watched as stars came winking on, far up in the sky. The sky darkened to the deep near-black shade of a dress his mother used to wear. He closed his eye and was asleep.

In the morning, which was brilliant blue as all previous mornings had been, Kyle packed the one horse and saddled the other, removed all sign of his camp, and set off up the cañon along the ditch bottom. The cañon opened out into a wide valley, and the ditch followed along one edge, keeping to the contour. The cañon closed in upon him again, bending to the right, and the ditch kept taking him farther and farther into the mountains.

The mystery was this: the ditch was carefully constructed and had been maintained, and yet it looked as though water had never passed through it. It was as though it lay in readiness for some future deluge.

Whoever had built this ditch, Irish or Asian, Kyle could see the hard work it had cost. He could narrow his eye and imagine hammers smashing into the rock, the drilling day after day, the blasting, the hauling of broken granite.

As he rode along to the sound of squeaking leather and steady *plop* of the horse's hoofs, Kyle thought of his father. Many of their Irish relations, his father had said, fled from the labor of digging ditches to drain the rotting meadows of Ireland. They came to America, only to be put to work on ditches again.

"Be thanking your lucky stars," his father would say, "that

your mother had the fine sense to learn the cooking, and more than the porridge and praties. And that your father found work for his hands and his mind with the telegraph company, and not just for the back. It's only thanks t' that you're not looking at life with the other shanty Irish, muckin' your way westward on the end of a shovel."

The shovel handle had not been Kyle's destiny. Nor, it seemed, was he destined to follow his father into the telegraph engineer profession. As a lad, waiting in the cold rooms for the early dark of winter to descend and bring home his parents, his mother from the restaurant and his father from the factory, he would sit and shiver and gaze into the last embers glowing in the stove and dream of that other story, that other destiny. In the story the Owen family were landholders of the old country, descended of folk who once owned a castle. In his dream, Kyle rode out on his fine horse, his sword at his side and his men at his back, and they covered the countryside, punishing the evil. It was what he had been born to. A lovely dream for a boy shivering through bitter winter nights in a city held hostage by darkness.

Once, waiting outside the restaurant for his mother to take him home, Kyle had sensed a shadow. He looked up from his cheap, thick shoes to see a gentleman standing there. The gentleman cupped the boy's chin in his hand, raised it, and stared into his eyes. He said something in a strange tongue; Kyle's house no longer had the Gaelic, as they were American now. The gentleman had turned to Kyle's mother, who had come up by then, and she had heard the strange words and had known the meaning. Years later, as he set his face to going West, she had told it to him. "That man was an earl in the old land, searching in America for children of his family who had made the crossing in the early days. Kyle Owen," she had said, "he saw you had the look about you." And because Kyle was going West, she had told him what else the gentleman had told her. "He said more . . . one of the landholding Owens, a woman with the Owens' look, went West with a fortune in gold coins and was never seen again."

After that, Kyle began to dream of some day running into a woman who spoke Irish, who had the strange dark eyes like his mother's, upsloping and heavy-browed, and the tall figure of the clan. He was sure that he would know her, or her children, and he would seem like kin to them. . . .

The horse stopped, and Kyle came back to himself. The ditch ended in a wide basin opening at their feet like a crater. It was useless to think of going farther, for the ditch ended against the cliff. High, high up the slick face of it, Kyle could see the pour-off where water would come down in a waterfall, if there ever was water. A waterfall would plunge into the basin, overflow it, and go down the ditch. But where would it go, and why?

He stood staring and imagined the water, cold and clear from the high mountain snow packs and glaciers, soaring off the lip of the cliff, making a fine mist, crashing and moving . . . where? Water is pulled by gravity, they had learned that in school. But was it to follow man-made paths? Was it the final and best end for mountain water to wind up soaking into some hay field on the flats?

Kyle looked left and right and saw no way to get the horses up and out of the cañon here. So he turned about on his tracks and rode east again, back trailing himself, watching north and south for a way out of the narrowed gorge.

The next morning was not cloudless. He could see a long way to the east where the clouds hung in long strips of gray and pink and streaky pewter color. Westward, broad bands of sunlight penetrated some of the cloud layers and left brilliant green patches on the high mountains where the forests were.

Kyle packed up and set himself a course, this time along the ridges where the riding would be easier. The ridges twisted this way and that, meeting each other across narrow gorges or wide valleys, and he kept a westward direction as well as he could. The clouds were down. He could not see the farthest range of mountains at all.

Riding the crest of one ridge where trees were sparse, he saw that the ridge off to his left consisted of cracked and broken blocks of stone like the ancient wall of a stone fortress. He crossed a divide, went down a sloping aspen grove and up grassy slopes on the other side, and started up another divide. Crossing a high hump of forest, he broke out of spruce forests into aspen groves and was riding in a fine mist. Kyle undid the slicker from its roll behind the saddle. He had ridden into a rain cloud snagged on the mountain, up where the rivers began their long, long journey to the sea.

And now he came out of the aspens, following a small creek into open and treeless terrain. It felt different to be there, and he felt more comfortable with the land. The creek was running west. West. The grass was deeper here, the flowers more prolific, the contours less sharp and hostile. He was across the final divide, riding down the western slope of the Rockies, the slope that caught the moisture from the westerly winds.

At camp that night, Kyle rigged the tarp like a lean-to over his bedroll and built a fire close by out of the drizzle. He had shot a fat rabbit that afternoon, and, while it cooked, he got out the penciled map Will had drawn. Will had seen high snowy peaks behind the miners' shacks, with the bed of a large river running north to south, and slopes so steep with rocks so loose that a man and horse couldn't negotiate them.

Kyle had seen no such country. He had found a ditch,

however, and it had led west and north. Now he regretted not having climbed to the top of that pour-off to see which way it went. Yet, he had stayed south of it for two days now and had not crossed it. Tomorrow he would start northward, keeping to the divide as much as possible. On the pack horse there was still flour and dry beans and coffee and salt. With some rabbit and venison, he could go on for two weeks or more.

Riding north and getting back down into the forests, Kyle came to the same ditch, or an identical one. There were a few inches of water running in it. A path, overgrown and unused, ran alongside, but it was easier to ride the bottom of the ditch itself. He rode along past dikes holding the narrow ditch against the mountainside, laid up of blocks of granite and buttressed with dirt and gravel. Once the ditch went through a tunnel, too low for a man to walk upright in, and Kyle made a long detour around.

Late in the day he came to the end. A creek came running down the narrow cañon, leaping boulders and fallen logs, making waterfalls and pools, nourishing river birch and willow and aspen. Somebody had diverted the flow by building a log wall with two heavy gates in it, one for the creek and one for the ditch. The gates were made to slide up and down between thick posts. They were partly open so some water would go down the creek and some down the ditch. He could see no way to close one and open the other; each log weighed more than two or three men could lift, and, besides that, they were soaked with water and wedged tightly between the uprights.

Kyle knew something about irrigation ditches and diversion structures, yet he couldn't figure out how anyone could open and close this one. No one had been there for a long, long time; that much was plain from the condition of the grass. There was a campsite with a fire pit, but grass grew in the charred remains. But surely someone someday would need to shut off the flow to the ditch, or increase it. How would they do it?

He got down to study the thing, his slicker dripping. The logs were spiked to each other. Iron bands were spiked to the logs to hold them together, and there were iron rings at the top of these bands. For lifting? But how? Each gate had to weigh a ton. There was no lifting mechanism, no hand winch, no windlass, not even a fulcrum. Short thick lengths of wood had been stuck under the bottom of each gate to hold it from sliding down, but if the gate couldn't be made to slide up again and release the chocks and then close tight, the thing was worthless. Maybe, he thought, maybe this giant rider of Will's was even bigger and stronger than he looked. There was nothing else to the structure, except for an empty post hole on the strip of rock between ditch and creek.

A kind of trail wound up the far side of the cañon, probably to haul logs to the diversion. Or maybe animals made it, coming down to drink. Whatever its use, it was a way out of the narrow place. There was no point trying to take the horses farther up the creek, which was tangled with birch and choke-cherry and willow growing tightly up against fir and spruce trees.

Kyle considered camping there at the flat campsite with the fire pit. The creekbank had good grass, and the water was clear, and the spreading spruce branches would make a shelter from the drizzle. But if the dim trail led out of the cañon, he would find some other place. It was not the cañon or the creek that bothered him. It was the head gate. The diversion structure. At first he thought he disliked it because it was crude and heavy and ugly. Men had spilled a lot of sweat cutting those logs and leveling them to make a watertight fit.

Digging those post holes through the rock and gravel must have taken weeks. All to stand in the way of a small mountain creek and force it to run another direction. To go elsewhere.

That disturbed Kyle. Up the cañon, the water danced on rocks, and made dragging willow branches spring back and forth, and bubbled against the banks, and whirled and swirled and churned over itself. But men had changed its destiny. Where it once sang, now it ran silently along a ditch toward its appointed use. Where it once gave life to the bushes and trees and grass along its course, it now went dutifully between barren banks of rock and gravel to become still and stagnant in some reservoir, evaporating beneath a summer sun.

Kyle's father had been a free-running spirit in his homeland. Unfit for pointless drudgery in fields where others broke themselves trying to scrape life from exhausted soil, he had crossed the border and taken up a job but found more starving. There had been a theft—he had never said what he had stolen—and three years at an Australian penal colony before he was free and had worked his way to San Francisco. But there he had found the old prejudice again—himself and the girl he had met at a cheap eating house were expected to remain silent about their needs and serve the food and wield the pick and shovel in the streets and so live out their destiny as American peasants.

But they had not. They were not cheap labor, not part of the stagnating pack of illiterates who were kept around to work on the streets and rails and sewers. With baby Kyle carried about in a basket, they had walked proud and determined until they had found better jobs. For him, apprentice in a factory making telegraph equipment, soon to be moving up to installation and engineering. And for her, decent lodging, being the mother of Kyle, until the lad could be left on his own and she could go back to the restaurant cooking.

Kyle's life took a path with many a stone in it, too. Harsh schooling, doctors with their salves for the eye that would not grow like the other one, his mother worrying he was too thin for his age, and the fights, and always dreading a day when his father would be introducing him to the factory foreman. Then the night of tears when he had read them the letter from his cousin, nearly his age. The cousin had enlisted and was posted to a cavalry regiment out West at a place called Fort Robinson. Young Kyle had his mind set to join him.

Kyle shook off the memories, then mounted and rode up the faint trail leading out of the narrowness, hat brim against the rainy drizzle. He paused once to wipe out the leather eye patch, then rode on.

Next he came into an old forest and rode upward through it. Dead trees leaned against the living ones, soaring dead-gray spikes, many with long zigzag scars from lightning. He found a dry creekbed in sight, but did not try to ride in it because of the rolling rocks and deadfall.

Late in the day the ancient forest came to an end, and Kyle halted the horses at the edge of a great meadow of dry grass. Another thick forest ridged the north side, to his right; cliffs like fortress walls barricaded the south. Directly ahead, the treeless flat plain flowed over a divide and vanished down the other side.

Halfway across, he could see over the divide. The yellow scar of a distant ditch ran around the mountain. It was the meadow where Will had seen the dark horseman.

Kyle rode on, wary. Shadows looked like figures of men. When he reached the farther edge, he pulled his Winchester from the scabbard. Far below, like toy buildings, he saw a few cabins scattered across a willow park. A faint sort of trail, probably used only by mountain sheep, went down across the

81

loose rock slope and was so steep it made him dizzy to look at it. But down he would go, to see who was there and learn what they knew.

He heard the pack horse slipping and grunting behind, but could not turn to see how it was doing, because his saddle horse was tripping on sharp angles of rock and stepping on loose ones that slid away under him, and Kyle needed all his concentration to balance his weight in the saddle and to watch where the miserable little thread of a trail was going. The whole slope might let go, any time, and the three of them would plummet to the bottom in an avalanche.

It was sheer luck that the rifle shot came just as he was upslope of two jagged boulders the size of corncribs. The sound of the explosion and the *zing!* of the bullet on the stone made the saddle horse rear up. Either that, or Kyle's involuntary jerk backward had done it. The boulders were all that kept the whole mountainside from going down. The pack horse bolted in terror, scrambling away across the cascading rocks. A leg down in a crevice, the saddle horse had fallen to its side, its breath spraying blood. Probably had a rib busted through a lung.

Another heavy-caliber shot *whanged* off the rocks as Kyle lunged for the Winchester he had dropped in the commotion, but he got to it and was back behind the boulder before another shot came.

The horse was crying now, blood bubbling with its whinnies and running from the mouth. Its eyes held nothing but fear and panic until Kyle rested the muzzle of the Winchester against the animal's head and sent a bullet through its brain.

Everything went quiet. The pack horse had made it to the far side of the boulder slope somehow and was somewhere in the trees beyond. Nothing was moving down below. The only sound was Kyle's heavy breathing. He huddled at the base of the boulder until the sun went down and coldness rose up the mountainside like an ocean tide. When it was dark enough, he dared to belly over to the saddle to get his slicker to wrap up in. That is how he spent the darkest hours of the night, jammed down against jagged granite, trying to get warmth from the stiff canvas, poked and prodded everywhere his body touched the rocks.

By first light he was stiff, a grotesquely bent figure huddling against the rock. He crawled to the dead horse and tugged the saddlebags loose from it, then began sliding and stumbling down the avalanche incline. Halfway to the bottom, and still nothing had moved below, and he hadn't been shot at. But he had cuts on both hands and bruises to his butt and forearms from sliding down the slope.

He reached the bottom before the sun had, and could see that all but two of the shacks were abandoned. These had jumbled piles of firewood and traces of smoke from the chimney holes. Kyle chose the nearest one and crouched as low as a tall man can crouch and crept up to the log wall. Inch by inch, he straightened up until he could see in through the rotten canvas covering the window.

In the dark he could make out two bunks and two shapes asleep on them. One was snoring. The smell coming from the window was overpowering. He saw a long-barreled Henry rifle next to the door. Kyle slouched down again to wait until they woke up. Sooner or later, one of them would come out alone, and he would get him. With his back against the wall, worn out from his night among the rocks, he rested and waited.

Chapter Six

Strange Brothers

Kyle had nearly fallen asleep under the window. The sun wasn't over the mountains yet, but the sky was getting light. He heard sounds in the cabin. His stiff muscles hurt as he got to his knees and pulled the Colt.

"Goin' out?" said a hoarse voice inside the cabin.

"Gotta pee."

"Light that there fire on yore way."

There was shuffling and clumping, accompanied by a loud belch.

"How's come you never gotta git up an' light the damn' fire?"

" 'Cause I kin hold my water longer than you."

Kyle slipped to the corner of the cabin, stepped over the pile of rusty shovels and picks and traps, and waited next to the door. He didn't have to wait long before he heard the wooden bar being lifted. The door swung open, releasing the pent-up stink, followed by the sound of boots coming out.

"Shut the damn' door."

Slam!

The owner of the boots lurched to the right and headed for a favorite bush a few yards from the cabin. A large man, in a stained undershirt and Levi's. With a loud *"ahhh"* he went about his business and got so intent on sprinkling every shriveled leaf that he didn't notice Kyle coming up behind him. Until he felt the cold metal of the Colt against his neck. "Uh . . . ," he began, starting to turn.

"Go on with your business," Kyle whispered. "You missed a branch there. Just don't make any sudden sounds, doin' it."

He grasped the back of the man's belt and with the Colt muzzle still against his neck turned him around to walk back to the cabin. When they reached the door, Kyle whispered to open it. As soon as the man lifted the latch, Kyle pushed him flying across the cabin where he crashed onto his partner, still wrapped up in quilts and blankets.

Kyle lifted the heavy rifle standing beside the doorway. He couldn't tell if it was loaded—or even worked—so he kept his Colt trained on the two.

The two men disentangled themselves and sat up, blinking in the glare from the door.

Then one spoke. "Yore turn to pee now, John. Mebbe light that there fire when y' finish."

"Light it yerself. I don't gotta go no more."

The other began to pull on his boots, every movement in the pile of bedding releasing a smell that would make a vulture lose his appetite. He acted as though having a cowboy with a gun come through the door was an everyday occurrence.

"Lookin' for grub, are y'?" he said to Kyle. "If it's money, we be fresh out. No horses, neither."

Kyle stepped inside. No use standing in an open doorway, in case some neighbor might take an interest in the situation.

"Funny you'd mention horses," he said. "Some son-of-a-bitch with a heavy rifle killed mine last evenin'."

"That'd be me!" said the first one, standing up brightly. "So I got 'im, huh? Never did hit 'em before. Never knew that ol' Henry'd carry that far. Y' hear, John? Hit 'em."

John had crossed over to the corner where a makeshift stove had been fashioned from loose stones and a sheet of iron. He got down on his knees, with considerable grunting and a massive fart, and blew into the ashes until there was a cloud of gray dust flying around his head. He shoved in bark and shavings and blew some more. A small red flame began to show. He gave the blackened coffee pot an experimental shake and set it on the edge of the iron sheet.

"Betcha didn't hit nuthin'," he said, and belched, squatting down to warm his hands at the little flame. He put in a couple of chunks of wood.

"Same as," Kyle said. "Spooked one into breakin' a leg and gettin' a rib through the lung. The other ran off. So you boys pretty much left me afoot."

John looked him up and down. He felt around in a box on the floor until he came up with a can of coffee, and dropped a handful into the pot. Putting the can back in the grub box, his hand came across a chunk of some kind of food, either prehistoric bread or ancient dried meat. Looking at it with sad resignation, John began to chew as he contemplated Kyle.

"Brother," he said to the other man, "I don' believe this here's the man. You gone and plinked the wrong one."

"Naw. I know what yo're up to, John. Yo're jus' saying that 'cause it wasn't you as shot him this time. Yo're jus' mad that I got him and you never."

"You never got him neither, brother. Man jus' said all y' did was spook his horses. You never got him, or he wouldn't be standin' there with a gun on y'."

Brother seemed to puzzle this out for a spell. Kyle swung the Colt toward him as his hand suddenly went into a greasy sack hanging from the window frame, but he came up with a piece of meat—or bread—of his own to gnaw.

"Well," Brother said at last, "we been shootin' at him ever' month since we got here, and this here's the first time he came tumblin' down t' the valley. Never done that afore. So!"

John replied with another fart that seemed to bend the walls out, and got up to his feet. He moved his fat belly toward Kyle, seemingly oblivious to the guns.

"You ain't the one what's been comin' ever' month, anyhow," he said to Kyle. "Brother, he didn't figure that." He went past Kyle, his belly brushing the Colt muzzle, and on outside the cabin. Kyle followed. John walked to his own favorite bush and gazed up the mountain slope while he went about watering it.

"Brother figured you for th' fella what comes along up there, regular-like, see?" He pointed with his free hand. "You seen the ditch up there, I guess. He comes along it, rides a ways down the slope there, and jus' watches us. Once we went up t' see about lettin' some water down. Y' can see there ain't any down here. Comes outta nowhere, he does. Big galoot, big horse, big gun. Don't say nothin'." John finished his business with the bush and turned toward Kyle. "Jus' come at us, drove us down them rocks, fallin', and damn' near to break our necks."

"You and your brother," Kyle said.

"He ain't my brother. Ain't nobody's brother, near as he knows. We jus' call him that."

"So this big man on the horse, he comes by about every month and shoots at you two . . . somethin' like that?"

"We shoot at him. He jus' sits up there like th' king of th' mountain, lookin' down on us. Like warnin' us. Makes th' skin crawl, the way he jus' shows up and sits up there. We shoot at 'im, but the Henry don't carry that far. Wouldna hit you, neither, 'cept you come on down inta range."

John waddled back to the cabin and squatted back down at

the fire. When the coffee boiled, he filled a dented tin cup and handed it to Brother. "You go t' the cache while that there coffee cools," he told him, "an' git that can of sourdough and chunk of that sheep bacon. Then y' can get up there and bring this man's saddle and such on down here."

Between the fire and the boiling coffee, the place had begun to smell bearable. And with the sun striking the roof planks and fire getting hotter, the chill went off and the cabin began to feel like the inside of an oven. Kyle took the guns and went outside, where he found a stump from which he could watch both the door of the cabin and the progress of Brother working his way up the steep talus slope.

John emerged after a time, sweating profusely, carrying a bent tin plate and a tin cup that he set down on a rock next to Kyle. The material on the plate looked like some kind of meat cut thin and cooked to the texture of a split pine shingle, and a lump of brown biscuit. But, out in the open, the coffee smelled even better than before. John squeezed back in through the door and came out with his own plate and cup and sat himself heavily on a section of log near the stump.

"Y' come over the top, then," he said, using a biscuit lump to point at the divide high above.

"Yup," Kyle said. "Came from the Keystone Ranch." He looked at the sweating fat man for a sign that he had heard of it, but the creases in his face showed only a stupid blankness.

"What's the minin' like, an' trappin', on that other side?"

"Didn't see any. Nothin' the last four, five days but irrigation ditches. Dry ones. Nobody livin' over there to speak of."

"Humph," John said. He volunteered that there were more people living down the valley, down the nearly dried-up river, a few days' ride, at a place where he and Brother went for supplies, when the wagon came in. "Not real often," he said. "Mostly what we get is beans."

"I noticed," said Kyle.

John made that humphing sound again and went on chewing at the meat and bread. Up on the slope, Brother was becoming a small dark figure inching his way gingerly toward the big boulders where Kyle had spent the night.

"Looks like Brother's 'bout there," John observed.

Kyle put down his plate and laid the Henry rifle across his knees, then drew out his bandanna and wiped the inside of his eye patch. John watched with bored disinterest. Kyle readjusted the patch, picked up the Henry, levered a fresh shell into the chamber, and checked the rear sight, raising it a notch. He aimed up the slope, and pulled the trigger back very slowly.

Whoomph!

He levered in a second shell. *Whoomph!* They could see where the shots struck rock, near where Brother was, from the white rock dust spraying up. They saw him throw himself down in the sharp talus and watched him slide down, with rock tumbling around him. After a time they heard his surprised shout of profanity echoing off the cliffs and the distant sound of rolling stones.

Kyle stood up and walked to the cabin to set the rifle inside the door again where he had found it, then returned to his breakfast.

"She pulls a little to the right," he said. And he finally smiled.

"Yeah," said John, "I know. But y'know, with a Henry, they jus' ain't a damn' thing y' can do about it. Short o' bendin' the front sight a hair, I mean."

"I'd try that," Kyle said.

"Well," said John, "I b'lieve I will."

They had finished their food long before Brother came struggling back down with Kyle's saddle and bridle and blanket. He dropped into the dry grass and lay there, panting and sweating.

"Somethin' been at your horse already," he finally said. "Look like a bear, maybe . . . maybe lion. They think that there horse meat's purty tasty. Good job I got your gear afore it got chewed on."

"Mebbe I oughta thank you," Kyle said.

"Seen another horse up above there," Brother went on, "looked like a pack animal. Had a pack on 'im, anyway. Jus' standing up there over in the trees, like."

Kyle had the empty rifle shell and was blowing into it, making the same low pitch tone over and over. Didn't sound like anything, but it was something to do.

"Suggest you go back up an' get that other horse, then," Kyle said. He smiled, but not warmly.

Brother sat up and mopped his brow with one torn shirt sleeve. "Maybe after I git somethin' t' eat," he said. "Maybe I kin get 'im then."

Kyle held the rifle shell between two fingers and put a third finger behind it, flipping it like a cigarette butt, and it hit Brother square in the chest.

"Maybe you'll go right now," he said.

"Guess I will," Brother replied.

Brother again crawled and slipped his way up the talus, becoming a smaller and smaller figure on the mountainside as the two men watched. He went up along the edge of the granite rubble, staying close to the trees. The footing on the loose rock was treacherous, but better than fighting logs and branches up through the forest. They made guesses at how he might contrive to bring the horse down, but neither one saw much point in worrying about it.

"Been to that ditch up there, have y'?" Kyle said.

"Once. Figured I'd find a way t' let water down here, so's

we could use it just t' pan out some o' this ore. Hell of a big sunuvabitch, that ditch. Got clear up over right about in there. . . ." John pointed to the place, which looked to be a mile or two beyond where Kyle had started down into the valley. "Big damn' gate up there. Logs . . . gotta be ten, twelve feet across, six foot high, at least. Couldn't figure out no way to lift it an' let the water go. Sure could use it, though. Nuthin' t' wash ore with. Not enough for trappin', neither.' "

"Why stay?" Kyle asked.

"Hell, who knows. The fella before us, he went. See that pile o' boards on yonder? That was his shed. Pulled ever' damn' nail outta it and took 'em with 'im. Ever' damn' nail. We seen him lightin' out, down the valley there, came up t' see if his cabin was better'n ours. Know what he done?"

"What?" Kyle said.

"Took ever' damn' nail outta that shack, and put him up a sign on that pile o' old boards. For sale, it said. For sale. Silly sonuvabitch."

"So this big rider up along that ditch, he never comes on down here, huh?" Kyle said.

"Nah. Hell, we got nuthin' he'd want. He wants that water, and he's got it. That ditch there, it goes on along f'r ten mile or better. That thing's so big she cuts off . . . hell, I don't know . . . a dozen bitty little creeks comin' inta this valley."

"Where's the water go?"

"Who knows? Look around y', here. See? Aspen, grass, spruce over there, everythin' just like here's water, only it's been a dry spell. It'll be back. Man just wait a season, and it'll be back. But it ain't comin' back, and that's what I told Brother. Don't care how much color's in that ore we're diggin' out, there ain't no way to sluice it. And there ain't gonna be. Tell you what else . . . one ol' boy from down valley, he went and spied him out that system, and he says it's all over like spider web up there, across the divide an' all. Says he thinks it's all goin' to a big ol' lake of some kind, one of them what-ya-call it . . . ?"

"Reservoir."

"Yeah. Anyhow, that big rider caught up to him and whupped him to a fare-thee-well and liked t' kilt him, and he took off down valley, and we ain't seen him since. An' there's three more men as has gone up there, and they ain't been seen again, neither. Least that's what some say."

Brother had disappeared into the trees up near the top of the ridge now, and Kyle and John exchanged guesses as to whether he had seen the pack horse. John waddled back to the cabin for something else to eat. Kyle got a can of saddle soap out of his bag and began to rub at the scratches and scars on the saddle.

"Ranches up there, somewhere, you figure?" he called to John.

John's head popped out the doorway, chewing on something. "You didn't see none, did y'?" John said. "Nobody here never did, neither. Don't believe there is. Brother, he talked t' some old guy, or so he says, once up in the woods there. Talked about there bein' a castle somewhere north up there. Brother also said this old guy disappeared while he was watchin' him, so . . . well, some of Brother's nails ain't clenched over real tight, if y' know what I mean."

"I'd like to talk to that old man," Kyle said. "Wonder how a man would find him?"

John just went on chewing and watching the spot where Brother had vanished. After a while, John got bored with waiting and went across the dry streambed and into the dead standing willows with a shovel, heading for his gold claim to do some pointless digging.

Kyle found a big patch of shade and lay down, his head on

his saddle, either to figure what to do next or to get in a nap. The high mountain air, fresh with pine scent and warm from the sun, made a man real lazy. Sleepy lazy. Before long, he drifted off to sleep.

He dreamed of being high in the mountains, too high for trees, with only moss and flowers on the ancient stones. The air was thin and clean, and it hurt to breathe deeply. He dreamed he was lying on the moss, breathing steady breaths, perfectly at peace. And although he dreamed and was asleep, he knew no one had been there before, that there was no trail and no direction to go and every direction to go.

He dreamed of thick winter snows and how they melt in springtime and run down thousands of watercourses. He imagined one flake of snow falling out of the sky and lying in a drift all winter and becoming a drop of water in spring, then pulling along with the rest down an animal's burrow and over rocks to meet a little torrent of water. And that torrent headed to some destination, some destiny, that the water drop knew nothing of. Just as it knew nothing of all the other possible destinies that might have overtaken it, had it come to earth elsewhere.

As he lay on the barren tundra in his dream, he heard breathing other than his own. He was alone, yet not alone, alone and yet watched. The breathing was as if a great bear had come along searching the tundra for something to eat and had found the cowboy there, far from cattle, far from cattle ranges. An odd thing, to the bear. To find a cowboy so far up there.

It was not a bear breathing, but breathing like a bear. Kyle lay perfectly still, in his dream, and knew he should stay as still as he could until the bear went away. The breathing made him tense, and no longer did he remember that flake of snow and the way it had gone without knowing where it was going or where it was not going. He only thought of the one who waited for him, for Kyle, to make a move.

Now he saw, looking into his dream at himself, his own breath rising and visible in the chilled air and mingling with the breathing of the watcher who stood invisibly over him, watching him. Then the other breathing went away, or stopped, and in the dream Kyle sat up suddenly and found he was looking down at the great ditch that captured all the water and ran off it to an as-yet-unknown purpose. At the same time Kyle came awake in the dry grass near the cabin and sat up suddenly and he was looking up at the great ditch, although he couldn't see whether it carried water and, if it did, which direction the water flowed.

John was nowhere in sight. Neither was Brother. Kyle rose, somewhat uncertainly, went to the cabin, found a water barrel, washed his face. He saw his saddle lying there by the log and stump and went to get it and find a place off the ground to put it. As he did so, his eyes fell on the Keystone patch on the front rigging strap. A simple design, stamped into the leather disk and sewed to the strap for decoration. It was just an outline of a keystone, like in the middle of an arch.

Kyle traced it with his finger and looked toward the ridge, toward the ditch. For the time being, he was bound to this brand. It was to him what a cross is to a priest, a reminder not only of responsibility and mission but of an alliance with the destiny of many. On other ranches it would be merely a brand, and a man might say he was "riding for the brand," meaning that he would do whatever had to be done for the good of the ranch. On Keystone saddles, bridles, and holsters, the symbol created deeper feelings in a man, sometimes like he was committed to some incomprehensible great cause.

A log jutted out from a corner of the cabin, and he hung the saddle on that. Neither of the two men had returned. Off on the western wall of the broad mountain valley, the sun flared brightly just before sliding down out of sight. The light remained. *Well,* Kyle mused, *at least some things haven't changed. She still goes down west of here and comes up east of here.*

John returned as the light began to fail and stirred up the fire and cut up something to boil in a pot. The trees across the valley were just a black border when Brother came up the long meadow, leading the pack horse and limping. The horse had not been hard to catch, he explained, near the talus slope, but, in order to get down the mountain again, they had had to go miles along the ridge and then down a shoulder of the mountain.

The three ate together, but without much talk. Afterward, Kyle hobbled the horse, spread his bedroll, and stretched out into a dreamless sleep, his breathing rising in the starlight like thin smoke.

A recognizable and very disagreeable smell woke him. John was standing there, tin plate in one hand and tin cup in the other. There wasn't a sign of a breeze in the crisp early air, but what air movement there was must have been coming from behind the fat man and wafting into Kyle's nostrils. Kyle adjusted his eye patch, sat up, pulled on his Stetson, and stretched.

"Ker f'r some breakfast?" John asked.

"Matter o' fact, yeah. I'm hungry enough to eat rattlesnake."

"Thet was yesterday." John grinned. "This here's some grits I found, and some sheep bacon."

John sat on the stump while Kyle ate, scratching at one armpit until it seemed like he would claw away the red cloth of his undershirt there. After a while he spoke. "Headin' out today, are y'?"

"Yeah," Kyle said.

"Got t' thinkin' last night about that Keystone outfit y' said y' work for."

"Oh?"

"If you was goin' back there, what about maybe takin' Brother along? He'd make a fair hand, y'know, just odd jobs around a place like that. Seems I recalled me hearin' yore boss there takes in strays like him, sometime. Brother, he kin wrassle a hammer pretty good, an' clean up horseshit . . . that kinda stuff."

"I ain't goin' back, not right away," Kyle said. "Maybe I'll check in with you if I do. When I do."

"Yeah. Sure. OK." John leaned sidewise to heave one ponderous hip off the stump and cut loose a gas explosion that startled the horse.

The silence then came back to the morning and the wide valley. High up in the sunlight an eagle called and circled where the carcass of the horse lay in the rocks. But that was the only sound. There was no river to mutter over the pebbles in the riverbed, no sounds of people, no wind.

"John?" Kyle said.

"Yeah?"

"What're you doin' up here? Lonely damn' place."

"Ah, that's me. Long time ago, I figured out I was a come-after. Somebody digs a shit hole mine tunnel, leaves it, I come after an' dig for the low grade stuff they didn't want. Trappers get the prime pelts, leave a cabin, I comes along after 'n' take leftovers. Still an' all, we get us some water down here, pretty soon the beaver be back, we'd wash us some ore. That water'll be back."

"What about Brother?"

"Brother? Ah, jus' another come-after. Had a family somewheres, moved off an' left him. Worked f'r a stage line a time. They up and left him. Me, I come after 'n' found him. Been sorta takin' care of 'im since. Gives me somebody at least t' talk at. Man like me, ain't many as wants to be around."

John pulled himself up off the stump and took the plate and cup back to the cabin. Kyle began to go through his plunder, figuring out what he could take and what he'd have to cache somewhere. It would be good to have a pack animal, but he'd often made long trips without one.

John's request touched him. If ever there was a man who couldn't afford to lose what companionship he had, it was John. And yet he had found a kind of comfortable life for himself, and had room in it for someone like Brother. Probably took care of him more than he let on. *Here I am,* Kyle thought, *ridin' all over the north of creation lookin' to help somebody and do somethin' big with my life before goin' to grass, and here's this John, happy enough to scratch up a little ore or trap a few stray muskrat. And take care of Brother. Maybe I'd oughta throw in with the two of 'em and stay right here. Wait for the damn' water to come back, take care of each other, not worry about who lives over the next ridge there. To hell with it!*

He went on repacking, in spite of his thoughts. This wasn't the place. He knew that. Pretty soon he had a pile of stuff on the packsaddle tarp. A jay bird flew down to sit on the cabin ridgepole where it could keep on eye on what he was doing, just in case there was going to be any food thrown away.

Kyle figured he would put what he needed into a pack behind the saddle and then cache the rest somewhere near here. Where he was bound, or when he would be back, he couldn't say—but somehow it felt good to him, the thought of leaving something behind to come back for. At least that would be something.

The cabin door slammed, and Brother headed for his favorite morning bush. That done, he looked around as if expecting to see something he had not seen every morning for the past months. He spotted Kyle kneeling over the packs and supplies.

"Figgerin' on gettin' goin'," he said.

"Might as well," Kyle said. "Won't get anything done sittin' around here."

"Well, I'm shore sorry about that horse," Brother said, coming near to look over Kyle's plunder pile for something he might use.

"Me, too," Kyle said. "Now I'm gonna have to travel light a while. Have to find a place to cache this stuff."

"Aw, y' kin leave it here. Me 'n' John, we'll look after it."

"No offense, Brother, but you and John don't strike me as bein' too permanent, if you know what I mean. No tellin' how long I'll be."

"Yeah, that's right," Brother said. "John, he gets enough water, mebbe in the spring, he says we're gonna sluice that ore an' get out. Find us a nice place somewheres."

"That's it," Kyle said. "So I'll just leave this somewhere I can find it again. Make a cache. Sure could use a pack horse, though."

"Mule?"

"What?"

"That crazy ol' guy down th' valley, he might could have a mule. Had one onct."

"What're you talking about?"

"There's that crazy ol' guy down th' valley might have a mule, that's all."

"How far we talkin' down the valley?"

"I don't know. On a horse, you'd be there by lunch time. Wouldn't get none, though. He don't talk so's you kin understand 'im."

"He don't, eh?" Kyle said.

"He's a furriner of some kind. Hell if I know what. Jabbers some kinda furrin talk. He's even got him a big furrin flag on a pole down there, flyin' over his house like he thinks this ain't America. Funny-lookin' red thing with blue."

"You seen any mules there? You think he's got a mule for sale?"

"Seen two, anyway. Made th' trip t' the store 'bout the same time as me 'n John, an' he packed 'em both with groceries and such. Me an' John, we gotta go do that again here pretty soon. He says he don't know what I do with all that food, but come first snow we're gonna be 'bout out."

"How do I find this place without wandering around half the countryside?"

Brother pointed excitedly, glad to know something someone else wanted to know. "See that there lump, yonder. That hill? Kinda like a big loafa bread?"

Kyle saw it, the knoll sticking out from the mountain that formed the side of the valley. It was where he understood Brother had gone to get the pack horse down off the talus slope.

"Jus' you ride up that a little, you'll see. See that damn' furrin flag, anyways. That's th' place. Reckon he's on the same river here, 'cept he ain't got no more water'n we got."

John verified what Brother had said, adding that the crazy "furriner" was probably a Norwegian or something like that. John had heard Norwegian spoken once, and it sounded like what the old man yelled. That was another problem with talking to him, according to John. Once he figured you couldn't understand him, the "furriner" increased his volume to make you understand. " 'Tween yellin' and gettin' mad at everybody, nobody kin figger out what the hell he wants. But I dunno, maybe show 'im some money an' point at one o' his mules, he might dicker."

Kyle wrapped his spare equipment and his canned provisions into the bigger tarp, and, with John supervising and Brother helping, he cleaned out a dilapidated little log dugout under a boulder up the hill. He hoped it would look like a caved-in prospecting hole to anybody curious. No other way to hide any kind of cache in this place.

John and Brother wished him well as he rode off. "Get back, now!"

"Oh, yeah," Kyle said. "I'll just see what this fella has by way of livestock, then I'll stop back this way. Main thing's to see about this big ditch project and this foreman with the handy rifle."

Kyle rode off, glad to have something to do, something that had a possible outcome. The horse seemed to have more energy, now that it was free of the dead weight of the packs and moving again.

Chapter Seven

A Fisherman Far from the Sea

Kyle slabbed the side of the hill, letting the horse pick the easiest part of the slope, until he came out on the crest and saw the flag, still far away, flying above the dark trees against the dry blue of the sky. All Kyle had to do was to follow the empty riverbed, take short cuts across the bends, and he'd be there.

One of the short cuts took him over a brown meadow that water could make into good pasture. The whole valley would make good summer cattle country, if there were water. Riding down again onto the river rocks, Kyle heard one of the horse's hoofs *clank,* and he knew the shoe was loose. He got down, hoisted the hoof, pounded the nail back in with a rock, clenched it, and figured it would hold. He thought about the blacksmith and about making his own shoe, and it seemed like a hundred years back that it had happened.

Through the next short cut, in the brittle grass, the horse spooked a good-size rabbit. Kyle halted and pulled the Winchester, although he'd never see that particular rabbit again. But there might be a chance at something. . . . deer, even. He jacked a cartridge into the chamber and rode with the rifle across the saddle.

The foreigner had seen Kyle coming for the past mile or more. He stood with his hands on his hips, waiting. Behind him was a cabin built right down on the edge of the river, and a shed of sorts and a corral.

Kyle got close enough to determine that the foreigner was short and bald—and hatless—and wore a homespun shirt under the bib of a pair of baggy wool overalls, or heavy pants that looked like overalls. A woman put her head out of the cabin, and the man screamed at her in some language Kyle had never heard. His voice was high-pitched and frightened.

The woman, even smaller than the man, came trotting to him as fast as her many petticoats and heavy shoes would allow, carrying a long-barrel shotgun. Kyle realized, too late, that he shouldn't be carrying his rifle at the ready across his saddle; it did look like he was riding up to their place ready for trouble. He held it up with one hand and slid it down into the scabbard.

Kyle put on his best apologetic grin and rode forward. And he kept grinning; a scared and nervous man with a shotgun is more dangerous than a cornered rattler. He stopped the horse at a respectful distance and slid to the ground, grinning so hard his face was getting tired.

"Nice mornin'," he said, although it was probably more like afternoon.

The foreigner said nothing. Kyle looked around. The whole farm seemed to consist of that one shed and corral, the cabin, and a kind of grain bin standing hopefully beside the dry field. The shed leaned, and the cabin and granary were pretty crude attempts at carpentry. A heavy plow stood in a furrow in a garden beside the corral. The furrows were as crooked at the fence posts. Not too promising. No feed in sight, no livestock. The house was built right next to the river, probably to get closer to the only water supply around, but it was not a smart place to put a building. The mountain rivers could flood, come spring melt. Then Kyle spotted a fishing net hanging on the cabin wall. A funny thing to have on a farm in the mountains.

The fellow waved the antique firearm and screeched something at Kyle, in a volume that surprised him. For a small man, he could sure make himself heard.

"Sorry," Kyle said, shrugging his shoulders, "don't know what you're sayin'." He pointed up to the flag flying from the tall pole. "What country?"

"Ha?"

"Country. Where you from?"

"Ha?"

"Farmer, are you?" Kyle said. "You a farmer? You know." Kyle began to make digging movements with his hands, then held his hands like he was guiding a plow. "What're you growin'?"

Kyle continued his pantomime, and then the woman, who had been peering out from behind the man, jabbered something and stomped back toward the cabin. She had understood, and it was apparently a sore topic. Then the man got it, too.

"Na," he said. He made motions as if he were washing out some laundry at a tub. Or using that fishing net. The fellow was a fisherman. For some reason, probably known only to God, he had wandered into this empty valley a mile above the sea. It was obvious he didn't know what he was doing. Equally obvious, he didn't have any extra horse or mule to sell; if he had a team, he probably would have fixed that old wagon and gotten to hell out of there.

"Anybody livin' below here?" Kyle said, pointing downstream. "Neighbors? A ranch?"

The small foreigner looked in the direction Kyle pointed, but, when he turned again to Kyle, his face wore the blank and gloomy expression as before. He did not speak; he did not even gesture or shrug. He merely stood staring at Kyle, dumbly.

"People?" Kyle said, gesturing downstream again. "Any people there?"

The reply was the same. Nothing. Just a slight, sad shaking of the head. The little man looked back toward the cabin where his wife had disappeared. Kyle understood—drawn here by some hope, these two found themselves alone in all the world, unable even to speak with passing strangers, with only each other to talk to. Kyle raised his hand in farewell, reined the horse around, and rode slowly back the way he had come.

A long time later he gained the rise of ground at the bend in the river and looked back to see the flag, a tiny rectangle now, lifting and turning to the movements of the cañon breezes.

John and Brother and Kyle dined that night on a young deer that had crossed Kyle's path. John made fresh biscuits, large and reasonably light. After John had finished off his third steak and second pan of biscuits, he belched contentedly and leaned back against a stump. Kyle, too, felt a great sense of ease coming over him. The early evening air, the high valley, the warm fire, coffee, and a bit of companionship could persuade a man to stay.

Brother was looking at the rim of the mountains as if he had never noticed they were there before. Brother spent a lot of his time staring at things.

"John," he said in a whisper, "John, I just seen it again."

"Same place?" John said, without opening his eyes.

"Yep, same place, John. Jus' a little bitty one, but she's a fire all right."

"Where's a fire?" Kyle said.

Brother came over, knelt beside him, and extended his arm so it pointed up the cañon, putting his head in front of Kyle's like maybe he expected Kyle to look through his head.

"Brother's got good eyes, he has," said John. "Good eyes."

"Right there," Brother said. "See that fire? That there flicker there?"

Kyle did see it, far, far up near the summit of the peak, far above the gorge that stretched up into darkness. It seemed to be a fire. Like a campfire, nothing larger.

"Know who it is, do you?" he said to both of his companions.

"I seen him," Brother said, "but John never. John, he tol' you there's that there big ol' gate holdin' the water back up there. Well, one night I seen that fire way far up over yonder and figger it's somebody works on that ditch or somethin'. Figger what the hell, I'd go up with a pick next day and make out like I's lookin' fer a job on the ditch. An' iffen I don't find nobody, I figgered to dig under it y' know and make some water come. Jus' enough for the sluice." He stopped, and his eyes went wandering the horizon again.

"So you saw him?" Kyle said.

"Hah? Oh, him? Ugly sonuvabitch. And big. Hunched like, but big. Shit, John's big and he'd make two of John, easy. And he was like you, only ugly."

"Like me?" Kyle said.

"Yeah, y'know, one eye. Only he never wore no patch. I couldn't' see that he'd ever had no other eye. Just the one. He's a cripple."

"Otherwise, he was just like me, then." Kyle smiled.

"Yuh, only black," Brother said.

"Black? Y'mean he's colored?"

"No," John explained. "Not colored. Black. He's more

like a white man . . . only one that got burned black, somehow. I seen him in broad daylight once."

Kyle looked at John thoughtfully, then back at Brother.

"So what happened?"

"He sics the god-damn' animals on me, that's what happened. I'm pickin' an' diggin' at one end of thet gate, not doin' too bad, and I hears a big laugh up above, so I climbs up th' ditchbank and there he sits on t'other side, like a big damn' toad on a rock. 'That ain't fur you t' do,' he says, and I gives him some argument, and he says it again. 'That ain't fur you t' do' . . . only he talks nice."

"This the same man as told you about a castle an' all?" Kyle asked.

"Yeah. Well, him bein' so black kinda takes me down a notch, but then I asks him who he thinks that there water belongs t', and he says the folks at the castle. Just like that. Like I know what the hell he's talkin' about. Folks at the castle. So I says to 'im, I figger just t' take a little of it anyways 'cause it belongs in this here valley an' not over yonder, an' so I slides back down that ditchbank with m' pick, see.

"So he says it again . . . 'that ain't fur you t' do' . . . an' he's got this big rock bar with 'im, six foot of steel, an' he bangs on his rock with it and, s' help me God, next thing I knowed he just ain't there. There's this here *clang*, and he ain't there. I start back down to where I left the pick, only now I starts to hear animal noises comin'. Growls like, and sounds of big feet. I got the hell outta there."

"And this really happened to you?" Kyle said. "You didn't maybe dream it or somethin'?"

"Hell, no. It happened. I kin show y' the pick I had with me. John, where the hell is that pick?"

"Brother," John said sleepily, "that pick don't prove nuthin. I seen him, too, y'know. I believe y'."

106

"Well, I wanna show that pick to 'im anyway. Where the hell is it?"

"I think we lost it. Or it's over to the claim."

"Well, damn," said Brother, staring into the remains of the fire.

Kyle rolled into his blankets and curled on his side to watch the flickering flames as they died. Presently John slumped to the ground where he began to shiver and snore, then jerked awake again. He got up, hugging himself for warmth, and lurched off toward the cabin to fall into his bed. Brother stood and stretched and followed, pausing to sprinkle his usual bush on the way. " 'Night," he said.

" 'Night" Kyle replied. A last spike of flame danced and wavered along the top of a charred stick until the stick broke and fell in glowing embers and all was dark save for the small ruby glow in the center of the ashes. Kyle looked toward the far, high mountain where the tiny glow of a fire had been, but darkness now covered it. *Come morning,* he thought, *I might go see this ditch.* And before the last glow of the embers was gone, his eye was closed and he was asleep.

The sky was light, but the sun was still below the eastern ridge when Kyle finished strapping his gear on behind the saddle. As he swung aboard, John came waddling out, scratching and yawning. He looked at Kyle curiously. "Comin' back anytime?" he asked.

"Figure to," Kyle said. "Want to see that ditch for myself."

"Hope you'll give thought to what I asked y'. About Brother. Takin' him outta here with y', when y' go."

"I will."

Brother made his appearance, frowning as he tried to figure why Kyle was already in the saddle before breakfast.

He finished his business with the bush and walked over to pat the horse on the shoulder.

"Goin' up there, huh?" he said.

"Yeah."

"Be a while?"

"Might. Dunno."

"Maybe I'll follow y' up, after a whiles," Brother said. "Maybe bring along that Henry. Give y' some ar-tillery if y' need it." He had a sudden thought. "Say! Careful what y' shoot at! Maybe be me, see, crawlin' up t' help."

"I'll watch it," Kyle said.

"Watch out f'r that Foreman," John added. "Sees y', he'll shoot y'."

"Thanks for the word," Kyle said.

He rode off up the gorge on a trail that was dim and little used. It took him around faint switchbacks and at times became so steep the horse had to hunch its shoulders and dig with all four hoofs as rocks and dirt rolled away down the slope. Three times Kyle dismounted and went ahead on foot to find the trail, sometimes marked by only a few piles of droppings from bighorn sheep.

The air up here was still. The heat of an intense sun put pine scent in the air and made the rocks radiate warmth. The trail doubled back around noon. There was an opening ahead that turned out to be rubble and slag from the great ditch. It made an immense slope of raw golden sand and broken golden rock where it slid down to the edge of the forest, burying part of the forest as it came, and it stretched along the mountain for miles.

Kyle found a flat clearing under the ditch where a seep of water ran and green grass sprouted, and there he picketed the horse while he climbed the embankment. His boots slid back down a foot for every two feet of progress he made, and he was soon clutching dirt with both hands to keep his balance and to keep going. But at last, breathless, he hoisted himself over the rim and stood on the broad top of the dike itself.

The air down in the forest had been still, but up here mountain wind flopped the brim of his hat and whipped at his sleeve. Far, far below he could make out the tiny cabins and a slender column of smoke rising. John had a fire going. He tried to see the foreigner's flag farther down the valley, but if he saw anything, it was probably in his imagination.

The ditch was wide enough for two wagons to be down in it, side by side, and deep enough to hide a rider. Water came up within a foot of the brim, moving so silently and undisturbed it seemed invisible, more like an illusion of water.

From the way the ditch bent around to follow contours, Kyle figured the log gate must be upstream. He walked that way, his hand on his Winchester. Be a hell of a place to get crosswise with that ditch rider and his rifle. Wide open target.

He came to a bend in the ditch from which he could see quite a way downstream. There didn't look to be any gates or breaks in the ditchbank. He kept on walking upstream, and just around another bend he came to the gate. Like the other ditch gate, this was a log wall. The logs were spruce, two to three feet thick and probably twenty feet long, held at either end by huge uprights. The center was buttressed by the thickest log of all. The gate was bound in iron bands with iron rings for lifting. But what force could possibly lift it? There was no winch, no mechanism. The whole road was entirely bare except for a flat round rock next to one end of the gate.

Kyle stood looking at the faraway smoke of John's cooking fire. John and Brother would be in the cabin, most likely, taking a *siesta* while a piece of meat roasted in the coals. Kyle looked farther down the valley and imagined the little fisherman hacking out a trench to his crooked furrows in hopes the river would come back.

The voice spoke from behind him.

"You'd be a Keystone rider," the voice said. "The second one!" It laughed.

Kyle turned, bringing the Winchester up. He would never doubt Brother again. The creature was just like Brother said: shaped like a toad and black as if he'd been burned, squatting on a boulder across the ditch. He wore a leather hunting shirt and leggings, and in one black hand he held an iron bar a good six feet long, like a man would hold a walking stick. His one eye was slightly to one side of his flattened nose; of his other eye there seemed no sign at all, not so much as a scar.

"How'd you get over there?" Kyle asked.

"How'd *you* get over there?" he retorted. "Thinking of trying to open that gate Number Six, are you?"

"Thought I would," Kyle said. "People down below can use some of that water."

The creature pointed eastward with his bar. "People down below there can use that water, too."

"You know how to work these gates?" Kyle asked.

"Don't you?" He squatted on his rock, his eye unblinking.

Kyle ignored him and kicked at the top log. If he could knock it loose, plenty of water would run over the top. If he got two logs loose it would make a regular river. If he had a long pole, like a fence rail, for a lever. . . .

"You could try to open it," said the squatting stranger in leather, "or you could try marching 'round it for seven days and nights, then blow your horn. They say it worked at Jericho."

"I don't have a horn," Kyle said.

"Too bad. Now, if you had my staff"—he indicated the long iron bar—"you might tap that round rock and make the water come, like Moses. It worked for him in the desert."

"I ain't Moses."

"Too bad."

"Where's all this water goin', anyway?" Kyle asked.

"Is that your question for the day? You only get one answer a day."

Kyle took out his bandanna and wiped the inside of his eye patch with it. It was hot in the open sun. "Have it your way," he said.

"All right. It goes wherever the ditch takes it, cowboy. Some to a lake, rather far from here. Some to other ditches, other destinations. Like life!!" He laughed and shook until it seemed he would topple off his rock. "But right now, this water from this side of the big divide goes . . ."—he pointed far to the east with his iron bar—"just into another river. Until needed. Water doesn't always know where it's best needed, does it?"

"So who figgers they know? Who's got the water rights to all this drainage here?" He heard the clang of iron on rock and turned, and the creature with the one eye was gone.

John and Brother were not surprised to hear Kyle's story. They had plenty of suggestions for his return visit to the great ditch gate, too.

"If'n we had blastin' powder, y' could blast 'er," Brother said. " 'Cept we ain't."

"Could y' dig under it?" John asked. "Maybe with a pick and shovel a man could make a hole under it, let the water do the rest."

"I wondered if those logs might float up if I got the iron bands off 'em," Kyle said.

And so it went into the night, around the fire, the three of them planning fantastic schemes like small boys plotting Halloween mischief. Use an augur to make holes in it; use a horse and rope to pull it over; get a big old pipe (if they had one) and make a siphon. Start a landslide across the ditch and that would dam it and make it overflow. Kyle took none of it seriously, but, sitting there with John and Brother, feeding small sticks into the fire, swapping lies and plans as the night around them grew dark and cold, he felt peaceful and at rest.

He waited a day, then rode back up the gorge to the ditch, back to the log wall holding the water from the valley, carrying a pick and shovel.

Kyle stripped off his shirt and began to dig, only to run into bedrock under the bottom logs. He shifted to the far end, where Brother had managed to start a hole next to the upright support. He thought about digging out the center log, but it was set into a hole nearly four feet across, bored into the solid granite of the mountain. How that had been accomplished he had no way of knowing. . . .

Clang! Clang! Clang!

The ringing of iron on stone. And again: *clang, clang, clang!*

Kyle dropped the pick and grabbed up the Winchester. He scrambled to the top of the embankment. Across the water, sitting like a huge toad, was the creature in leather hunting shirt and leggings, with his one eye and iron bar. Seeing he had summoned Kyle and made him climb the bank, he gleefully struck his bar on the rock again. *Clang!*

"Keystone man!" he shouted across the running ditch. "More questions for today?"

"Same question. What's all this water bein' used for? What's it good for?"

"What's water good for?" the other one mocked.

"Could run a mill," Kyle said, thinking out loud, "but

there ain't any down in that country east of here, not that I know of. Not that big."

"No grinding grain nor sawing logs, then!" The other laughed. "Good! Try again!"

"Maybe it runs clear to the Platte, so's boats can come up. But who'd ride on 'em? Nuthin' around there for miles. Could carry logs, I guess, but who'd want 'em."

"Just right, just right. None of those things!" He laughed and clanged his bar on the rock.

"So what *does* it do?"

"That your question, what does the water do?"

"Yeah."

The black shape laughed again. "Cowboy, it follows the course made for it. Of course . . . hah! . . . some of it evaporates and escapes the ditch, but the clouds bring it back. It will water a acre of oats for your horse. Or drown your horse. Or you. Then it comes back on the wind to do it all over again."

"You said it goes to a lake."

"Ah! Once a beautiful valley of grass and flowers where the deer grazed. Living things, you understand. Now the grass and trees and flowers and bushes are dead muck drowned under water. Hah! But it could make life, if it would."

"That ain't much of an answer. Why don't you just tell me how to get this gate open, at least a little ways?"

"One answer a day, Mister Keystone, one a day. Tell you a secret, though. You'll never lift it because that isn't the way it works. Hah!" And he rose and went off, clanking his bar on the rocks. "Not the way it works!" he called back, shaking his huge head as if he had just heard the best joke in all the world.

The next day, Kyle ambled up to John's gold diggings and politely admired all the work that had gone into it. John and

Brother had accumulated a great pile of ore to wash for gold, when the water came in spring, or whenever it came.

The following day, he again rode up the gorge to confront the gate. This time he carried a steel pry bar he had borrowed from John's diggings. If anything was logical about this irrigation deal, and nothing was, it might be that the one-eyed man somehow used his steel bar to regulate the gates and the ditch flow.

Kyle hobbled the horse and left it in a good patch of grass a safe distance from the log gate, just in case he did make the water flow. He clambered up the bank and walked up the current to the gate. There was no way to get a purchase on any part of it with his bar. He could stretch out and just about reach the iron band nearest him, but had no fulcrum to rest the bar on. He admitted that he was just killing time, waiting to see if the creature showed up. He stuck the tip of the bar under the round flat rock, the only thing loose on the road or near the gate, and began to move it closer to the edge. Might use it as a fulcrum. Under the rock was a deep hole. It ran down out of sight next to the log barrier. It looked like a post hole. If a man had a long post to put down there and a long beam like a hay derrick, he might hook onto that ring and lift that gate.

"Ought to watch your back, cowboy," came the voice from across the ditch. "Men have been shot."

Kyle turned. The one-eyed man had settled his bulk on a rock, toad-like, as before; he was sipping from a bright metal cup the size of a saucepan.

"You're talkin' about the one they call The Foreman, I guess," Kyle said. "Been wonderin' if he'd show up."

"A wonder . . . if he would show up," the other mocked. "If he showed up."

"Not around, is he?" Kyle said. "Dead, maybe?"

114

"Not yet," said the other. "He may be with The Lady. He may be at the headwaters, thinking about his fate."

"Knows his fate, does he?" Kyle asked. "And what would that be?"

"Ask The Lady."

To Kyle, the conversation made no sense, except to tell him that the rifleman would not be showing up any time soon. This other character was probably taking over the job of keeping an eye on the ditch.

"The other day you said you knew how to open this gate," Kyle observed.

"Is that your question? You want to know the key, now that you found the keyhole!" He rocked his fat body back and forth at his own humor, banging the tin cup on the rock in great glee. "Last question!" he chortled.

"OK. Where's the key, then?" Kyle said.

The dark little man did not reply, but leaned out and scooped up water from the running ditch. He drank it in three gulps. "Care for some?" he said, hurling the oversize tin cup toward Kyle.

Kyle caught the cup. The sun was hot, and he was thirsty. He knelt at the side of the ditch, dipped water, drank. The chill of it made his teeth hurt. A man could freeze to death in that water.

The one-eyed man heaved himself to his feet and began to melt away into the trees.

"Hey!" Kyle yelled. "You said there's a key. A way to let some water out of this ditch!"

"In your hand, Mister Keystone! It's in your hand!!" His laugh boomed out and seemed to bend the trees in his path, and then he was gone.

Chapter Eight

Blood for Water

Kyle once more dipped the cup, which held almost enough to fill a canteen. He sat on the round rock and looked down the valley and drank. The water chilled his teeth. He poured the rest of it over the embankment, watching it soak into the loose gravel.

The key. Quite a joke on him, all right. The key. "Now you found the keyhole, you want the key." The cackling toad must have escaped from some asylum somewhere. "Found the keyhole."

But maybe the hole *was* the key. It didn't make any sense, but neither did anything else around here. He went over and knelt by the hole, then tried to fit the tin cup into it. It almost fit. Almost.

"Horseshit," Kyle said.

He rose and walked the ditch, back and forth, watching the gleaming sheet of water flowing, gazing down the valley, trying to figure out where the ditch was headed. Made sense that it would end up dumping into a river, eventually. Even a reservoir could hold only so much. But what river? It must be one that was farther north than he'd ever been.

He returned to stare down into the hole. Could be a drain of some kind? It could come out down below somewhere. If it did, and a man dragged some logs down to block the ditch, it might divert water down that drain. It sat lower than the top of the gate, that was for sure. You could dig a shallow ditch to get the water to it, except that it was in solid rock.

Kyle took a pebble and dropped it into the hole. There was a clatter as it bounced on the sides, but he didn't hear it hit bottom. He needed a way to find out where it went. It came to him. Just like the black toad had said. He had the answer in his hand.

The first cupfuls of water wouldn't do much, but if he poured enough water down the hole, he'd be able look around and find where it had run out. If it did.

He dipped the first cupful and poured it, listening as it gurgled down into the darkness. Another cupful, and another, and still another. And then it happened. He was scooping more water from the ditch when there suddenly came the sound of slabs of granite scraping together. The ditchbank trembled. The grinding got louder and louder, and the ditchbank shook harder, and the grinding sound gave way to a deep rumble.

The gate was turning, a groaning inch at a time, pivoting on its center post. The rumbling noise kept up, and the opening became a hand's span wide, and water was pouring through. The gate kept edging outward. The flow of water became a waterfall. When the opening got to be a foot wide, the ground jumped and shook under Kyle. There came a heavy thud from down below, and the gate stopped moving.

Water rushed around both sides of the log barrier, tearing down the steep slope, sweeping up broken rock and hurling it into the trees. More and more water dislodged more and more rock to go careening down toward the cañon. Kyle could see treetops shaking as their trunks were hit by the boulders. One tree and then another toppled, their old dry roots undermined by rushing mud and silt.

He was glad the gate had stopped pivoting. There was more than enough water plunging down toward the dry riverbed. John and Brother and that foreigner of a farmer would be tickled to see it coming, and so would those settlers John had said were living farther down the valley. It was a good thing the horse was picketed in a clearing a safe distance away.

Kyle looked over the edge and down at the gate's foundations, down where he and Brother had dug some of the rock and earth away. Rushing water was finishing their job. It was washing dirt and gravel out of the hole, lifting big rocks and toppling them down the slope. The force of it undermined an enormous slab of granite that gave way with a crack echoing off of the peaks like a cannon. The flood scooped the ground from under another heavier slab, and it fell over and bashed the end of the gate farther outward. Logs groaned like living things and then split as they were twisted. The entire structure began to lean.

The power of the water now went to work in earnest. Kyle heard the awful cracking of heavy wood breaking. The ditch current pushed the gate farther, a few shrieking inches at a time, bending the barricade. More and yet more water went roaring through the gap.

Kyle dropped the cup and ran along the embankment until he was above the patch of grass where the horse was. The horse was heaving its hobbled forelegs up and down and whinnying in fright, and Kyle knew that he should try to calm the animal, but he couldn't do anything except stand there, watching, as the water plummeted out of the broad ditch with awful force and went racing through the forest, throwing trees aside like matchsticks, making a howling din as if all hell had been turned loose.

Far below, on the cañon floor, the riverbed was already a

writhing serpent of mud pushing tons of débris in a thick gumbo of silt and rock and shattered trees. The monster hit the bends of the old riverbed, where it heaved upward and came crashing down full length. Trees along the banks shuddered and fell into the current, adding their weight to the weight of the muck, becoming battering rams.

Kyle saw it hit John's and Brother's mine tunnel, and it took it out, all of the stockpiled ore, the slag pile, the timber props, tools, tunnel and all, all of it gone in a second. And the brown force flowed on. He caught a glimpse of the tiny dot of their cabin an instant before the torrent flowed over it.

The valley grew more quiet. The flow of escaping water settled into a steady, dirty river pouring down through the fresh gouge. Every creek and snowmelt trickle and stream that the ditch intercepted was now flowing down into the valley. Kyle imagined John and Brother being caught in the flood and carried away, drowned. His eye stared, unblinking, down at the spot where they had once lived. The stinking cots, the hearth deep in old ash, the hanging deerskin bags of meat and bread. John's outdoor fire pit, Brother's favorite pee bush. One tear, and then others came hot to Kyle's eye and ran down his cheek. How had John died? With a sudden lungful of silt-thick water, or a broken neck from a floating tree log, or a cracked skull from a rock?

He imagined the hellish mass taking the boys with it when it boiled around the river bend below their place and sweeping down on the Norwegian and his wife and their poor cabin, taking them down to God knows where. The pitiful little man had probably stood there with his old rifle, watching it come, and helpless to defend the old lady.

Kyle turned away and sank to his knees. His stomach heaved and heaved; bitter vomit choked off his breath until he was pale and gasping and shaking. The dry earth soaked up his vomit without concern, without pity.

How long he remained there on his knees, he could not say. The spasms clenching at his stomach ceased after a time, and the cloudy, sour spittle stopped running down into the stubble of his beard and began to dry. It was stinking, like the puke on his shirt.

The sun had moved a good distance in the afternoon sky when Kyle finally lurched up onto his feet and stood, weak and shaking. When he moved forward, one leg seemed to drag on the gravel. Automatically he drew out his bandanna and wiped the inside of his eye patch.

His eye fell on the oversize cup shining in the sunlight where he had dropped it. A few sips of water remained in it, but, when he drank, he found it even more bitter than his vomit. Before the flood, the water had been sweet and cold and clear as crystal; now it looked cloudy and tasted like acid on the tongue. He drew back his arm and hurled the damned thing as far as he could into the black forest.

Kyle scanned the woods for the one-eyed man, but he was nowhere to be seen. Just the dark shadows of the spruce, the whisper of the mountain breeze in the top branches, the steady burbling and hiss of the water flowing through the gate and down the valley.

He heard the clattering scramble of hoofs on loose rock. The horse had broken its hobbles and was clawing its way up the angle of the ditchbank. It reached the flat expanse on top, where it stopped and stood with its head down and its breath coming hard, eyes wide and staring stupidly at Kyle. Kyle walked slowly forward, making soothing sounds to the horse until he could put out a hand and take hold of the halter. Both his hands and his voice were still shaking.

Kyle was too empty and his muscles were trembling too much even to think of riding, so he took the reins and, leading the horse, walked down the ditch. After a time they came to a place where the ditch builders had engineered another log wall into the earth embankment. It was twenty, maybe thirty feet long, and was topped with a narrow catwalk made of halved logs. They had made a narrow trail down into the ditch at that point. Kyle led the horse down it, knowing that the animal would never go across the catwalk.

The bottom of the ditch still had a little water in it. The horse tried to avoid stepping in the deeper places and did not stop to drink. The walking was easy, and Kyle began to recover his strength. He wiped sweat out of his eye patch and swung up into the saddle. The horse moved forward again.

Something was there. In the trees, off to his left, something white, gleaming for just a split second in among the dense shadows. Kyle pulled the horse up and dragged the Winchester from the scabbard. There it was again. Just a quick flash of something white, something moving.

He held the Winchester across his left arm and wondered how many shots were in the magazine. And how many he had with him, altogether. There was a box of Winchester cartridges in the saddlebags, he knew that; his cartridge belt probably had a dozen or more for the Colt. All of his remaining ammunition, equipment, spare clothing, everything, was in the cache down at the cabin. Gone, now. Everything Kyle had in the world was in the saddlebags and in his pockets. All else was gone, washed away. Whatever he had now, and it wasn't much, he had with him. Kyle suddenly thought of how Will had come back to the Keystone with nothing.

Another glimpse of the white thing in the trees. Kyle had never seen a Rocky Mountain goat, but he had heard about them, that they were stark white. But this figure was upright, like a man. Smaller, like a boy.

There was no way to get out of the ditch, so, if this was an ambush, they had him dead to rights. Ever since the last log wall, the ditch had become very gradually deeper, the sides more perpendicular. It cut through a big shoulder of the mountain, and he guessed that was why it got deeper in through here.

If this was an ambush . . . there was no cover, none. Kyle swung down and put the horse between himself and the last place he had seen the flash of white. He put a hand in the halter and led the horse along that way, the rifle ready in his other hand.

He walked slowly. He expected a shot to come out of the trees at any moment. But what came from the dense shadows was not a shot, but a voice. A high, faint, feminine voice. It was more of a whisper, but Kyle heard every word clearly.

"He is coming," the voice whispered. And again, without pausing: "He is coming."

Kyle stopped and tried to see who it was.

"He is coming."

Kyle aimed the Winchester in the direction from which the voice seemed to be coming.

"You want to show yourself?" he said.

"He is coming. Be ready."

"OK, who's coming?"

"The one to fear."

"One to fear. You mean that Foreman character?" Made sense. Whatever this ditch was, wherever it went, it had suddenly stopped running, and somebody was certain to come to find out why.

"Where's there a way out of here?" he said to the trees. He could see a little bit of white and knew that she—whoever she was—was standing behind a thick pine.

"You cannot," she said.

"No, I mean how to get outta this ditch. Too steep to climb the horse out, and I sure ain't leavin' him here."

"There is a way," she said, "but it is closed to you. It opens to The Guardian. You must ride to the end. Except . . . except that The Guardian is coming and is between you and the end."

"I appreciate the warning," Kyle said. "I'll just have to get past him, then. Much obliged." He stepped to the stirrup and into the saddle.

"No!" She moved from behind the tree, but stayed in the shadows. She was young and small, with long loose hair. Over her long white dress she wore a thick cloak, also made of white material. "No," she said softly. "He is strong. You will only prevail upstream from him. His power is from the way the water runs . . . if you allow him to pass you and come at you from upstream, he will prevail over you. He will prevail. Keep the flow at your back, Keystone rider."

"Prevail?" Kyle said. "You mean kill me?"

But she was gone.

Well, this was interesting. If he turned tail and made a run for it, this Guardian character would back shoot him for sure. According to the weird woman, if he let the *hombre* get upstream, he'd "prevail" which probably wasn't good. And as long as he was in the ditch, Kyle didn't have a speck of good cover or any way either to run or make a stand.

Down the ditch he had a glimpse of her standing in the open on a rock outcropping where the ditch turned a corner. Kyle rode there and sat on his horse, looking up at her.

"Who are you, anyway?" he said.

"I live with The Lady who owns the water, that is all. I am no one important. She is important."

"Owns the water. Lady, there ain't nobody owns the water. It oughta be free to go anywhere, and folks who need it oughta be able to have it."

"She guides the water to greater ends than you can imagine. Therefore, she owns the water."

"And The Guardian?"

"She owns him. And me. Should you be alive tomorrow at evening, she will own you."

"Nobody owns me! So you gonna come down here? How you gonna get home?"

"That is of no matter. She sends the water and gives it purpose. She will send you where she will, should you be alive tomorrow evening. Should you be alive."

Kyle would have asked how she knew all this, except that the horse whickered, jerked its head up, and set its ears. The wet sand was thrumming to a far-off thud of hoof beats—the hoof beats of a very heavy horse coming toward him in the ditch.

"Tell you again," he said to the figure in white, "I go where I want. We'll see about this tomorrow stuff, but I'll tell you right now, I don't belong to nobody. And I go where I want to. Even if I don't know where the hell that is," he added this last under his breath, but she was already gone, vanished as completely as before.

The beat of the heavy hoofs came on. The bend in the ditch offered him the only chance of protection he had, so Kyle urged the horse to the side and hugged the rock, held his breath, and waited. The rider wouldn't see him until he was maybe ten yards away. And that's when the fun would start.

If Kyle had the ancient gift of backward sight, he might have looked back through untold generations and seen one of his forebears creeping through a mist-cloaked moor in ancient Ireland. His ancestor, also, had known the sound of hoof beats approaching; his ancestor had known about goblin men and faerie maids, and he had known the thing that was happening. A wyrding it was, a moment in the life of a fighting man. It came out of nowhere and passed on into song. Wyrdings caught the fighting man unaware and always alone, and in the wyrding he could see what others could not and could hear more keenly than a hound or a hare.

That Irish ancestor had gone to his grave, and centuries had rolled by, and now another strange fight was poised to happen in a wide, deep ditch cutting the spine of the Rocky Mountains. It would be between two men entirely alone, watched only by the trees and the soaring hawk. No words would pass between them, not even to give the reason for the battle. They would come upon each other in terrible remoteness and with awful antipathy, he who sought to know the destiny of the mountain water and he whose fate had made him Guardian of the source.

The hoof beats were farther away than they sounded. Everything sounded louder, down in the ditch, from the call of some remote bird in the forest to the little *whush* of a breeze pushing at a treetop. Kyle changed his mind about the advantage of being mounted; he dropped out of the saddle again and looked around for somewhere to tie the horse. In a niche in the corner of the ditch there was a jagged rock sticking out, large enough to tie the reins to.

He dug into one of the saddlebags and brought out his Bowie, a thick-bladed knife he rarely carried on his belt because it was heavy and got in the way. Mostly it was a camp knife, good for slicing a deer open or for cutting the chine to make a venison roast. He stuck it, sheath and all, into the back of his belt. He eased his way back to the corner of the rock and listened.

He heard talking a long way away, a long way down the ditch, loud talk like somebody was mad. Then there was silence, then more of the raised voice. Next he heard a banging noise, the noise of that iron bar hitting against the rock. Three times. Then a laugh, followed by silence. The Guardian must have been riding up the ditch and come across the black toad-shaped one, maybe blaming him for the ditch losing its water.

Kyle flattened himself against the cool granite. He couldn't judge the distance to the voice, for some reason. He reckoned that, if he stepped out into the middle of the ditch, he'd be able to see The Guardian. Get the first shot off, too. Take him by surprise.

But he didn't step out. He wondered what he was doing there. He wondered what would happen if he stepped out with his hands up and empty and tried to grin an apology. Use his big smile, act friendly, and just let the other man take him to the boss, or this lady, or whoever he worked for. He was sorely sorry the ditch had broken out, he could say, and that he had caused it, and it wasn't what he had come for.

The hoof beats began again. Kyle thumbed back the hammer on the Winchester and held his breath. The thing to do was to get the drop on this Guardian, tie him up good, take his horse, and get a long way from this place. Kyle kept remembering what had happened to Will, and knew by some instinct that this enemy did not accept surrender or take prisoners. He knelt down and got ready to brace the Winchester against the rock corner and take his shot as soon as the other came into his sights. The gravel under his knee was soggy and cold.

This wasn't right, either. Somebody was too damned sure he had come here to kill this Guardian *hombre*, but maybe that wasn't what he was going to do. Nobody was telling him what to do. Not murder, and not from ambush.

Kyle rose to his feet, used his finger to wipe the inside of the eye patch, held the Winchester at hip level, ready to fire, and stepped out into the middle of the ditch.

He was just in time to see the very broad back of The Guardian as he rode away, fast, down the ditch, the horse kicking up damp sand and gravel. Must have suspected something was up, because he was sure hightailing it out of there. Kyle raised the rifle halfway to his shoulder; he still had time for a shot. He didn't take it. He hadn't turned back shooter, not yet.

He might have yelled or fired over the fleeing man's head to make him turn and fight, but he couldn't even do that. He stood there until the hoof beats receded around the next bend, then slumped against the rock and eased the hammer down.

Now what to do? Ride back to where the gate had washed out, try to get the horse down the mudslide there and into the valley, except then he'd see where the boys' cabin had been and he might find their drowned and battered bodies in the flood wreckage and he didn't want to find them and be the one who had caused that. He might just go as far as that one log wall and get back up on the embankment road and ride there, but then he'd be an even easier target for somebody up in the woods opposite. He could get real crazy and follow after The Guardian. . . .

Kyle hunkered down, his back to the rock, butt on his boot heels, and, as the rigid muscles went soft, he felt the shaking and the sweat begin. When he could move again, it was to cup some water from a standing pool to ease his dry mouth, but the water was as bitter as before. He drank another handful and another, but then could not take any more.

His ears were ringing, all the noises of the forest like one high wailing. They again picked up sounds coming from far down the deep ditch. This time it was a scrambling, the clatter of a horse clawing up a steep bank where the rock was loose. The Guardian was climbing up out of the ditch. What if that toad man with the iron bar had told The Guardian where he was? Hell, yes. He had to. One of those two, the toad or the girl, had to have told The Guardian where he was. OK.

What would he do, if he was The Guardian? He'd get up out of the ditch, first chance he had, and circle up above, cut through the trees maybe even on foot, get above the ditch. Or get upstream by cutting through the woods and come down from the opposite direction.

That girl had said The Guardian needed to get his back to the upstream side, but, of course, that was just some kind of crazy talk. She didn't seem to make a whole lot of sense about anything. But the important thing was that The Guardian knew where he was and had gotten up out of the ditch. Kyle thought he could follow, climb out himself, and make it a hunt, except that The Guardian could lay him an ambush just about anywhere. No, it had to be up the ditch. And fast. Kyle had nothing to lose by riding up the ditch, nothing. He untied the horse and swung into the saddle, Winchester still in his hand and knife still in his belt, and pushed the horse into a gallop along the damp sand. Within two hundred yards, he heard the sound of the other horse crashing through branches above him, racing to get ahead!

Kyle passed the log wall, then came to the broken gate where the water was still coming down the ditch, running about half full, and pouring through the washout. He went on in a chilly stream of water up to his stirrups. The horse lunged and pushed for all it was worth, but the water made the going slow. Up ahead, the ditch turned with the valley and curved inward, to his left, a lucky break for him. The Guardian would have to ride one hell of a lot farther to get ahead of him, once he reached that big curve.

Branches crashed close by somewhere, and Kyle caught the movement out of the corner of his eye, the big man on the big horse heading down through the timber and coming so fast the horse hardly had time to see the deadfall timber and jump it. Kyle swung the rifle up and around, and the sound of his shot was sucked up by the heavy forest, and the slug went way high. He saw the big form of The Guardian riding straight at the ditch, straight down the mountain through the trees, and he fired again, but the horse was surging under him, fighting the current of the water.

The Guardian hadn't seen that the ditch had been dug through a rock shoulder of the mountain, there, where it turned so abruptly, and that the drop-off was impossible. When he did see it, he reined his horse to the left, viciously hauling on the reins, and Kyle got off another shot that went wide because The Guardian's horse stumbled down the last few yards of slope steeply angling away from the shoulder of the mountain and then crashed down into the water. By some miracle, it kept its feet.

Kyle pulled up, a hundred yards away and upstream, and turned to face the pursuer. The Guardian was fighting his horse, forcing it to turn into the current, and pulling his own rifle from its scabbard at the same time. He twisted backward to get the long gun out.

Kyle had time for a careful shot, and he took it. *Whang!* His bullet drew first blood. The Guardian jolted to one side and let go of the rifle he was trying to get loose of its scabbard. He rose in the stirrups and drew his revolver, and Kyle heard the *blam!* of the report and heard the *chang!* of a bullet hitting rock behind him at the same instant. He replied with the rifle. The smoke hid The Guardian for an instant, but he thought he had hit him.

Another *blam!* brought lead caroming into rock right next

to the horse. The hammer of Kyle's rifle came down on air, and he knew he had emptied the magazine. He shoved it back in the scabbard.

The Guardian must have figured to retreat, because he swung his horse around and rode, lying down along its neck with his right hand hanging down and the horse churning and clawing down the current. But Kyle still wasn't a back shooter, not yet, and with Colt in hand he followed as fast as he could get his horse to go. The water was bitterly cold and flowed past the two desperate men with indifference, troubled not at all by horse hoofs churning and frantic bone and muscle cutting the current, troubled not at all by drops of blood from the dark rider striking the surface and dissolving invisibly.

The Guardian passed the destroyed gate and turned halfway around to take a shot. At the *whoom!* of the heavy revolver Kyle's horse shied sideways, but kept pawing through the water. Kyle could see the man was both shooting with his left hand and holding the reins, and that the right arm was hanging. Everything was moving either too fast or too slow to be real, but whichever it was, he seemed to see the next bullet coming, and he dodged, ducked, and heard it distinctly as it ricocheted on a rock and down the ditch. At the same moment his Colt was up and aimed, and he watched his bullet fly through the gunsmoke and smash into The Guardian, the same arm as before.

Kyle's heels pounded at the horse's flanks like a man in a hurry for his own execution. Later, he even thought he'd been yelling like a maniac as he charged through the last of the water, up the washout, and after The Guardian, who was heading out of sight down at the next bend of the ditch, riding for his life.

Kyle put the Colt back in the holster and lay down along

the neck of the animal and did something he had rarely done. He talked to the horse.

"Let's catch him now," he said.

The horse made no answer, not so much as an extra movement of the head.

"We'll do it," Kyle said. "You're a good horse. We'll do it." There was nothing to show the horse heard him. "One more corner," Kyle assured the horse, "one more after that, and we'll see 'im."

The horse ran on with gravel and wet sand flying from its hoofs, plunging across the standing pools, taking the inside of each turning of the ditch. Even the horse did not know when it had ever been able to run so fast and so hard.

The Guardian pulled up in a straight passage of the ditch—a mistake—and waited to fire another shot, but he fired too soon, and the bullet plowed gravel several yards ahead of Kyle's horse. By the time he steadied his horse again to take another shot, he had lost the range and the lead went screaming off the granite to Kyle's left. Kyle considered how many shots he had left and decided he had only two and that this was not the right time to use them. He kept on charging instead, staying low on the horse's neck and telling the horse that the man could not hit them and, besides, his gun was probably empty.

The Guardian raced ahead, around another sharp corner, and, when Kyle came riding fast around it, he saw The Guardian's horse standing sideward in the ditch, blocking the way. The man was on foot, making a run toward another log gate. He was carrying something in his left hand, but not a gun. More like a shiny bar or long knife or something, and he thrust it into the embankment somewhere near the log gate, which began to make that grinding noise as it opened.

Kyle reined back his horse when he saw the other blocking

the way, and pulled out his Colt and cocked it, but he didn't want to hit the big horse. He rode forward, slowing down so as not to spook the horse, but The Guardian got to it first. Although Kyle took a shot at him, he managed to get himself back into the saddle. Kyle's next shot—and his last cartridge—slammed into The Guardian's leg and probably through it, for the horse gave a sideways jump that nearly unseated him.

Suddenly it was Kyle's one desire, his one overwhelming task, to keep that man from going through the opened log gate in the embankment. He was closer to The Guardian than The Guardian was to the gate, which left The Guardian with only one choice and that was to attack. Attack first, flee later.

He came at Kyle so viciously he seemed to grow in stature, face horrid with pain and flushed with blood, holding the shining blade aloft and forcing the great horse into the narrow passage on Kyle's right, his blind side, The Guardian's only good side. Kyle held his ground and made his own short charge so that The Guardian might not get upstream of him. The two horses crashed together, breast to breast, hoofs flailing air and thick necks bending. Kyle shoved the Colt back into the holster and grabbed for his Bowie. Time seemed again to slow for him so that he saw every movement of the blade upraised against him, and he could see his own knife rising to meet it, and even the clanging of steel meeting steel sounded long and far-off.

He kicked back and in with his left heel, making the horse dance its haunches around into the chest of The Guardian's horse to stop it from getting past him. He had to swivel around in the saddle so that his good eye could see the big man, and he slashed out and felt the Bowie cut into something. Kyle was no knife fighter. He had never been in a knife fight in his life. But by some instinct he knew what he felt was his blade slicing leather and cloth and human flesh.

The Guardian screamed and slashed back with his knife, but he only cut Kyle's jacket and shirt and left a shallow wound over the ribs. The horses plunged and whinnied against each other. Kyle was again talking to his horse, telling it to stay against The Guardian's, telling it all this was nearly over. He backed up enough to see the huge dark figure next to him again, and again he made the hacking motion, like a man using a cleaver to cut kindling, and he felt the edge as it found The Guardian's muscle and bone.

Sweat was in his eye. His breath burned his throat. Time kept slowing and hurrying, making him dizzy. His horse rammed The Guardian's horse again, but this time its momentum carried it around in a full twist, and Kyle thought he had lost track of the other man, but as the ditch stopped spinning and he turned his head downstream, he saw the big horse with its big rider bent low and holding his side riding out through the log gate.

Kyle paused to forearm the sweat away from his eye and put the Bowie back in his belt. He drew the revolver to reload it from the shells in his belt, but as he ejected the fourth empty cartridge and shoved the fourth fresh one into the cylinder, the log gate groaned and rumbled closed. He was trapped in the deepest part of the ditch.

Chapter Nine

Iron in the Fire

Kyle dismounted and studied the gate, using his Bowie knife to probe into every crack. He tested the logs, heaving his shoulder against them, but they held solid.

"You cannot open it." It was the girl in white who spoke, keeping herself hidden in the lengthening shadows.

But he had to open it, he told her. He didn't have time to ride back to a place where the horse could climb out. There was a man wounded, he told her, the one they called The Guardian. He had to find him, like you would a dangerous wounded animal.

"Or maybe you already know where The Guardian's headed for?" Kyle asked.

He went to his horse and held it by its headstall. It looked like he was talking to the horse, instead of talking to some pale spook of a girl hiding in tree shadows.

"He has returned to the house of The Lady. He is badly hurt. Now you must wait."

"Wait? What for?"

"You must wait."

"Hate to argue, but this is a poor place to be waitin' on anybody. Trapped like a. . . ." He managed a sort of smile, but there was no charm in it.

Her arm, draped in white, rose from the shadows of the

tree branches, and she pointed down the ditch. "That way," she said in her whispering voice, "you will come to a place to ride up into the forest. There is a path to a place where others have stayed, and there will you wait. You will see the manor lights, at night, and you will hear sounds, but you must wait until I return."

"Return from where?" he said.

But the silence told him that he was once again alone. He listened for footsteps, but heard only the horse's shifting hoofs and an evening breeze coming up. The air down in the ditch was chilly, and the place had a bad feel to it. He thought of going back to what remained of John's and Brother's place after the flash flood and maybe salvaging some of his equipment, maybe getting lucky and shooting himself some meat on the way.

John and Brother. Dumb as they had been, it was a wonder they hadn't died years ago, one way or another. Kyle stopped himself short. Why was he thinking that way? He'd killed them, and now they were just a couple of bums. To hell with even thinking about it. Right now he just wanted to think about getting up to some higher ground where he could see the lay of the land. Maybe see where that sliced-up, shot-up son-of-a-bitch had gotten to.

As the woman had said, farther down the ditch there was a place he could climb out, a faint trail going into the trees on the upslope side. It was mostly grown over, but it got him to a wide-open park with old fire rings showing where campfires had burned at one time or another. Kyle figured this was where the men who had dug the ditch had camped. He rode from fire ring to fire ring and found one protected from the wind by a log lean-to with three walls. A deadfall tree nearby would provide his firewood supply.

Kyle thought about all the men who had lived in this camp

and who had worked here. It was hard, lung-busting work to be digging through rock at that altitude, and they must have been desperate for wages to do it. Married men, with women needing money for food. Somehow he couldn't feel much pity; after all, if they were hard luck cases, it was their own fault.

As Kyle went toward the lean-to, a spike buck came out of cover and stood watching him. Kyle's hand came smoothing up along the holster to slide the Colt out and cock it, and with one shot he dropped the buck where it stood.

"Venison supper," he said to the horse. "We'll be all right here."

He picketed the horse to graze, set the saddle in a low fork of a tree, tossed the saddlebags and blanket into the lean-to, then dragged the spike buck off to a tree on a rise of ground where he could hang it, gut it, and let it bleed. From the rise he looked down across the dark ditch. Beyond it, he could make out distant lights. Lights in windows. Windows in a tall building, far off in the gathering gloom.

That night, he dreamed about the day he had met the blacksmith.

In the dream the blacksmith was darker and larger than when Kyle had come upon him all that time ago. The blacksmith, at first, paid no attention to this Keystone rider who came into his camp. The blacksmith's boy silently took the reins from Kyle and solemnly tied the horse to one of the two wagons, and the mute woman came up to him with her two hands holding out a cup of water to him. Kyle drank and watched the blacksmith at his work.

The boy returned to his job of pumping the double bellows. Up and down the handle went, in the rhythm of a man breathing. The coals glowed red. With long tongs, the smith turned a bar of iron in the coals, studying how the color was changing from dark to cherry red.

"The thing is," he boomed in a heavy voice, without looking away from the metal, "that it heat evenly. Its heat must be even. See the color now . . . you know from that color it's ready for the hammer."

He drew the glowing rod of iron from the coals, holding it by the end. He laid it along the anvil and hammered it into a U-shape, plunged it back into the coals, took it out with another pair of tongs, struck it twice, returned it to the coals. While it was heating again, the smith hoisted the end of a long, heavy chain onto the anvil. Each link, like the one in the fire, was a foot long.

Again the metal came glowing from the fire, and again the blacksmith's hammer rose and fell. The boy ran forward to pour white powder on the new link, and again it went back to the fire. Now the critical moment was at hand. With the tongs, the smith seized the cherry-red link, and in one continuous motion brought it to the anvil, looped it through the last link of the chain, twisted the link closed, and smote it with his heavy hammer. Sparks flew in all directions. The color faded from the iron. The weld was good; the new link was made.

The boy brought a wooden bucket so large he could hardly lift it. Kyle expected him to pour it on the hot metal, but instead the blacksmith seized it and drank from it deeply, letting the water run down over his beard and chest.

"Coincidence, findin' you here," Kyle finally said.

The blacksmith looked at Kyle's face for the first time. "It always is," he said. His voice seemed too loud to be coming from just one man. He tossed the empty bucket to the boy. "Wine."

"Thing is," Kyle went on, "my horse there dropped a shoe somewheres back in the sagebrush this mornin'. I backtracked quite a ways, couldn't find it. Maybe you got a new one that a man might buy off'n you."

The boy brought two deep cups with wine in them and a little wooden box that the smith opened. He drew out a palmful of the contents and poured half of the amount into one cup, half into the other. He took a glowing rod of steel from the forge and plunged it into one cup and handed that cup to Kyle and did the same with the other cup, handing it to the blacksmith. He put the rod back into the forge.

The wine was thick and warm and sweet.

The smith opened a wooden chest. "Do you know these tools?" he asked.

"Some." Kyle pointed to the tools in the tray of the chest. "That there's a Hardy, for cuttin' metal on the anvil." The blacksmith took the Hardy and dropped its tang into a square socket in the anvil. "And that thing there's a creaser. For puttin' the nail groove along a horseshoe. That other thing with the handle's probably a swage. You got a punch there, too."

They finished the wine in silence. Kyle asked again if the smith had a horseshoe. In his own good time the smith finally went to the horse and studied its hoof, then returned to the forge and anvil. He selected an iron bar from a keg and handed it to Kyle.

Kyle examined it, like a man considering buying it, and it puzzled him. "Figured you might have some ready-mades on hand," he said. " 'Course, I see you're on the move here, might not carry such things with you." It looked like the bars that the smith beat into links for his chain. "Good job of weldin'," Kyle said, indicating the chain.

"The secret's the heat. And the flux," the smith said, "the flux to purify the steel when it's ready, the heat to bond the ends. Do you ever watch the sun rise?"

"Some," Kyle said.

"That's the color."

There was another long silence as both men drank more wine. They looked off into the distance as if both were seeing the sunset at that moment, although the sun was still high over head.

"When you ride west," the blacksmith said, after a time, "where is the sunrise you saw the day before?"

"Ain't there."

"It's already gone west ahead of you. Somewhere west of you, it's rising again for somebody else. The sun is always rising, somewhere west of you, until you see it in the east again. You think it's a new day. Because of where you are, you think it's another dawn. You think it a new chance, a new day to do your work or do your riding or take your ease. You think the coming of the dawn should make things new, bring something already made for you that day. But by the time you see the new dawn, it's already headed west."

Kyle wasn't sure he knew where this was leading. Never was one for these philosophical conversations. Art, he liked them. Will used to, before he took to the bottle too much.

"Go ahead and toss your iron into the coals. Sunrise color, that's what you want."

"Me?"

"You, rider. The metal is a gift, me to you, but you have to forge your own shape of it. There is the forge. The coal is there, and the boy will bring water. He can also work the bellows, some."

The blacksmith went to the pole and canvas shelter where the woman sat sewing, and he lay down and went to sleep.

Kyle stripped off his shirt and got on the bellows and blew the coals into white heat. Then the boy took over to keep the forge hot. Kyle took the blacksmith's nippers over to his horse and nipped off the remaining hind shoe and brought it back to the anvil to use as a measure. The two shoes should be the same general size and shape, Kyle thought. Good thing he had one for a pattern.

"This'll be our pattern," he said to the boy.

"Hah!" the blacksmith roared, seemingly in his sleep.

The work was slow and took more strength than he had thought. At first the steel wasn't heated evenly and Kyle couldn't hammer it into the same bend as the other shoe. Then it got too hot, and, when he tapped at it, the metal went in directions he didn't want it to and twisted. He puzzled over how the steel would warp and twist when he hit it, and, when he bent it one way, it would get a bulge on the inside of the curve. He got it pretty close to the shape he wanted, eventually. He heated it again and again, turning down the ends to make the caulks, punching down a bit of metal for the toe caulk. He even did a decent job of creasing the groove and punching out the nail holes.

By that time he was sweating like a pig, and his skin felt scorched, and he silently cursed the blacksmith as a crazy bastard for making men shape their own horseshoes when it would be quicker and easier for him to do it. He knew how to do it right and how to get the exact fit. Kyle knew what he wanted from his bar of steel. But he didn't want to be the one to forge it.

He finally lay the shoe in the coals to turn sunrise color and went and led the horse over to the anvil and tied it there to a wheel of a wagon.

This part he had done before, with ready-mades. He got the tongs and retrieved the hot shoe and laid it against the hoof, letting it burn there a few seconds, fitting the hoof to the steel, and looking to see where it needed more shaping, then bent part of the shoe over the anvil's horn, just slightly, and put the shoe against the hoof. It fit.

The boy had lugged up another bucket of water. Kyle drank, and, when the shoe had turned blue-black, he plunged it into the bucket to cool off so he could handle it. After that it was only a matter of nailing on both shoes and trimming the hoofs with the rasp and clenching and cutting the tips of the nails. The boy brought thick black tar that he painted on the hoofs so they wouldn't crack, and then the job was done.

Kyle washed in the bucket and put on his shirt. He looked at the sleeping smith. He fished four bits out of his jeans and handed it to the boy.

"For the use of the forge an' all," he said. "As for bein' any help, when he wakes up, you can tell 'im I said he could go straight to hell."

In his dream Kyle rode back to the Keystone with the late sun in his eye, wishing there was another direction he could ride. He pulled his Stetson down to shade his face and thought about the sun just now coming up on somebody else out there somewhere. When he got back, he might tell Art about that and see what he thought. He leaned over the shoulder of the horse and looked at the new shoe. He spit into the sagebrush.

"Horseshit," he said.

The morning broke cold and clear. Kyle rose shivering and stomping to get the warmth back in his body. With trembling fingers he laid a fire of twigs, duff, and larger sticks, and lit it. He got out his knife to slice some meat from the deer.

When he got to where the deer was hanging, he found a bulging grain sack hanging alongside it. In the sack he found coffee, flour and soda for biscuits or johnnycakes, a clay bottle of honey for sweetening, a package of salt, a frying pan.

In the bottom of the sack there was a couple of pounds of beans.

He ate handsomely and slowly that morning, enjoying the process of mixing batter and greasing the pan with deer tallow and gently toasting his johnnycakes golden brown. He cut venison strips thin as bacon and grilled them on green sticks.

Kyle rigged new hobbles for the horse and let it go to graze. He kept the Colt on his hip and the rifle nearby, but no one came to the mountainside, no one came to the ditch. He gathered firewood, walked around, exploring, stood and looked down toward the distant house; he slept when the sun was high and afterward walked up the slope and found a trickle of water where he filled his canteen.

He slept through the next night and did not remember dreaming, woke to the mountain coldness, and made his fire for warmth and cooking. Around noon he was looking at the deer carcass, wondering if it would be worthwhile to try to scrape and tan the hide, when, in the distance, he saw tiny specks moving toward the house. Lots of specks. Some looked like wagons moving, some seemed to be horses, some were men walking. Dozens of people coming from somewhere. All going to the house.

That night he heard the sound of many people wailing. It came from the direction of the big house, and it must have been loud because the house was a long way off. It reminded Kyle of a night he camped in a cañon down in Mexico, when he heard spook voices. It might have been the wind in the rocks, but it sounded like a whole bunch of people wailing. The noise from the house was clearer; it was human voices and not wind or spooks.

He lay under his saddle blanket looking at the stars slowly moving across the black skies and listening to the breeze bring the rise and fall of the wailing to him. Kyle thought about Brother and John and their cabin but couldn't remember what they looked like. Except that John had been fat, and Brother had been stupid.

That third morning he woke with the feeling that he was not alone, and, when he turned over, the woman was standing there. She was wearing an ordinary green dress, now, and a homesteader bonnet that put her whole face in shadow. She was holding another grain sack.

"Food for you," she said in her whispering voice. "There is a shirt also for you, and a blanket." She put the bag down.

"What's goin' on down there?" Kyle asked. "Thought I saw a whole bunch of people goin' to that house."

"The man is dead," she replied. "His widow does not know what to do. The ditch water has stopped flowing. No one wants to come to the ditch to find the reason. They are afraid because someone . . . *you* . . . killed the man."

"So what am I supposed to do about it?" Kyle asked. "They got any kinda law down there? Supposed to ride down an' give myself up?"

"He kept the law. He was the only law."

"Well, look. I think I'll just ride on then, an' let you folks sort it all out. Maybe when I tell Art about it . . . that's the owner of the Keystone Ranch, if you know what that is . . . maybe he'll want to send somebody."

She turned and gazed toward the park where the manor house stood. There was something in the way she was standing there that made Kyle stand the same way, and they both gazed in that direction as if they were reaching some decision separately.

"You have been sent," she said at last.

"To do what?" he said. "Get down there an' get killed by his friends?"

"They are not his friends. They labor on the ditches, grow some food, that is all. Most have no guns and no wish for any. The Lady who lives in the house . . . The Lady who owns all of this . . . will need you." She turned then and looked into his eyes. Even though her face was hidden under the dark bonnet, Kyle could see that her eyes were pale and did not blink, and he could not look away.

"Remain here. Tomorrow I will tell The Lady that she must have another guardian . . . someone to protect the ditch and to tell the workers to do this or do that, to be here or there. To make repairs and bring the water back. I will tell her tomorrow, although she will be very angry. Today she buries The Guardian."

"And after you tell her, then what?"

"I will have more food brought to you. Whatever you want. After three days or four, I will be able to return and bring you with me to The Lady. I will tell her you are the one, and that I found you and brought you."

She turned and was walking toward the forest as if the whole deal was done and he had agreed to it. She had made it clear that he was to stay here alone until she came back. Alone. That *did* remind him of something.

"Wait a minute," he said, as she was about to vanish into the shadows. "What about this fat *hombre* with the iron bar I seen up here? Where's he gonna be all this time I'm sittin' on my haunches waitin' for you?"

The woman stopped to look back at him. "He is a bad one," she shouted in her light little voice, "a very evil bad one! Ignore him. Or if you can, kill him."

And she was gone.

The next day passed, and he saw nothing, except that late in the day he could make out that same tiny line of people moving in the park, this time away from the house. Kyle paced his clearing, gathered more firewood than he needed, skinned out his deer, fashioned a scraper, Indian-style, from a flat stone, and scraped on the hide. Afterward he found a hill of ants and put the hide near it so the ants would finish cleaning the scraps of flesh off the skin.

The next day he got down into the ditch and walked until he found a good pool of water where he stripped down and took himself a bath. The water was warm from the sun, but made his skin prickle just the same. Sitting there with water around his hips, he looked down and saw himself reflected in the water, surprised at how rough he looked. A week's worth of scruff on his face, fire soot on him, his hair all shaggy.

Back at camp, he began to fancy himself up. Kyle boiled some water and soaped up his beard and razored it down to clean skin again. He took care to square off his sideburns, real nice. With the frying pan full of water for a mirror, he carefully combed his long hair back and cut off stray pieces with the razor, then combed and trimmed it until it flowed back over his ears. He left it long, down over his collar in back, and, after he washed it and it dried in the sun, he ran his hand through its soft waves.

The next day he took deer tallow and soot and polished his boots and holster and gun belt. He spit on a corner of his bandanna, dipped it in fine fire ash, and used it to polish the metal studs on his belt, and on his saddle and bridle as well. He washed his pants and shirt at the little spring and spread them on a big sun-warm rock to dry.

The following day it occurred to him to make a stiff brush by binding a bunch of horsetail grass with deer sinew and with this he brushed and brushed his hat, vest, and jacket. He spent most of the day doing this, after he fed himself and gathered wood and rubbed down the horse with one of the grain sacks.

Two more days passed, and the woman returned and found him at the small trickle of the spring. He stood up when he saw her, and he knew that she was looking at his trimmed hair, his clean clothes, his shaven face. He felt taller, larger, more important than before. Kyle acted as though he had expected her but did not really care whether she had come or not.

"This here spring," he said, smiling indifferently, "I was thinkin' some of those workers of yours could get up here an' divert it into the big ditch. Just goin' to waste, dribblin' off in that direction there."

They walked back to the clearing. She led the way to the rise where he had hung the deer.

"When you are ready," she said. "I will wait for you there." She pointed to a pair of stone cairns standing like a gateway at the edge of the plain beyond the ditch. Her saddled horse nibbled at the grass near one of them.

"And then?"

"And then," she whispered, "you must come to the manor, and I must convince my lady you are her new guardian."

He turned to go back to collect his things and saddle his horse, and, as he did, he saw the black shape waddling as fast as he could for the safety of the trees, clutching the sack of food. Kyle calmly slid his Colt up out of its holster and thumbed back the hammer, but, after he had drawn a bead on the figure, he sneered and let the hammer down again. He took out his bandanna and wiped out the inside of his eye patch.

"Enjoy the leftovers, you fat toad," he said under his breath. "I got better uses for my ammunition than to plug you. But when you see me up here again, better stay clear."

146

Chapter Ten

A Bully and a Back Shooter

Kyle found the woman, as she had said he would, between the two cairns. Her horse was a small, pale buckskin. Under the saddle skirt was a soft leather scabbard with a longbow and a quiver of arrows. He couldn't see that she carried any other kind of weapon.

He rode close behind her, off to one side, without speaking, and they came to a low treeless hill overlooking a mountain park. It reached out as far as he could see and dropped over a swelling horizon into trees again, and from side to side it was an open plain that would take a man half a day to ride across.

Not far from the near edge was the manor. As a boy he had seen pictures of manor houses—one time his father had taken him into a gloomy library smelling of old musty paper and shown him a book about Ireland. "Your people," he had said. "Your people came from houses such as these. Before the hard times came upon us all." One time at the Keystone, Kyle had told the Pendragons about his long-vanished aunt, and Art had dragged out a big book with pictures of family trees and coats of arms and huge stone houses.

The woman reined up. She pushed back the hood of her riding cape and motioned toward the house with a gesture of her head.

"Crannog," she said flatly.

"What's that?" Kyle said, puzzling the word on his tongue but not saying it.

"It's what The Lady chose to call the house. Or her first husband called it that. I can't remember which. I wasn't here at the time. It's the headquarters of The Great North Reservoir Company. You will oversee the raising of the cattle, the ditch digging and repairs, some haying, possibly the horse breeding although that is in very capable hands and needs almost no supervision."

"I don't recall askin' for a job," Kyle said. "This one you've been callin' The Guardian, he ramrodded all this?"

"Yes. Very capably," the woman whispered. "You will find yourself quite able to carry on."

"Like I said, I'm not askin' to. How many of these guardian foremen have been here, anyway? I get the feelin' he wasn't the first."

"I am not sure. Two I have known, but, certainly, there must have been another one or two before that. The house and the settlement are quite old. The irrigation scheme, it is not so old."

Kyle looked over the vast open park, but his gaze kept returning to the tall stone house with its surrounding houses and barns, stables and storehouses, corrals and paddocks. He wanted just to laugh off the idea of ramrodding it, and ride away, but a kind of curiosity held him. He wanted to see this *Lady* and find out more about the irrigation. A mysterious feeling kept running through him, a feeling that this was what he had come here to do. It felt like the time when a mean Roman-nose snake of a bronc' had kicked hell out of three good men, and Kyle had gotten up early one morning and went to the bucking corral and looked at that devil and he knew he was going to get aboard and ride the outlaw to a finish. He

148

had stood there knowing that he was going to do it. And it had been a good feeling.

"So this Lady of yours got a name?" he asked. "An' while we're at it, what's yours? How you figurin' to tell her I killed her man an' I'm here to apply for his old job?"

"You can call me Luned," she said. "Everyone does. When you say *this Lady of yours,* you must think that I work for her, but that is not the case. At times I do. I live in the house, that is all. She is my patroness. She lets me live here . . . she and I talk and keep each other company. Most of the time. She is somewhat eccentric, as you will discover. When she came here years ago, she learned that some states are divided into counties, and her ambition is to own . . . or control . . . such an area. She even calls herself a countess because of that. Her family name is Fontana, and you will not be surprised to learn that her family named her Felice, after the lady who loved the out-of-doors."

"Never heard of her, but the name's a pretty big mouthful," Kyle said.

"You will not find yourself using her name very often," the woman whispered, almost smiling. "But as for your other question . . . I will speak first and tell her I found you on the plains and brought you here. She will enjoy calling me a liar and will pride herself for seeing the truth. She will argue that she cannot accept a man who killed her husband. . . ."

"Husband?" Kyle interrupted. "Christ, I didn't know. . . ."

"She will not want you to stay. I will point out that you must be a better shot and a stronger fighter than her husband had been, and that she cannot hold the ditch for long without someone to fight for it. The primary ditch is not ready yet. It is vulnerable in too many places. When she sees you"—as she said this, the woman looked at Kyle, and he could see now in the sunlight she had green eyes that were sweeping him from head to foot—"she will make some other argument, but she will not be able to resist. You will be our guest for a few days, but, by this time, in a week, you will be the new foreman, the new guardian of the Great North and of Crannog."

She pulled her hood over her head again, kicked her horse into motion, and wordlessly led Kyle down to the park and across it until they came to a wide roadway that they followed, riding abreast, to a long stable and corral.

The small man who handled horses met them, taking the reins as they got down. Kyle used the tip of his finger to wipe out his eye patch as he followed Luned to the house.

"What!"

The voice came through the paneled oak door, reaching Kyle and echoing on down the empty hallway. He could not hear the faint whispery voice of Luned, only the shrill tone of the other woman, which seemed to rattle the windows.

"My husband . . . not dead these three days . . . you *dare!* No! It is impossible for me . . . and we do not know who he. . . ." And the voice calmed somewhat, and he could no longer hear.

A half hour passed, then another. Sometimes Kyle heard a loud word or two from behind the door, but for the most part the house was a tomb. Two servants came down the hall together and went up the stairway past him, but they didn't look at him or speak. He thought of going, but something made him want to stay and see what this Lady of Fontana, or whatever, looked like. She sounded like a screaming banshee.

The door opened, but the small woman was holding it as if she were making up her mind whether to leave or not.

"You must talk to him one time or another," she was saying to the other woman, hidden behind the partly open door. "I'll see that he is given a bed."

"You will *do* no such thing!" came the scream from within.

The accent was English, like the bunch of English lords who came through the Keystone once on a big game hunt. The door slammed shut again, and the argument went on. For Kyle, it was enough; he walked out of the house and headed for the stables and corrals.

He had a foot on the bottom rail of the gate, studying a barn big enough to have a bunkhouse in it. The hostler slept there, he figured. Maybe some of the hands. Place like this would take a lot of. . . . Kyle's thoughts were busted by the sound of a horse coming fast, and, when he turned toward the noise, it was a big roan being ridden by a big man. The rider was sawing at the bridle, the horse trying to pull its head away from the vicious pain.

"Open up, dammit!" the man yelled. Kyle hesitated, then pulled the latch pole out of the iron hasps and gave the corral gate a shove. It swung open just as the horse reached it.

The cursing rider spurred the foam-covered roan at a run through the corral and over to one of the smaller stables. The small hostler met him there and caught the bridle of the plunging animal. The rider jumped off, grabbed his broad black hat from his bald head, and began whipping the horse's head with it. He gave the handler a few licks with the hat for good measure, then shoved him and sent him sprawling.

The man was big enough to hurt a horse seriously—a bearded, bald man with a paunchy belly and little eyes like a fat marmot. He came straight at Kyle.

"Where the hell they got 'im?" he said. "Prob'ly up in that damn' chapel of hers. I was clear the hell up on Boar Ridge when that skinny sunuvabitch came an' told me." He sneered. "Missed the party, I reckon. Who the hell are you?"

Kyle looked at him steadily. When the man had come storming at him, he had unconsciously shifted the latch pole to his right hand. He carried his Colt on his left hip.

"Owen," he said without any warmth.

"Yeah? What happened to your eye? Hey! Mebbe you're the road turd that got that ol' bastard at last. You th' one?"

Kyle let his left hand drop down to rest on the butt of the Colt. "Guess I am," he said.

"Now I find y' studyin' the place like y' was fixin' t' buy it, huh. Gonna hang your gear in there with them other trophies a' his, huh? Shit, serves him better'n right. But I bet I'm a problem y' never counted on."

"How's that?" Kyle said.

"How's that, One-Eye? Tell y' how's that. I'm in line f'r his job, not you. It's me what's gonna move into th' manor an' sleep on them fancy sheets. With that fancy countess. Good y' got that big ugly bastard outta th' way f'r me, but now I want y' to get your horse an' punch a hole in th' breeze. Outta my way."

Kyle was right-handed, although his bad eye made it easier to shoot with his left, and in that right hand he was still holding the four foot long latch pole, thick as a man's wrist and worn smooth. Kyle held it by one end, letting the other end rest on the ground.

Without a hint of warning, he swung the latch pole upward, catching the loudmouth dead center between the legs. Kyle pulled the pole back again, level with his waist, shoved it forward into the fat paunch. The bully had groped his gun out of its holster, but Kyle brought the pole down full force on his wrist and smiled grimly to hear bone breaking as the gun dropped into the corral dust.

The man held his gut with the broken hand and groped with the other, clawing into Kyle's shirt. Kyle punched the pole into his stomach again. And he kept punching, making the fat man step backward with each blow.

Kyle ended it by bringing the pole down on his skull,

sending the man to his knees. He wobbled there like one of those toy clowns with lead weight in the base, and finally fell over sideways in the dirt.

Kyle calmed the horse and got the rope from the saddle. He put the loop around the man's ankles and tied the other end to the saddle horn.

"Where's your honey pile?" he asked the hostler.

"Over there," quavered the small voice. The hostler pointed toward a heap of horse manure scraped from the stables. Beyond it was a pond.

"Drag yore friend here through that pond, then you can drag him to the top of the honey pile an' leave him. Then cool that horse down and take care of it."

"Yes, sir." The hostler set out to follow instructions, but Kyle didn't watch. He crossed the corral, picked up the gun, shut the gate—checking to see that he hadn't cracked the latch pole—and went back to studying how the barn was put together. Somebody had done a heck of a good job on it.

"She won't see you," came the whispery little voice behind him.

"Didn't sound like it when I was waitin' for you inside," Kyle replied. "I decided to come out here and beat up on your help, instead."

"I saw. He is called Blair. The others do not like him. He imagines himself to be The Guardian's successor."

"We had words about that," Kyle said. "Well, if your countess won't be havin' company, I guess I'll be goin.' "

"No! You must stay. She is so helpless in these things. No. This barn has several rooms where some of the . . . what do you call one who supervises, but is not the foreman?"

"Ramrods? Oh, you mean *segundos?*"

"Yes. Sometimes they come in from far parts of the ranch and stay there. You will find all you require there, and I will

153

bring meals to you. One or two days more, and she will see you. Show yourself in the corral, or out on the road, where she can see you from her window. She will give up her mourning and do what she must. Two days."

They stood there with the late afternoon sun warm upon them, the lanky cowboy with his Stetson pulled down to shade his good eye, the tiny woman in the white dress. There was a comfortable feeling about it, but there should not have been.

"What's her story?" he finally asked.

"My father built this house," she replied, "and made the first of the ditches, a small one through the solid rock. He is a mason. He hated wasting all the hard granite that he quarried from the ditch. So he gradually built this house with it. Father does not do small things, as you have seen. It was he who designed the ditch gates.

"There was a small lake. North of here. French trappers had named it Lac d'Espoir . . . Lake of Hope. Father saw that with some dams it could become a great lake. He could fill the whole basin with water. Reservoir, the French say."

"So where'd the countess come in?"

"I am explaining," Luned said. Kyle looked over her head and saw Blair rousing himself on top of the manure pile and glaring in his direction. The man's better judgment prevailed, and he stomped off into the distance, bareheaded and filthy and holding his broken wrist.

"Might have to kill that one," Kyle said.

"I do not doubt it," Luned said. "But the countess. She knows that she came to America on a ship when she was little, and it has been observed that she speaks with the accent of Ireland, a little, and that her French is that of a small child.

"Someone took her to the other ocean . . . the Pacific . . . in a big group of people who traveled in wagons, but she does not know who they were or where they were. You will soon find that her grasp of geography is very limited. She also remembers crossing a jungle and being in a sailing ship.

"When she had nearly reached the age of her womanhood . . . perhaps you do not know what I mean by that? . . . she was being cared for by a woman who lived rather far from the ocean and who one day walked off into the desert and did not return. Thereafter, nuns in a convent school cared for her and taught her many new things about books and religion. One day she heard that her friend, the woman, had been seen. And so she, too, walked away into the desert. My father was returning from a search for the salts with which to make blasting powder and found her senseless."

Kyle kicked at a pebble and looked around. "So he brought her here, and she just took over the place?"

"Father has no use for such a house. I live there, with my two sisters, and she . . . well, she is The Lady of the house. It was she who found what to do with the water, with the ditches and reservoir. Her first guardian went out and brought back men to make a sawmill, carpenters to finish the house as she wanted it. My father only likes to quarry ditches and build walls . . . he has no head for business in irrigation. It was she who knew that The Guardian had to protect the ditch. Men come to break into it. But you know."

As they were speaking, Luned had been leading Kyle toward the grand barn. Inside, she showed him doors that opened into a series of rooms, each with a wide cot, a dressing table and mirror, an oval carpet on the pine board floor, a washstand and a clothes press.

"Choose any one," she said.

He chose. And later, with twilight dropping dark shadows between the buildings and behind the corrals, Luned returned to him with hot food and sat with him outside the barn while he ate and told him more about the extent of the manor properties called Crannog and The Great North Reservoir Company.

"Sleep well," she said at last, standing up and taking the empty plate. "Tonight you may sleep peacefully. Perhaps tomorrow Blair will come back to kill you, and there is another man who will come when he hears The Guardian is dead, another one who feels he is the successor." She put her hand on his knee and peered at him intently from under her bonnet. "But you know, only he who has overcome The Guardian of the Water can become the next guardian."

"What if they overcome *me?*" Kyle said. "Then do they get the job?"

"Later, perhaps, someone will. But if Blair or the other man kills you before that, it may be that the irrigation company will be no more."

She seemed to float away into the dark. Kyle went inside and found a lantern and made sure the room he had picked was the one with the strongest door.

It was more than a week before The Lady of Crannog sent for him. He had seen her three times, each time from a distance, as she went riding out from the small stable behind the house. She always went in the same direction. He could not tell if she was young or old, beautiful or ugly. Her posture in the saddle showed her to be slim and straight, and she rode with control and ease. Even from far away, it was clear that she was one for whom saddle horses were created.

One afternoon, seeing her return to the manor, Kyle had an urge to see where she had been. He saddled his horse and went riding in the direction he had seen her take. After a time he came to a chapel built of stone, like the manor house, and there was a small graveyard with a fresh grave, but he did not approach it.

He left that place and rode on southward across gently swelling hills covered with good grass. He saw steers up to their knees in it, and guessed that they were the meat supply for the house. He saw a few horses, mostly old ones that had been put out to pasture. One came limping up to him as soon as it saw him. It dipped its head, greeting his horse. From its sagging red-shot eyes and the gray around its muzzle Kyle knew it would be wolf food before too many more winters.

The evening was one of those when winter seems to be hanging around over the next ridge, waiting its moment. The warm autumn air came down the slopes, bringing scent of dry pines and the aroma of leafless aspen and dead grass and dust. It felt good to be wearing a jacket. In such a twilight a man on a good horse could go on forever, if the twilight would last forever. No place to get to, nothing to find. Just open parks, a light evening breeze, and the loneliness. A man could ride and watch how the high mountains were turning purple, or the string of geese spread out across the darkening sky.

Into the loneliness, into the quiet, came a sharp hit on his shoulder, followed by the sound of a shot. Kyle recovered his balance and twisted his head to look at where the jacket was torn. Red blood was soaking the ragged edges of the denim. He thought the shot had come from behind him and from down close to the ground, and he leaned low and kicked the horse into a run, waiting for a second shot to come whistling after him.

Another shot did come, but later than he thought it would, and he was surprised to hear the whistle of the lead and then the *boom*. It was a rifle, and must be an old one. With a good Winchester, anybody could have gotten three or four shots off by now, and Kyle wouldn't have heard the bullets going past.

He pounded the horse on another hundred yards and turned. There was nothing back there that he could see, not a horse, not a man, just a wide park of grass. Kyle swung to the ground, wincing at the pain that was starting to set in. He took out his bandanna, wiped his eye patch with it, then folded it and stuffed it between the wound and his jacket, buttoning the jacket up tight to hold it there. His arm was tingling. Or going numb.

The rifle boomed out again, and again the shot went wide. Kyle saw from the flash and the smoke that the bushwhacker had done a stupid thing—he had hidden in a wallow in the park, a shallow hole. He must have been hunting, when Kyle rode into sight, and his rifle must be something like a Sharps, judging from the sound of it and the amount of time between shots.

The light was failing, which was in his favor. The park was full of rises and shallow swales, which was also in his favor. Kyle mounted again, gritting his teeth against the pain of hauling himself into the saddle, picked out the terrain he wanted, turned the horse, and made a charge straight at the wallow where the bushwhacker was hiding. He counted under his breath: "One . . . two . . . three." He visualized the other man rising up, realizing that Kyle was coming straight at him, sighting the gun, squeezing the trigger. . . .

Blam! it boomed out, sending an echo across the land. Just as Kyle had figured, he came to a dip in the ground just as the gun went off again. Now he came up out of it, riding hard, counting the time it would take the shooter to reload, swerved with a half second to spare, began a big circle in the dim light around the wallow, narrowing the circle, keeping the shooter turning and off balance. Kyle took advantage of each rise to ride faster down each slope; he lay low along the horse's neck in the swales and gulches, totally hidden, each time emerging much closer to the wallow than before, still going in a circle. A long time went by without a shot.

Maybe the bushwhacker was out of ammunition, or maybe the gun had jammed up. Kyle would never know. Didn't matter. He came to a dome of ground, rode the horse halfway up it, then turned hard and rode around the dome instead. Another shot came *whooming* from the wallow, much nearer now, and kicked dirt where he would have been if he had gone on over the dome.

This was the time. Kyle drew his Colt and kicked the horse straight at the shooter in the wallow. The light was bad, but, as he pounded down the last twenty yards, he could see the other man desperately fumbling in his overalls pocket, a Sharps carbine under his other arm with its lever dropped and the breech open. Kyle saw why the shooter was so slow at reloading. His mistake was to be carrying his cartridges in a pants pocket so he had to dig around to fish out one without spilling all of them.

The shooter came up with a cartridge, and still had time to shove it into the breech. The rider was coming at him fast now, very fast. The back shooter palmed the rifle up. The cutter caught momentarily on the twisted paper end of the cartridge, then the breech closed with a click. The man could see the foam around the horse's mouth, and that the rider had a patch on one eye, but that the other eye was cold and dark. His hand went to his pocket again, his fingers closed on a percussion cap and rolled it until it was between thumb and forefinger. He pressed it to the nipple, but his finger slid off of it, and the cap dropped to the ground.

Instinctively he bent down for the tiny copper cap lost in the grass, then realized how close the hoof beats were. He straightened up just in time for the horse's right shoulder to catch him full in the face. He was falling backward to the ground when the hind hoof clipped him in the head.

Kyle hadn't even used the Colt on him, but had run the horse directly into him, knocking him down beneath the hoofs. He stopped the animal and rode back, dismounted, and studied the unconscious man, trying to figure out if he was a ranch hand or just a stray range bum. He stripped him of his clothes, boots, hat, gun, everything but his long handles and socks. These he wadded into a bundle and strapped on behind his saddle, his shoulder getting more painful every time he moved it.

Son-of-a-bitch, Kyle thought. *Probably out there hunting, saw me, knew who I was, figured to make some points by killing the man who killed The Guardian . . . something like that. Seems to be a pretty popular sport around here.* Kyle got up into the saddle with a grimace, and after he had made a wide circle looking for the horse—if the shooter had one—he rode back toward Crannog in the dark.

The man in the wallow woke with pain screaming through his skull. Gradually and stupidly he realized he was stripped and cold and alone in all the darkness. He may also have realized, somewhere in his subconscious, that his mistake had been in thinking that the rider would be afraid once he heard the sound of the Sharps. Some men said a man who is afraid is more dangerous, because you don't know what he'll do. The man in the wallow subscribed to the idea that the most dangerous man of all is the one who isn't afraid of you. If he isn't, you'd better get the hell out of there.

As far as anyone knows, the bushwhacker was never seen on that range—or anywhere in the territory—again.

Kyle was shivering by the time he got back to the barn. He found the strength to dump the shooter's belongings into an empty stall, to strip off the saddle and blanket and bridle, and put the horse in the adjacent stall for the night. In his room, he lit the lamp and stripped to the waist and cleaned the wound with water. The blood was crusted and dry; the furrow in the skin had stopped bleeding. He lay back on the bed to figure out if he had something to dress it with. The next thing he knew the morning light was leaking in at the window. He could smell the oily soot in the air from where the lantern had burned out.

When Luned brought him his breakfast, she found him at the mirror, a wet bandanna wrapped clumsily over his shoulder and under his armpit. She set down the tray, left, and returned with dressings, witch hazel, and a thick balm that smelled like a lady's bedroom. She made him sit on the edge of the cot while she swabbed the wound until it stung, then soothed it with the balm and bandaged it again.

She gathered up his blood-soaked clothes and said she would see that they were washed and mended. Kyle went to get another shirt and found Blair's revolver still in his saddle-bags. Thinking of the bald man topping off the honey pile, he held it up for Luned to see.

"S'pose I oughta give this back to Baldy?" he asked. "Ain't much of a gun. Smith and Wesson, and he didn't take no better care of it than he did that horse of his. Look at that. Must've dropped it on a rock somewhere."

Luned took the revolver and held it while Kyle buttoned his shirt. Still carrying it, she led him out of the room and down through the barn to a corner room. By standing on an upturned pail and stretching, she was able to reach a key hanging, hidden, in the barn framing. It opened a thick lock on a door; the door opened into a room with high, barred windows, a room in which more than a dozen saddles and bridles hung on one wall and countless rifles and pistols hung on another. Wordlessly Luned simply carried the Smith & Wesson to the wall of guns and hung it by its trigger guard on an empty nail. Kyle could only stand there, taking it all in.

He didn't need her to tell him what it was. It was The Guardian's trophy room, the place he put all those things he had stripped from men he had beaten. Soon the bush-whacker's Sharps rifle would be hanging there on the wall. Kyle figured to burn the clothes and boots.

Luned stepped over to one of the saddles, which was not dusty like the others. It had seen recent use. Someone had cleaned it, but there were stains on the skirt and fender. They looked like blood and looked new.

"Guardian's?" Kyle asked.

She nodded and left him there, alone. Next to The Guardian's saddle was a model he'd never seen before, light and simple like it was made for racing and not for working. Next to that, a scuffed one with makeshift girth and curled edges to the leather, like something a farmer might ride. And next to that . . . next to that, a very good quality saddle for cattle work, double-cinched and high toward the cantle, the horn wrapped in rawhide to protect it from a dally rope. It had once had leather *conchos* attached to leather thongs on either side of the fork, and they had been torn off, both of them. The remaining bits of thong were shredded and stretched, not cut. Kyle knew such saddles well. He rode one himself. Those missing *conchos* had carried the Keystone brand.

What if he did take on this ditch-guarding job for a while, and another Keystone rider came to bust it down or some-thing? He didn't figure he could ever draw down on a Key-stone man. . . .

Luned reappeared at the doorway. "Lady Fontana has fin-ished the time of mourning," she said. "She asks that you come to the house."

Chapter Eleven

Successor to the Guardian

Luned silently led Kyle through the foyer, and pointed up the wide staircase. As Kyle went up the steps, Luned vanished down a hallway. Upstairs, he found six doors facing the landing, one with the door standing open; it took him into a small anteroom and then into a large sitting room furnished with heavy chairs and small tables. An open inner door showed a bedroom beyond.

The Lady of the Manor was standing in the sitting room, quite tall and even pretty in a cold and reserved way. Her stiff posture reminded Kyle of one of his schoolteachers. She was slim and straight, her narrow waist made even narrower by corseting; her blue satin skirts cascaded in long folds and pleats to the floor. There was one difference between her and his schoolteacher: instead of a pointing stick, The Lady held a small nickel-plated revolver.

Kyle stood still and said nothing. The silence weighted the unmoving air as if they were both part of a ceremony, and he felt as if he had been through this ceremony, somewhere, long ago.

She walked around him like a horse buyer considering the purchase of a horse, her every movement underscoring her poise and dignity. Her gown whispered along the waxed pine floor, the sound of her footsteps scarcely audible. She completed her tour of him and again stood in front of him, holding the revolver as casually as if it were a teacup on a saucer.

A single drop of sweat itched its way down along Kyle's brow and crawled beneath his eye patch, but he kept his fist closed to fight down the impulse to wipe it away with his finger. He tried bestowing The Lady with one of his charming and beguiling smiles. It felt odd to him, though. He had been smiling at people all his life, but since he had first stepped foot onto the Crannog land a smile no longer seemed to be any natural part of him. Nevertheless, he forced the corner of his mouth upward.

"Why are you doing that?" she said. "Why do you smile at me like that? It is ugly. I don't like it."

He looked past her and saw himself in the mirror. She was right. Compared with the mirror image of her straight shoulders, her slim bare neck, and the proud way she carried her head, he was a dark, sneering figure. The comparison made him feel ugly. As she had said.

She slid the dainty revolver into a pocket of her dress and again the stiff fabric swished on the floor as she walked to the opposite wall. Most of the wall was taken up with a map. On either side of the map were rifle cabinets.

He followed her to the map. A sinuous line of green marked the **Great Ditch** with its irrigation gates numbered, including the one marked **Gate #6**, the one he had wrecked. Small twisting blue lines showed the creeks that the ditch intercepted, with names like **Willow Creek** and **Elk Creek** and **Boulder Rapids**. At the site of the manor house was a little picture of a house, three stories high, with a square turret on one corner, and there was a little square speck that was the chapel. The map showed roads and other ditches, the expanse of lake a few miles to the north, and the way the ditches led water into the lake and then out of the lake to a river that stretched far out to the east, off of the map. Large blank spaces were labeled **Horse Pasture** and **Bull Pasture** and **Hay Fields.** He also saw a square with a dozen or more little crosses in it. A graveyard? Not far from it was another square with tiny boxes, probably representing the settlement where the workers lived.

"It is all familiar to you, of course," she said.

Kyle said—"Yes."—but without knowing why. Because it was familiar somehow. She, too, seemed like someone he had known for a very long while. He thought it was because of knowing Gwen, Art's wife, but Gwen was younger and had golden hair. This woman's hair was black. She was taller. She was more mature, and she could even have been more beautiful than Gwen, if she would smile and if her eyes were not as cold as ice.

She stood there, saying nothing while he looked at every word and line on the wall map. Then she walked into the bedroom, and Kyle knew he was expected to follow. It was large and furnished with two heavy armchairs and a round table, besides the bed and nightstands. A decanter and two glasses stood on the table; she poured dark red wine into the two glasses and handed one to him.

The ceremonial silence went on and on. Kyle swallowed some of the wine, carefully so as not to make any sound doing it. The wine tasted odd, like crushed cherries and bitter flowers. She set her glass back on the table and once more took out her revolver.

"Luned has told me that you are a traveler who happened into our valley, but she is lying. You murdered my husband. And there is nothing I would like better than to kill you in turn. Nothing I would like better! Besides the fact that . . . well, of who you are and what you are . . . you are quite unattractive."

She put the revolver on half cock and began tapping its barrel against her open palm while she studied Kyle from head to foot. When she brought the barrel up and pointed it, Kyle thought she was aiming it at him, but she was indicating another door, behind him.

"That leads down behind the kitchen and out to the rear of the house, where you will find a stable. Your horse will be stabled there, not with the other animals. I believe that you will find it more comfortable to use this stairway than to come and go through the front of the house."

"Come and go?" Kyle asked. His glass was still half full, but he felt as though the wine had made his tongue thick and useless.

"These are your rooms. This is where you will live while you continue the protection of the ditch and the overseeing of the labor. It would not be fitting for you to live with the hired persons. For now, you will take your meals alone, either in the kitchen or in your rooms . . . once I become more accustomed to you, I will expect you to dine with me downstairs. My own rooms," she added, "are on the floor above this one. You will not go up there."

He looked into her eyes to see if she were serious about all of this; she held her head cocked ever so slightly like a challenge, elegant and superior, one eyebrow raised slightly as if daring him to ask a question. And there the two of them remained, cowboy and lady, silently confronting each other, measuring each other. It was time for questions, but there were no questions. Each fully understood the other. She allowed the silence to go on for what seemed like many minutes before she turned away from him with a swirl of her skirts and left him alone.

Kyle returned to the first room and stood in front of the map a long time, finishing the strange-tasting wine. His memory of the Keystone was flickering like a dying candle flame, vague and uncertain; images of his friends' faces were blurry and indistinct. He could remember one thing since leaving the Keystone—a smelly low cabin he had been in— but not how long ago it was. The rushing flood of water through the broken gate seemed to be just a quick flash in the mind, more like a picture he had seen somewhere than like something that had really happened to him.

Kyle put his finger on the map where the gate was. *Need to get some men up there to fix that,* he thought. *No need to keep an eye on that bunch of pick and shovel miners down in the valley below the gate, though, not for a while. Nobody left down there to try any ditch breakin'.* His smile came back, but it was crooked. And he didn't care.

That same day Kyle personally put his horse in the corral behind the manor house and opened the door to an empty stall so that the horse could go inside if it wanted to. In an adjoining stall he found The Guardian's horse, a tall, heavy animal, and let it out into the corral with the other. The hostler came and cleaned up the few fresh piles of droppings and spread clean straw in both stalls. Except for removing his hat and telling Kyle his name, in case he was wanted, he said nothing.

Kyle started for the trophy room, carrying his old Keystone saddle to store there because he preferred The Guardian's longer and lighter one. By the time he came to the trophy room door he had forgotten the hostler's name.

He adopted other belongings of The Guardian as well. A clothes press in the bedroom held clothes far more in keeping with the manor house: gabardine trousers and linen shirts, dark vests of brocade, tailored coats.

As Kyle's first days stretched into his first weeks, he became accustomed to wearing shirts with collars and a string tie, rather than his open-necked homespun shirt and kerchief. His comfortable Levi's seemed faded and shabby, and so he wore the dark gabardine trousers. His boots scuffed and heel-worn, he wore the dead man's patent ones.

A woman from the kitchen brushed his Stetson and steamed a graceful sweep into the brim. The same woman saw to the washing of his clothes and the keeping of his room, although he did not know her name. One day a week— Sunday, he assumed it was—The Lady ordered the dinner table set with places for himself, Luned, the two women who kept the manor house clean, the cook, a girl who helped the cook, and the hostler. She said grace and carved the meat— Kyle had never heard of a woman carving meat at the table before—and asked her hired help questions about the animals and linens and such. She had no questions about Kyle's doings.

One cold day when the clouds were lowering and it seemed that flakes of snow were about to appear in the air, Kyle was standing at the window in his room when he saw a man walking toward the barn, a man looking all around, cautiously, like he didn't want to be seen.

By the time Kyle got on his gun belt and had shrugged into The Guardian's sheepskin coat, the man had disappeared into the barn. By the time Kyle got down the steps and through the corral and over to the barn, the man was on his knees in front of the trophy room door, picking at the padlock with a bit of wire. When Kyle's shape darkened the barn doorway, the man froze in that position.

Kyle brushed back his sheepskin coat to show the Colt in its holster. "Go on ahead," he said, closing the space between them, "I wanna know if a man can pick a lock like that. You go on ahead with what you're doin'."

"No," the man said, "I just . . . I didn't mean t'. . . ."

"Go on ahead," Kyle growled. "Who are you?"

"Name's Spigo, but I ain't nobody." The man's hands were shaking, but he was still picking the wire at the lock. Probably to his great surprise, it snapped open. "Oh, God," he said. "Look, I don't want no. . . ."

"Go on an' open it," Kyle said. Spigo opened the door. Kyle gave him a shove that sent him sprawling into the center of the room. He stared around at the saddles, the bridles fancy and plain, the hats on their pegs, the gun belts and rifles hanging from nails.

"See what you want?" Kyle challenged. He drew out a white handkerchief and wiped out the inside of his eye patch.

"Listen, this ain't my idea, at all," Spigo said. "I kin jus' be goin' now, and you won't be seein' me no more."

Kyle latched the door. On the wall next to the door hung a saddle, and on the saddle horn hung a plain hackamore braided out of rawhide. Kyle took down the hackamore and began pulling it through his fingers. It bent heavily, the way that greased rawhide does when it's tightly braided. There was a horsehair lariat on a peg, and he took it down as well. Spigo cowered back against one wall, but, when he put out his hand to steady himself against the wall, he was horrified to find his hand touching a rifle standing there, an old Henry of heavy caliber.

"Look," he said, "I jus' work on your ditch, that's all. Pretty good sawyer, some say. Sawyers ain't that easy come by, way up here, neither. Maybe I'd jus' better. . . ."

Kyle's face was without expression, but the look of it was starting to make the other man babble. It was as if he believed he could stay alive as long as he could keep talking. He made a fist with the hand that had touched the Henry rifle, felt the wetness of his palm, had an urge to take his shirt sleeve and clean his sweat from the barrel of The Guardian's rifle, but he was afraid to move.

"M'wife, she works in the big house there, see. It was her idea. Her idea is that maybe you ain't the right one, after all, maybe The Lady wants to get rid of y', see?" Fright and babbling were making him leer and blink, as though he were Kyle's confederate all of a sudden in some conspiracy. "She's thinkin', why don't my man get into that room and get him a gun, see, and take care of y'. Stupid idea. I had t' pretend I was goin' along with it, see, that's why I done this in broad daylight! Hell, who'd try t' get in here in broad daylight if they was serious about gettin' to a gun, anyway?"

He began to cringe his way toward Kyle, intending to bow and scrape his way past the glowering man in the sheepskin and sort of sidle out of the room.

Kyle stepped sideways in front of him. "Well," Kyle said, "I guess you didn't really take nothin' here."

"No! That's the thing! Didn't touch nuthin'. I better get back t' work."

Kyle's fingers opened, and the lariat dropped to the floor at their feet.

"Aw, here, lemme get that," Spigo said, and he bent over to pick it up for Kyle. When Kyle spoke again, Spigo was crouched in front of him, his hand on the lariat and his face turned upward, looking for Kyle's approval.

"Now you done it," Kyle said, "now you went and touched somethin' that ain't yours." He brought his fist up into Spigo's chin.

The blow was so hard that Spigo came upright, standing but tottering on his heels. Cool and methodical, Kyle punched him in the belly and then in the chin again, dropping him until he was crouching on the floor. Kyle gave him the point of his boot in the face and then in the ribs, and, when he rolled onto his back, he gave him a boot heel to the chin.

Spigo woke up with his head full of spinning blood-colored shapes and singing noises. He didn't know where he was. He was on his stomach, but he was looking down at the floor. There was something in his mouth, and he was swinging slightly, and the motion was making him sick.

Kyle had suspended Spigo face down with his hands tied behind him. He had looped the lariat over a rafter and tied it to the hackamore. The rawhide nosepiece was between Spigo's teeth. Kyle had hooked Spigo's hobbled feet onto a saddle peg so that his head hung down. Even to his groggy brain, the situation was obvious—if he moved his head much, or if he opened his teeth and spit out the braided nosepiece, or if his feet slipped off of that peg, the nosepiece would go down around his throat and strangle him. It was only a matter of time until his muscles would give way and he would end up hanged.

Kyle opened the door, got the heavy padlock, and hung it in the man's mouth by its hasp.

"Tell you what," Kyle said gently. "From now on, we're goin' to leave this room open. Any time you or your friends figger to try an' see if I'm the right man, why, you just come on in here. You bring 'em on down here from their work, why don't you, and show 'em all this stuff. See if it makes 'em want to try me, or just piss their overalls, instead."

And he went out, leaving the hanging man wondering how many minutes were left him in this life. He did not close the door.

Kyle walked through the snowflakes that were beginning to fall and up the steps and into the front door of the manor house. One of the cleaning women and the girl who helped the cook were in the front hallway. As he went past them, he saw a second cleaning woman on the landing at the top of the stairs. She was talking with Luned, who slipped into her room and shut the door the instant she saw him. Kyle paused before starting upstairs. He laughed a cruel laugh, like he was about to share a funny little story with the two women.

"I just now left a man hangin' by his neck," he advised them, and grinned crookedly. "The one of you that knows where he was goin' could save 'im, if you got there in time."

The older servant started to scream, but then choked the scream in her throat and rushed out the door. She looked like the kind who'd have goaded her man into doin' something stupid, like stealing a gun and trying to kill him. Kyle sneered and went on up to his room.

Sawyers, he thought. *Well, we'll have to keep them sawyers busier so's they won't have time to sneak around tryin' to shoot folks. Wonder how they'd like a job snakin' heavy logs through the snow this winter?*

Winter came down as hard as any winter ever had in that north country, and for weeks at a time nothing moved either at Crannog or along the Great North ditch. The temperature dropped and dropped until it would freeze exposed flesh instantly. A few times, Kyle rode to the collection of huts over the hill and ordered the men out to saw timbers and to clear the trails along the ditches, but finally, in their faces, he saw that they would rather face his guns than face that skin-searing, tortuous cold.

At times the winter would let up for a few days, and, if the snow was not too deep, Kyle would saddle the big horse and bundle himself into a half dozen layers of clothing and ride up to and along the ditch, looking for trouble. But the ditch was always the same: empty except for a few shallow patches of ice. The feeder streams were frozen solid. In the forests above the ditch the snow lay deep, and the whole land was hushed.

One morning seemed warm. It was not time for the thaw to begin, but that one morning a warm wind came down off of the backbone of the Rockies, and water began to drip from the eaves of the house, and, where there had been a thin crust of packed-down snow on the roads, there was something you could almost call mud. Kyle rode out in his sheepskin, carrying an extra blanket behind the saddle, just in case. Within a mile of the manor his coat became uncomfortably hot.

That day he rode all the way to the Number Six gate and sat in the saddle a long, long time, feeling the warming wind in his face and studying the way down into the valley. Thick snow cover hid all traces of the flood and the way it had gouged the hillside and tumbled the trees. Snow filled the valley below, burying the willows out of sight so that it looked like a vast park of smooth whiteness with only the fir and pine planted in it.

Far down, as far as he could see, there was a poor thin line of smoke rising and then bending east in the breeze. It had to be down near the Norwegian's cabin, or where the cabin had been, before the flood. Maybe past that. Trappers, Kyle thought, or hunters. He'd have to come up here more, now, and keep checking for strangers. He would bring the big Henry rifle because it would carry farther than the Winchester.

Kyle looked at the repairs on the gate, nodded, and rode back again, the warm wind behind him. The crew had put it back the way it had been, but he didn't know if the secret trigger, or whatever it was, had been fixed, too. He got to thinking about it, that gate and the other one farther down. Somebody knew how to make hidden pivots and hidden latches for those gates, and it occurred to him he ought to know that secret himself. Might be that the fat black toad with one eye knew. Might even have invented how they worked, for all of that. Son-of-a-bitch.

He could not remember what he had done to pass away long cold winters before this one. This one he whiled away time by reading books from The Lady's library, and by target practice with his guns when the weather was not absolutely freezing. He also went out for short rides, which took a long time. It took time to get bundled up against the cold and longer to rub the horse down afterward and to see to its bedding.

Kyle went to work, weaving a headstall for the horse, using The Guardian's old headstall as a guide to get the size right, but putting his own designs to it so that it would be his. He spent time searching for different colors of horsehair for it from the Crannog herd, even riding to the far ends of the horse pastures to find a lighter or darker shade, then roping the horse and grooming its tail by pulling it through his gloved hands until he had enough hair of a particular color. The gathering, alone, took many days; he would lay out the long strands and match them, sometimes going back just to get a few more of the right shade. He went at the weaving just as methodically, sometimes unweaving the whole thing to change the pattern.

He made the brow band from the horse's own tail, so the almost black color matched that of the horse, but patterned it with white slashes like lightning bolts and a white border from the tail of a white horse. The earpieces were of roan and bay color woven in the pattern of a diamondback rattler. He left long tassels of buttermilk color horsehair hanging from braids on either side.

One day Kyle went by the stables and saw his old horse standing there, head down, back drooping, like it was asleep. Funny. This horse had given him all it had during that fight in the ditch. He had figured it would be special to him all his life. Now here it was, and he didn't really feel anything about it, one way or another.

Some days Kyle and The Lady would try to play cards together, although he did not like learning her card games and she did not care for his. During these games she would speak of the man who had built the house, and how the ditches were dug, or she would tell him of the great plans for the place.

"The Company," she explained, laying her king of clubs across his jack, "has friends in the government. All of the region east of here, below the foothills, is declared to be wasteland, to be desert, not fit for farming. It is for this reason that the government has not opened it to those who wish to homestead. However, certain laws are in process of being passed . . . do you know anything about how laws are passed? . . . no? . . . suffice it to say that, when these laws are passed, all the land that has been declared desert and waste will be made available to those who can bring water to it."

She laid down a ten, followed by a queen, and gave him a triumphant but reserved look that could have grown into a smile with a bit more effort.

"You do realize what I am saying," she said, spacing her words carefully as if explaining to a four-year-old. "Those who provide irrigation for the land will, under law, be entitled to claim legal title to all of the land which they render productive. Thousands of square miles of land are waiting for those with enough water to sustain agriculture upon them for a period of five years."

Kyle shuffled the deck. He understood, right enough. Her scheme, her dream, was to own a territory the size of a state, or a small kingdom. If those laws passed, she could hardly miss. It was what she had set out to do, to control land and people.

As for himself, he had already found what it was he was needed for. He looked at The Lady across the table and saw only an employer. He thought about farmers coming to build their houses and churches and stores and the like, hoping to raise families on the newly irrigated land they'd have to buy from The Great North Reservoir Company, and he didn't give a damn. If they tried to squat on the land or steal the water, he'd shoot them down and bury them in their own damned vegetable plots.

At times he tried to think about the Keystone, but he couldn't remember much about it, or what he had done there. He remembered Will, but only as a pathetic drunk who had quit the ranch. Will had quit on everything. He thought about the men at Crannog, men who got together of an evening and drank the home-brewed beer and laughed and played poker, and he didn't give a damn about them, either. Catch one of them trying to stake out a claim somewhere on Great North land, or letting some relative steal water, and he'd take the hide off them with a rope's end. They were nothing to him. Nothing had any claim upon him now except the big horse, the guns, and the job of keeping Crannog running and the ditch running. It had become the only thing he could imagine Kyle Owen doing; it would always be there for him to do. It was his. It was he. He had already proven that he was the only man who could do it.

The cold gradually let go of the land in mid-March. In a few weeks he would be able to ride the whole ditch without seeing snow. Water was flowing again, muddy with the run-off. He found places where the winter freeze had forced rocks apart and made the dikes leak, and he ordered crews up to fix them. He stabbed his Bowie knife into the logs of the gates, checking for rotten ones. He put gangs out on the big ditch to clear away the winter débris, and he already had other groups digging the next series of delivery ditches out of the reservoir.

It was while riding one of the minor ditches, one cold windy day, that he saw the fat one-eyed man again, his face black as charcoal. As before, the ugly blob was sitting on a rock, probably the only warm place for miles, where he was out of the wind and facing the morning sun. On the other side of the ditch. Kyle figured the showdown was overdue; the toad would either tell him who he was and what he knew about the way the irrigation gates worked, or he'd get shot down right where he sat. Kyle rode straight toward him, drawing his Colt, wondering what it was going to feel like to blast the toad-like bastard.

But the little man sat with a smirking gleam in his one eye while pointing his iron rod down the hill. Kyle barely had time to swivel around to see what he was pointing at, when he heard a shot and felt something grab at the sleeve of his jacket.

A man was behind a horse below, standing on the ground, sighting his rifle across the saddle. *Wham!* came the next shot, and the toad-man laughed and banged his iron bar on the rocks with great delight. Kyle swung off the big horse and grabbed the headstall and began running with the horse toward the shelter of a ponderosa growing next to the ditch. More shots followed him, kicking up gravel under the horse's belly and then whistling overhead.

Kyle kept moving, putting more distance between himself and the shooter, cussing all the while. He rounded a curve of the ditch and got out of sight. He mounted up, took the Winchester from the scabbard, shucked a shell into the chamber, and listened. The sound of hoofs was not long in coming. He lay low along the horse's neck, reins in one hand and rifle in the other. He listened, and, when his ears told him that the other rider was just the other side of the rise, Kyle straightened up in the saddle, kicked the horse forward, and began firing the instant the other man's head was in sight.

The rifle slug took his attacker in the temple, just where the nose joins the forehead. His body jerked backward and somersaulted over the horse's haunches and landed flat on its back while the horse trotted on.

Kyle caught up the loose horse and went back to the man, lying spraddled on the ground where he had fallen. He studied the face that still had a surprised look on it. His head seemed to be lying in a hole in the ground, a hole that was a deep pool of steaming blood; the exiting bullet had taken off the back of his skull.

Kyle got down to collect the rifle and the gun belt and Schofield revolver. He stripped the shotgun chaps from the corpse and recovered the broad-brimmed hat. He searched out the dead man's wallet and knife, and wrapped everything up in the jacket the man had been wearing and strapped it behind the saddle of the riderless horse.

The toad man was still perched on the rock when Kyle rode back, leading the other horse.

"I'm sendin' some men to bury him." He scowled. "See the wolves don't get him till they get here. And next time I see you, there's gonna be a reckonin' between us. You can count on that."

In return, the fat black creature aimed his finger at Kyle and dropped his thumb on it like the hammer on a pistol, and he winked his eye and grinned widely as if he knew something Kyle didn't know. Kyle rode away wondering why he hadn't shot that pile of shit while he had the chance.

Back at Crannog, Kyle gave the horses to the hostler to

take care of and put away the rest of the equipment himself. Later, after supper, he took his jacket to the downstairs woman so she could sew up the two holes that the shooter's bullet had punched through the sleeve. Then, rather than return to his room, he drew his heavy sheepskin coat around him and went outside to smoke a cigar and have a look around before it got dark.

The tobacco smoke helped to get the smell of steaming blood out of his nostrils. The peace of the evening somewhat stilled the echoes of gunshots in his ears.

Kyle looked off over the peace of Crannog and the parks and forests beyond and felt a feeling of ownership, a feeling of having finally come to what his life was for. Ever since leaving that stinking place over the divide. . . . where those two hopeless cases lived. . . . what the hell were their names?. . . . he had made no mistakes. Nothing was easy, nothing was safe, but he hadn't made mistakes. A lot of strange stuff yet to figure out, like that one-eyed toad in buckskin and this strange Fontana Lady, but he knew it was only a matter of time.

The sun was a half hour over the divide now, and its last crimson and silver rays were slicing the clouds into long wedges. *Nice sunset,* he thought. *Nice red color to it.* A furrow appeared between his good eye and the eye patch. *Somethin' about sunsets I'm supposed to know,* he thought. *Sunset color, and, for some reason, horseshoes.* But the cigar was burned short, and the dark was spreading across the yard and buildings. Time to get inside.

Chapter Twelve

The Bridegroom

"For the love of God, Luned!"

The woman's voice carried like a bugling elk, Kyle thought. Right through the walls. He opened the door to his room and looked out into the hall, but the women were upstairs. Luned made some reply he couldn't hear, and then Fontana's voice echoed through the house again.

"I wish you would stop denying it!" she said. "You don't think I know your ways, but I know. I know all about you. You followed me. Me! And what makes me so angry is that the man was harmless. He was the only one, of all the people around me, the only one to offer comfort to me. And then you . . . *you!*"

Luned's answer was too soft to hear, but it was pretty clear that it wasn't what Fontana wanted to hear.

"A lie! His only *desire* was to follow me and speak with me. Do you think I was so eager to be loved, this soon after my husband's death? The man found me at the grave, spoke to me when no one else would. He stood for hours in the meadow, waiting for no more than a chance to wave and smile. *Why* did you . . . ?"

Kyle heard Luned's soft voice again. Then Fontana's.

"And what if I did want his love . . . any real love with some human joy to it . . . what is that to you? Was that a cause to shoot your lethal little arrows at him, drive him out of the valley? Because he *is* gone. No one has seen him since the last day I saw him. He is dead, or he is gone, and it is your doing. Yours.

"Don't take that posture with me, either. I know your ways. My husband said you tried to interfere with his work. But to do this! And a woman, to do this to another woman!"

Kyle got his jacket and gun belt and went out, down the back stairs. Wrangling females were real high on his list of things to stay away from.

The hostler wasn't around, but Kyle didn't mind. He took his time, rubbing the horse with the saddle blanket, easing the new bridle over its ears, placing the bit gently in the big mouth. He was just swinging the heavy saddle up onto the horse when Luned came to the stable door. She wore the tight-lipped expression women have after they have been in an argument.

"Did you kill him?" she asked.

"Who'd that be?" Kyle said indifferently.

"I don't know his name. He worked around the settlement. He became infatuated with Fontana, spent days watching for her to come out of the house. He followed her every time she rode to the chapel. And that grave."

"Have a horse?"

"I doubt it. Few of the shack men do. Most traded away such things to keep themselves in food and clothes a few more months. Now they live on the hope of having homesteads and sharing the wealth when the land under the ditch starts getting water. He is one. He obviously had some idea The Lady would marry him when the claiming time comes. A fool."

"And he showed up dead?"

"He hasn't been seen for a while is all."

Kyle was silent for a moment while he pulled the cinch tight. "Probably that back shooter," he said. "If you know what kind of gun he carried, there's one hangin' in the trophy room now. Belonged to a man that tried to kill me, up in that big meadow. But I didn't kill him, not unless he died of the cold. Prob'ly took off with his tail between his legs."

"Did you give him a beating?"

"Yeah. Why? You get the blame for killin' him?"

Luned ignored the question. "It was good that you gave him a beating. The Lady Fontana actually might have left with him. And without Fontana, the entire project would almost certainly collapse. Any stranger could come in and take it over, and all the workers would be left with nothing. As things stand now, they have no claim on any of it, except her word that they will have the first filing on the farming land when the ditch water reaches it.

"She is angry now, and will be angry and pity herself and be sorrowful throughout most of the night. In the morning, be ready. She will call you to come to her."

Kyle only nodded. Then he mounted up and rode out of the stable, ducking under the doorway.

His need for solitude drew him again toward the high meadow and the low pine hills bordering it, but in truth he was not fully aware where he was going or why. That wyrding feeling was upon him again, as if he had drunk a power of liquor and was feeling the fog in the brain, as if he were drifting along above himself, watching himself and the horse moving rhythmically over the grass and up the faint trails. Something, he felt, was going to happen to him, something beyond his ability to control, and beyond whoever he was at this moment.

Kyle's sleep that night was fitful. The pillow seemed full of lumps rather than feathers, and became damp from his sweat. The blanket twisted around him as he rolled to one side and the other. Short dreams came all through the night. He woke from each one with every muscle tensed. He was on his feet before sunrise, staring out the window. In his last dream he heard the blacksmith again: "What one man sees as sunrise is another's nightfall."

He washed in the basin. He paced the floor, watched the morning rise, even sat on the bed and looked at a book without remembering what was in it. Finally he heard the cook clanging the stove lids, and, beginning to smell bacon and coffee, he went down the back stairs to fortify himself for the meeting to come.

Lady Fontana was brief and to the point in telling him what was on her mind. Her eyes were red from crying, and, while she held herself as straight and dignified as ever, he could tell the perfect lady-like posture was costing her extra effort this morning.

"It is not fitting that we live in the same house and are un-married," she said with stiff lips.

"Well, I seem to recall that was your idea," Kyle said.

"It is needful. Your job is to protect me, as well as the project, and you must, therefore, remain near. But it is time we marry."

" 'Scuse me," Kyle said, "what was that you said?"

"Marry. As guardian, you have a share in the land claims and in the revenues once the water reaches the farming land. Luned did not explain this? But for that, you must be my hus-band. Without that, you would be seen by the workers as only another hired man."

"Kind of a strange marriage, seems to me."

"You must. If the people agree, of course."

"The people? You mean that ratty-lookin' bunch of

hunkies livin' over in that collection of calf sheds they call their settlement?"

Lady Fontana stiffened and ignored the remark. "Tomorrow we will go to the settlement. In the hallway closet on the second floor you will find suitable clothing. We will leave the house at mid-morning. And one thing more," she said.

"What's that?"

"This marriage will have nothing to do with being man and woman, you understand. It will change nothing while we are inside this house. Nothing. Outside, you will escort me or will appoint someone to escort me if you cannot. A married woman in my position should be escorted. When the time comes for the water to be released to the homestead land, your share will make you a wealthy man. Should I die, you will also have my share. But from this day on, you will protect the water project as if it is your own."

"You think I'd just take off on you otherwise, is that it?"

"I think," she said, "that this is the way things must be."

Just after midday, Kyle Owen, the Lady Fontana, and Luned rode together into the central square of the settlement. It made a curious picture: Kyle, all in black, even to the scarf drawn up around his chin, sat in his saddle scowling and glaring around with his one eye; Luned, in a white jacket and white riding skirt split so she could ride astride, looked more like she belonged in some equestrian park in St. Louis; Fontana, in black dress, hat, and veil, sitting her mare sidesaddle, looked as if she were waiting for an English fox hunt to begin.

The working people were bunched up in front of this mounted trio, some standing in awkward stances and some sitting on stumps or the ground. Some sat in a wagon bed. All of them were dressed in rough cotton and wool, many wearing homemade shoes and homespun coats. The women wore shawls; most had their hair pulled back under scarves or homemade bonnets. A few kids squatted together, playing with a mound of fine dirt at a gopher hole. Some of the people studied their shoes or the ground or picked at their fingers. Some looked boldly up at Kyle, with dislike and distrust plainly written on their faces.

Lady Fontana sat calmly erect. *You could use her backbone for a ramrod,* Kyle thought. She watched the people until they were all quiet in the coolness of her steady gaze. Only when they had been motionless for several minutes did she speak:

"The mourning time must now end, and the project must continue. Our Guardian is buried and can no longer protect our interests. For this there is no help, no remedy. But we . . . you . . . must continue the work. You have worked hard and faithfully, and, in the spring and summer to come, I expect to see the control ditches completed. A year from now we will be turning the water into the feeder ditches and out onto the land, onto our own land. Your land."

Approval rumbled through the rag-tag bunch of hopefuls. Kyle suppressed a sneer. People like these never got hold of land, he was thinking. Never got a break. They'd do the work, but his bet was they'd never own the big irrigated farms they were dreaming of.

"Until now, you have kept our agreement of secrecy. And you have done well. The Guardian kept faith with you, ensuring no outsider would interrupt the flow of the water or discover the extent of the Great North project. He had no ambition for himself . . . he wanted no lands, no rewards. He served us all because of his allegiance to me. I was to share my portion with him.

"We have held his wake, and he is buried, and it is over. Now we are without protection except for the man you see here, a man able to take on the duties of The Guardian. Some of you men are already working for him, and I have not heard complaints. With the approval of the settlement, of all of you . . ."—she brought a gold ring from her pocket and held it aloft for them to see—"I shall marry him and endow him with half my share, as I endowed The Guardian, so that he will stay and protect the interests of us all. If you disapprove, say so now . . . if not, then I intend to marry. After harvest, men will gather the cattle and drive them down out of the mountains to the buyer . . . they will return with a minister to perform the service."

She saw no movement in the crowd. No voice was raised. Most of them had gone back to looking down at the ground or were looking at each other with blank expressions like her announcement had nothing to do with them. She waited. There was no movement. Finally she reached over and took Kyle's left hand and placed the ring on his finger, then held his hand aloft as if he were a prize fighter who had just won a fight.

Still no one moved. They stood there stupidly, some looking at Lady Fontana, some at Kyle, most of them looking at the ground and at each other.

Luned finally broke the spell, wheeling her horse around and trotting away from the settlement. Kyle and Fontana followed, not looking at each other and not speaking.

He did not know why and he did not know how, but this move of Lady Fontana was already working on him. He felt a new responsibility, for the ground they were riding on, for the forest stretching up the mountain beyond the big house, for the ditch project. For the people. His mind began forming plans. Now that he was a partner in the deal, he had ideas he wanted to carry out. Like fencing in big parts of the park for horse and cattle breeding, once the settlement people had gone off to be bean farmers with their new water. He'd get the workers to do the fencing now, then he'd use it later. In the years to come, with settlers moving into the region, somebody was going to make a real pile of money selling beef and horses.

And the timber. There was money in that, too. He meant to check to see if the control ditch would carry logs, if it was straight enough and wide enough. Maybe even rafts of sawn lumber. A man could make a fortune selling lumber out there on that open flat land beyond the foothills. It was just a matter of owning the trees and getting them out of the mountains. With the water he could have a sawmill, a good one. Not like the ramshackle lash-up that Fontana's sawyers used for their beams and boards.

Mining, too. Now that he was the water boss, he'd sell placer water to jackass miners back over the divide and take shares in the gold in return. Maybe stake out some mining claims over there himself, and sell them.

"Your mind is elsewhere," Lady Fontana said, breaking into his musings. It was not an invitation to start a conversation; it was merely an observation.

"Just thinkin' about what needs to be done around here," he said.

"Good," she replied.

A cloud rose above the western mountain range and drifted across the afternoon sun. Within minutes the air was chilled. Then the cloud moved on, and from under it came bright streaming streaks of gold. As the trio rode toward the house, they saw the gilded evening light glinting off the west side of the house like a summer morning sunrise.

In the high Rockies, May is the month in which the word "park" takes on full meaning. They are not fields, those mile-wide treeless expanses of grass and willow-margined streams, nor are they meadows. They are parks in which deer stroll and browse the new grass while fawns dash away from the does and back again, in which the elk lie down in the warm sun and chew their cuds. Above, eagles endlessly circle. The parks are ribboned with clear-running streams meandering through lush grass and willow thickets, streams dotted with dimples where the brook trout make leisurely lunch of floating bugs. Patches of flowers abound in surprising numbers; the blue and purple of wild iris and aster, pasque flowers and lupine; the yellow of golden banner and bushy penstemon and rabbitbrush rising above the new green grass.

There are smells in the air, smells of fresh earth burrowed up by marmots and gophers—those rodent residents whom the circling hawks and eagles watch—and from the high snowfields above timberline come the spring smells of rushing water from snowmelt and of damp granite gorges.

Musky smells, too, like unexpected whiffs from a damp winter den still warm from the bear who lay there all winter. Or like the musty scent that makes a coyote suddenly stop in his trot across the upper end of the park to raise his nose and search for the source.

The Guardian felt it, riding across the park late one afternoon, trotting the horse just because it felt good to feel the solid thudding of muscles jarring him and just to feel the breeze on his face. Even if he had been blind in both eyes and even if he was not aware of the warmth of the late afternoon sun, he would have known it was spring just from the smells. The earth. The grass. The willows. The stream.

The next morning he started down the back stairway for breakfast. The narrow staircase had a dark and lonely look. Not that he gave a damn about seeing anybody—except that cook with a plate of hotcakes and eggs and a pot of coffee. But he decided he would rather go down the main stairs. There was no reason he shouldn't. He belonged in the house, and he was no damned servant.

The Lady Fontana had been in the hallway recently. He could smell her powder, a faint sweet flowery aroma left drifting in the air just at the top of the stairs. It reminded him of her hair. A few days earlier he had been outside and coming toward the house, when he had caught a glimpse of her standing at her window, brushing her hair. She had seemed to be looking off into the distance with a dreamy look. Her scent stayed with him through breakfast and was on his mind as he went to make his morning check of the stables and barns.

He and the hostler were talking together behind the stalls about whether there would be enough bedding straw to last until they could get more when they heard Fontana's voice calling for the hostler. He bowed apologetically and hurried back into the barn where she was waiting to go riding.

The Guardian heard her tell the hostler to get her mare from the stall and saddle it, and, when he put his eye to the crack between the boards, he could see the hostler smoothing the blanket across the mare's back while Fontana waited in the center of the aisle. Now that she was through with mourning and warmer weather had come, she wore lighter colored dresses, like the one she had on now. The bright morning sun was pouring through the doorway behind her.

The hostler finished and held the mare next to a mounting block so that she could place herself in the sidesaddle and adjust her legs and skirts. The Guardian stared at a glimpse of ankles and bit of calf; as the curved leather-covered pommel disappeared beneath her skirts, he caught his breath.

Fontana rode out into the sunshine and waited for him to saddle up and join her. Together they "took exercise" as she liked to call it, riding up across one arm of the park to inspect the ditch building, then around a rock outcrop and up to a spot where they could look down on the settlement shacks. She was every bit the picture of a countess inspecting her lands. She did not make conversation. She did not ride near any of the shacks or acknowledge any of the working men. She remained aloof, detached.

Her Guardian could only ride beside her, not talking. It was a kind of routine by now. The only indication that they were aware of each other was because of his eye. As they turned and went one way and the other, he would drop back and then bring his horse up on the other side of hers so that his good eye was toward her. At times Fontana seemed to get on his blind side deliberately. Just to make him uncomfortable?

On this particular morning, he kept her on his good side and slightly ahead of him, and he watched her as they rode. It seemed to him that her figure had more profile than usual. He noticed her mouth more, particularly the slight pout that she made with her lips. She didn't do it when she was aware of someone watching her, but sometimes she let her guard down, and her lips would part just slightly and form a sugges- tion of a pout. Once, when a new calf from the meat herd dashed in front of her, he even saw those lips open into a smile.

A few days afterward, The Guardian was across the hall from his room looking through a storage closet when he thought he heard singing. Or humming, at least. At first he thought it must be the woman who cleaned and took care of the upstairs, but then he realized that the closet was directly beneath Fontana's rooms. He listened hard and heard splashing noises in addition to the soft singing. A lead drain pipe came down one corner of the storage closet; her bath was just above.

She was no more than ten feet above him, in her bath. Looking up at the ceiling boards, he imagined her with her hair drawn up off her neck and her shoulders bare, and her arms bare, too.

When he left the closet, he shut the door quietly. He crossed to his room, got his hat and gun belt, and took a walk in the sun.

The Guardian walked a half mile or more, to the old gateposts marking the entrance to Crannog's grounds. Not once did he look back at the house. One gatepost was leaning dangerously. He figured he ought to send a couple of men out there to take the whole damned thing down before it fell on somebody. He didn't know why he hadn't noticed it before.

Walking back, the whistle of many wings and the staccato wharking of flying ducks making conversation made him look up at the flock going over. They were headed for the pond on the other side of the hill past the chapel. He had not tasted roast duck for a long, long time. The old man who was lame, the one who was married to the cook back where he used to live on the . . . the Keystone, that was the name of the place . . . that old guy used to get ducks, and the cook would roast them.

The idea of shooting some ducks grew as he walked back. He didn't want to go back into the house. What if he was going up the main stairway and Fontana was coming down, and what if she had that fresh damp smell around her to remind him of what he had imagined that morning? No, he didn't think he wanted to go back inside, not for a while yet. He would go and shoot him some ducks, instead.

He strode into the barn, yelling for the hostler to saddle his horse while he collected some baling twine to hang the ducks on the saddle horn. Then he decided he would use a grain sack. By the time he found one, the hostler had the horse tied by the reins to the whip socket of a buggy standing in the barn aisle.

"Been shinin' the brass, I see," The Guardian said condescendingly.

"Yeah," the hostler replied. "The Lady thought she might be takin' a buggy ride this afternoon or tomorrow."

Maybe tomorrow, The Guardian thought. *If she expects me t' be goin' along.*

The hostler rubbed the horse's back and smoothed the blanket onto it. The Guardian had polished the dark saddle the day before, working over it until he could see himself in the leather.

As he opened the trophy room door, there was a rushing flutter of wings over his head. He had disturbed a small hawk sitting on the top of the door frame waiting for some mouse to go scampering toward the grain bins. The hawk flew on up into the rafters.

Kyle only muttered—"Damn' bird."—and went into the trophy room. One of the former guardian's trophies was a good shotgun, a Greener, and a canvas shoulder bag of shells. Kyle wiped off the dust with his bandanna and checked the barrels, then cocked the hammers and pulled the triggers. Worked smoothly. He wondered what the story was, about this gun and bag of shells. It looked like his predecessor had surprised some Englishman on a bird hunt. Didn't matter. There were lots of stories on these walls, if the guns and saddles could talk. He picked out a couple of shells he figured had the right size pellets for ducks and loaded them into the gun.

Out in the aisle of the barn, the hostler was just tucking in the girth strap. The Guardian glared at the polished buggy and pictured himself and a smiling Fontana riding along with a picnic hamper and a blanket in the back, she in her white spring dress and that scented powder on her. He gave the saddle horn a pull to test the girths and was sliding his hand down over the leather, to feel the good job he'd done polishing it, when the hawk in the rafters decided it was time to let go. The blob of white bird shit was too wet to make much sound as it hit the leather, but wet enough to splatter on his hand and spread out on the seat of his saddle.

The Guardian swore and jerked his head back to see up toward the roof. The hostler ducked back against the horse stall. Kyle swore again, and, when his eye had located the hawk sitting up in the shadows, he brought up the Greener and cocked both hammers as the barrel swung up. He didn't wait to aim but fired from the hip straight up into the rafters. And if hell ever broke loose in a barn, it broke loose in that one. Chunks of boards and shingles and rafter came raining down through the cloud of gunsmoke while the roar of the two barrels seemed to keep on reverberating forever in the barn. The horse plunged and reared and crow hopped and knocked The Guardian onto his butt, then headed out the open door, dragging the buggy along until it caught on a stall and turned over. The whip socket and part of the dashboard went with the horse.

Looking up from the floor through the fog of choking dust, he saw a shaft of light coming down upon him in the haze. It was as if the heavens had opened and a holy radiance were touching him. Or as if two simultaneous blasts from a ten-gauge Greener shotgun had torn an opening in the barn roof big enough to throw a sow through. The hawk had either gone out through the hole propelled by two loads of birdshot, or it was sitting unharmed some place, laughing itself to death.

The hostler cowered, crouched down against a stall, trying to make himself invisible behind a post and knowing much better than to make a run for it. The Guardian rose to his feet, drawing himself up to his full height, seeming to tower in the shaft of sunlight pouring through the dust. He ran his finger inside his eye patch, and, when he brought it back and looked at it, it was covered in rafter dust and bird shit. He glared around at the overturned buggy with the broken dashboard. The horse was nowhere to be seen. He walked across to the crouching hostler, and with his free hand he gripped his shoulder and hauled him to his feet.

The Lady Fontana, who had just dusted herself with her scented powder and who was brushing her hair and admiring her own eyes in the mirror, heard the twin explosions and rushed to her window. When she looked out, she saw something strange. Incomprehensible. Dust was rising from the barn roof. Her Guardian's horse was standing a distance from the barn, dragging some kind of trash from its reins. Walking toward the horse were two men, The Guardian and the hostler, and The Guardian had a shotgun in one hand and the other arm around the hostler's shoulders. Both of them were laughing and appeared to be enjoying a great joke.

It took two workmen the better part of a week to cut new roof boards, shingle the hole, and splice the joist that the shotgun pellets had blown in half. The Guardian stood in the corral looking up at the fresh new shingles of the patch on the roof. His thoughts of Fontana didn't bother him as much now. When they went riding, he talked to her and even smiled a few times. She didn't ask about the hole in the roof, and he didn't volunteer to tell her. He did, however, smile behind his napkin when she complimented the duck dinner.

Spring gave way to summer very abruptly, as it does in the mountains, and The Guardian stepped up his patrols of the irrigation works, especially the big ditch. One day as the horse was clopping along the ditch embankment on the way to the Number Six gate, he saw something move in the distance. It seemed to be a man running away. Probably another one of those damned miners, looking to get some water from the ditch. Probably heard him coming and was hightailing for home. The Guardian dismounted and slid the long Winchester out of the scabbard and threw three shots in the man's direction, just to hurry him along and discourage him from coming back.

On another day he surprised a trapper heading for the divide. This smelly individual in stained buckskins was leading a pair of mules—not burros, but big mules—packed with all sorts of junk. Even his gun was junk, just an old percussion cap musket. The Guardian let him keep it, but rammed a half dozen lead balls down the barrel, along with a handful of sand, and busted the nipple with a rock. With the trapper tied to a tree, he went through the packs and threw out the shabby cooking gear and a sack of provisions and then left with the two mules. Back at Crannog, he didn't bother putting the stuff into the trophy room, except for the keg of gunpowder and the bar of lead and bullet mold. The rest, including the beaver traps, he gave to the hostler. The mules would be put to work on the rock sled.

He still smelled Fontana's flowery perfume in the house. He still watched for moments when he could gaze at her figure without her being aware of it. Sometimes he would be stirred by the way she caressed a wayward lock of hair back into place or the way she sometimes touched her finger to her lips when she was concentrating. But the tension was gone. No longer did he feel his gut all tied up with a sense of expectancy when he saw her or caught her scent.

The days got warmer and the nights became softer, with long twilight evenings that brought the shadows slowly stealing across the park toward the house. He would sit outside until the mountain air took on a chill, listening to the nighthawks and the coyotes singing the moon up, listening to the softness of the mountain breeze passing the tips of the pines, sometimes bringing him muffled sounds of people over at the settlement.

One evening, sitting on a chunk of log in the shadow of a corral post while the darkness gathered, he looked up at Luned's window and saw her putting her hair up for the night. Fascinated, he studied the way her breasts lifted upward and outward when she swept both of her hands up behind her head. His pulse hammered when he saw her reaching behind her back for the buttons of her dress. Had she not suddenly seen the open curtains, and had she not closed them, God knows what he would have seen. He knew, though, and the thought of it pushed away all the evening whispers and scents.

He slept poorly that night, waking at times to stare at the ceiling and imagine the slender body in bed just above him. He hardly remembered where it had been, or the name of the woman, but he remembered a white nightgown from long ago, how it clung over the thighs and breasts of a sleeping woman.

Some mornings, Luned went out to the lawn beside the manor house to practice with her bow and arrow. The Guardian would watch from his window. She shot with her arms bare, except for a leather protector on her left forearm, and she wore an ivory-colored skirt that came to mid-calf. She was like a statue from a picture book standing in the sunlight with her back straight and her breasts lifted as she took the bowstring with three fingers and drew it back to her cheek.

One day she was riding out just as he was leaving the

corral, and she asked him where he was headed. She had never before spoken to him when she saw him going out for a morning look-around.

"As long as you're not going near the pond beyond the trees," she said, "I wonder if you'd mind watching to see that none of the men go that way. When the weather is warm, I like to go swimming there. I like sunning myself afterward. You understand."

He understood. In his mind he saw the whole picture. Sun-warmed grass bordering the pond, the tall lodgepoles sheltering it like a stockade fence, the quiet and the sunshine everywhere, and Luned walking naked out into the water. Luned, later, lying naked on the grass. Oh, yes. He saw it very plainly.

The following day, he rode clear to the lower end of the ditch leading out of the reservoir, and it took all day. He told himself to bring blankets and food next time and stay overnight. No reason always to be sleeping in that house full of women. It made him nervous. It made him want some action, somebody to beat up. Down off the end of the ditch he found where some nester had planted stakes, and these he pulled up. He made a bonfire of them, and, while it was burning, he searched around until he found the small stone cairn he knew would be there, and dismantled it until he found the tobacco sack with the claim note in it.

I Jakob Swansen, it read, **herby clame this here 160 acres acording to law. Trespasers will be shot.**

The Guardian sneered and looked in his saddlebag for a pencil stub. **Your the trespaser,** he added to the note, **and will git shot.** He stuck it in the remains of the cairn and rode away, figuring he ought to come back in a month or so and see if ol' Jakob was a big as fool as he sounded.

The Guardian thought about doing some deer hunting, or maybe shooting himself an elk, but the weather was too warm and the venison wouldn't be any good. The animals would have bugs in them until the first hard freeze came. But he could check on the meat herd and maybe shoot a yearling for the cook. He found the herd lying down near one of the ponds. Some of them were standing in the water, drinking. He sat on his horse and watched them. It felt good just to do that. He didn't need to shoot any meat. Come fall, he told himself, he and some of the men would go on a roundup and move the other herd to pastures farther down in the foothills. It would be nice, riding along in the cool fall days, moving the cattle, watching the men and horses at their jobs.

He needed to get a crew together and build some new fences, too. It was good to work with men. There wasn't this tight feeling all the time, like when he and the two women spent time together, like they were holding their breath waiting for something.

Coming over the last ridge that rose between him and Crannog, The Guardian felt the trees pressing in close against him. It might have been because it was getting dark and he was hungry and tired, but the branches seemed to grab at his clothes and slap at his face on purpose. The pine forest was dark and hostile, and a cold wind came to blow up his back and chill the sweat soaking his shirt.

Chapter Thirteen

Four Rifles Ride North

The Keystone Ranch slumbered. In the big house, the hallway clock ticked away the dark hours. It was just after midnight; the sable gloom made a black shroud across the pre-dawn land. Gwen was sleeping like a cat, curled against her husband with her head pillowed in the hollow of his shoulder. Art snored softly, oblivious to the loving little weight that made his arm tingle.

Mary, the cook, and John, her husband, were the only other people in the big house. They slept in separate beds pulled close together. The quilt over Mary's heavy form rose and fell rhythmically. John had thrown off his quilt sometime in the night and now twitched and shivered from time to time as phantom drafts stole through the room.

From the black shadow of the bunkhouse across the ranch yard came a steady cacophony of every sound the human respiratory system could possibly make while sleeping. Once in a while a deep sigh issued from the dark, above the ongoing snoring, as some cowboy dreamed of a Kansas girl he might have wooed. Other sleepers groaned from time to time as if grappling with heavy weights in their dreams, while still others lay relaxed with open mouths, exhaling the raspy racket of dead branches scraping a corrugated tin roof.

A rider came out of the east, moving gingerly through the shrouded dark, letting his horse pick its careful way along the ruts of the road. From time to time the rider would dismount and skyline the horizon, which was all but invisible to him from saddle height. Bending close to the ground, he scanned the faint change of shadow where the black opaque night met the dense and featureless strip of land. He looked for shapes of buildings, outlines of fences or gateposts. But for two hours he had seen nothing on the dark horizon except where the two ruts of the road crossed over it.

About to dismount once more to skyline for landmarks, he stopped abruptly. He had caught a scent. He leaned over to pat the horse's shoulder as if the horse needed now to be quiet so the man could smell the air. It was the smell of wood smoke. Just a light aroma on the motionless air, but it was the smell of smoldering pine. Like the banked embers of an overnight fire, a cooking fire. A cooking fire in a stove. He had arrived.

Man and horse together followed the scent, careful not to run up against any fences. Soon they came to the back wall of a Keystone building. He led the animal along rail fences and around sheds until his hand felt a corral gate. He opened it, took the horse in, lifted the saddle and blanket and saddlebags, and left the horse there in the corral where it would be safe until morning.

He carried saddle, blanket, and bags back along the rails and came to the corner of a building and moved around it until the ground felt clean underfoot, and there he threw down the saddle for his pillow. Huddled in his sheepskin coat and with the saddle blanket over him, he went to sleep to dream of Mary's thick flapjacks and strong coffee. He'd have cream in his coffee, he decided. And bacon. He'd have bacon with those flapjacks.

"Gwen?"

She stirred softly, purred herself more deeply into the pillow.

"Gwen!"

"Mmmm. Mmm?"

"He's back. Look at this."

Gwen sat up, stretched, and put both hands up into her yellow hair to sweep it back over her shoulders. Still half asleep, she swung her legs off the edge of the bed, and shivered in the chill morning air. "Cold!" she whimpered, her feet feeling for the slippers. "What is it?"

"Come look," Art said. "He's back."

She tied the strings on her wrapper and went to where Art was standing at the window, snugging up against him. He put his arm around her waist and drew her close for warmth. She lay her head against his shoulder and looked down from the window. There was a man sleeping on the ground against the wall down below. His head was pillowed on a very good saddle and over him was spread what looked like a new sheepskin coat and Mexican saddle blanket. His boots were dusty from travel, but not battered. He was no range bum.

"Who is it?" she asked, looking up into Art's face.

"Hard to tell, isn't it?" Art said. "It's Will. Will Jensen."

Gwen could be forgiven for not recognizing a man who had once lived on this very ranch, since she had not really known him well and because the last image of him she had had was of a skinny, pale shadow of a man wearing dirty clothes and a torn hat, a man whose shirt and trousers hung on him like a scarecrow's. She recalled a man who walked with his head down, his face toward the ground. The man below the window moved, and the sheepskin fell off his face, and she saw that he was quite strong-looking, quite handsome, in fact. She would not have known it was Will Jensen.

Will took a late morning breakfast with Art and Gwen. Over helpings of Mary's biscuits and preserves followed by grateful gulps of the hot coffee, he told them such parts of his story as he thought might seem interesting to them. Some of the places he'd seen, especially in the first year, he did not remember. Nor did he care to. Sometimes he remembered episodes of his booze-haunted odyssey only because nameless men and loveless women, temporary and insubstantial companions, had told him about them. Mostly what he remembered was that he worked at various jobs while staying "perpetually intoxicated."

Gwen smiled at him, tilting her head slightly to let her hair fall away from her perfect neck. "You may use the word *drunk* you know," she said, "I don't mind."

OK, drunk all the time. If the drunks and derelicts he hung around with could be believed, he had done outlandish things and had fought a dozen forgotten fights in bars that were now only blurry memories. Of any bar in any town, he could remember only the same smell of stale beer soaking into the same filthy wooden floors, and the same stink of tobacco swill in tarnished brass spittoons. His memory knew the smell of whisky being poured into a glass while he slouched with his face nearly on the bar, his nose close to the glass, watching with dull eagerness for the amber liquid to reach the top.

He said very little about his recovery or how it had come about after all those months of fog and whisky. He said even less about his recent jobs and the fine horse and expensive saddle. When Art asked, Will only laughed and grinned and said: "Oh, I woke up dead one morning and saw I'd killed myself. Even tried to embalm my own corpse in alcohol. So I

said . . . 'Well, Will Jensen, that will be just about enough of
that! '"

In reply to Gwen's direct and none-too-diplomatic question he said: "A lady? Well, if it was a lady that set me on the
straight path, I don't recall her. Ladies I ran into never
seemed to know what a straight road looked like."

Poor women, Gwen thought, eyeing the outline of Will's
chest and shoulders under his snug store-bought shirt. They
missed a catch.

"No," Will continued, "just by sheer luck I finally fell
down . . . drunk . . . at the feet of a man of Christian charity. A
man patient enough to put up with me while I got back to
bein' worth my hire."

After lunch, Art and Will took horses and rode around
looking at the improvements and at the places that still
needed work. They talked about cattle and men they both
knew, and land, and the future of the West. They went
looking for men who were culling cattle or cutting fence posts
and moving hay so Will could say hello to his old *compañeros*
and meet some of the new men.

"Pasque is even around here somewhere," Art said as
they rode through a patch of chokecherry so he could show
Will a spring they had dug out and rocked up to make a
pond.

"Pasque? No kidding!"

"Yeah. Road up from the Cimarron River country, oh,
about three, four days ago. Things down there were as quiet
as they are around here, I guess. So he thought he'd just make
a little *pasear* up here and pay us a visit. I thought maybe we'd
do some hunting, 'cept it's not cold enough yet. But I was
'way up in the peaks last summer and saw this big ol' ram and
thought I'd sure like to have that head for my wall. Full curve
on the horns, all the way around to here."

"That would be the peaks north of here?" Will asked. He looked at Art.

Art looked off to the northwest. It was the direction Will had ridden three years ago. And it was the direction Kyle had taken two years ago.

Kyle was the first one Will asked about during breakfast, and he knew why Art wanted to go hunting in the northwest mountains. He knew why Art said it so indirectly, calling it a hunt for a trophy bighorn, not asking the question that was already in the air. Art believed in finishing things. He believed in getting back aboard a horse that tossed him. He also believed in letting a man choose his own way to go.

"Yeah," Art said. "North and west. Never really had a good look at that country, except for that one time. And it was short. Thought I'd like to go back and really look around."

"Sounds good to me," Will said.

"OK."

Three words. Sounds good. OK.

Three words, and Art Pendragon and Will Jensen sealed a covenant men have been making with each other since the beginning of time, a covenant to travel together for an unforeseen time into an unknown wilderness in pursuit of a unspoken need or an unconfessed discontent with the domestic hearth. Each man was promising to protect the other's back, even if it meant putting himself in Death's way. If Death were to take his comrade somewhere in the beast-haunted lawless wild, he would go to the end of his own strength to bring the body home.

Those are the terms of the masculine pact; understood and unambiguous, they go unspoken.

Sounds good.

OK.

Neither Art nor Will realized it, nor did Pasque or the Pinto Kid who came along for the hunt, but a sort of invisible magnetism drew them north by west. It seemed to control the horses, to keep their heads straight into the light northwest breeze blowing day after day. Art reckoned they might find even bigger trophy sheep farther north along the Divide, and Will figured he could recall some of the terrain from his earlier trip.

"Y' suppose Kyle came this way?" the Pinto Kid asked.

"Could be," said Pasque, who rode beside the Kid. "Seems natural."

"I think I recall a camp site up ahead," Will said. "Good creek there, if it ain't dried up."

A week out of the Keystone, the high Divide grew nearer and the four riders became increasingly watchful. Each of them fell into his own way of scanning the trees, the edges of the dark forest, the open parks. And they especially watched the craggy mountain range looming on the western horizon.

One night as they lounged on elbows around their campfire, Will told of his encounter with The Guardian. He did not embellish, nor did he take any pleasure in the telling. The other three remembered hearing it after he had come back to the Keystone looking like a skin-and-bones ghost. His voice now sounded the same as it had then, hollow and sad and haunted.

If any of the four riders had actually believed that they were going up to hunt the Alpine slopes for bighorn sheep, he no longer believed it after hearing Will's story that night. As they packed up in the morning and rode on, they no longer talked about seeing big elk and trophy sheep. It was The Guardian that was on their minds.

To the Pinto Kid, The Guardian was just something curious he had heard about second-hand. He couldn't believe any man on a horse was much more dangerous than any other, but he was curious. It was like going to look at a bear somebody had caught. Dangerous, but not to him. What the Pinto Kid didn't know was that at least two of The Guardian's victims had gone there just out of curiosity about the big ditch.

Art was deep in thought. As he mulled over Will's story of the hired gun defending a ditch way back in that remote country, he couldn't help but figure there was some big organized outfit behind it all, or some kind of settlement that maybe hired themselves a shootist. Or more than one, maybe. And while it was a damned far way from the Keystone's range, it wouldn't hurt to know what was going on. If he could get this Guardian to talk to him before starting any gun play . . . well, maybe when he saw there was four of them, he'd figure he should think it over before starting any shooting.

If he did start shooting first, it would mean that he was crazy, seeing as how all four of them were carrying rifles. It wasn't like when Will rode up there with just his Colt and a saddle carbine; this time, the stranger would be looking into the muzzles of four rifles built to bring down big game at long range. The Pinto Kid had blown in a couple month's pay on a '70 Sharps in the .45 caliber, complete with a long range "peephole" hind sight and double-set hair trigger. Pasque packed along a beautiful Winchester, an 1866 .44 Rimfire given to him by his father-in-law.

Will, too, had these rifles on his mind as the horse string wound its way up into mountain parks and through heavy stands of trees. Art, Pasque, and the Pinto Kid had put their hunting guns into long boxes strapped to the pack animals. Will's carbine was in one of the boxes, too. He had put it there in order to use his scabbard for the rifle he'd borrowed from Art. The scabbard wasn't built long enough for the big .45-70 Winchester, so the butt was always snagging his reins, but he felt a lot better having it right there under his knee.

"You s'pose Kyle came through here?" Will asked as they rode.

"No idea," Art said. "I just hope he's all right. But we got to figure maybe that gunman got him. Or maybe he got . . . well, you know, robbed and left in the woods same as you. I was thinkin' maybe he made it to one of the Mormon settlements 'way west of here."

The Pinto Kid put in his two bits' worth. "Might be some one of those good-lookin' Mormon gals snared him!" He tried to laugh, but no one else did. "Well, it could might be. Art?"

"Yeah?"

"I could've hit that bighorn we saw yesterday."

"I know it."

"You didn't want me to shoot."

"Too small."

"Art?"

"Yeah?"

"We're not really lookin' for sheep, are we? We're lookin' for Kyle."

"Probably."

Toward evening, Will left the others to make camp while he took the .45-70 and climbed up the bare knob of a peak behind the small meadow. He was gone a long time, and, when he came back, he had a plan.

"I think we're just about in that bastard's back yard," he said. "And I figure he's gonna get us spotted directly. If not tomorrow, the next day. Up there . . ."—he indicated the bare knob behind camp—"I think I was lookin' over at the valley I ended up in, so I got a pretty good idea where we are now. I'm thinkin' we ought to bear south in the mornin', and get down into that valley. For some reason, that shooter doesn't seem to go down in there. I remember a couple of squatter cabins. One was some kind of crazy Swede or Norwegian, didn't talk English. There might be somebody down there could tell us about the situation. Somebody might know what's going on. Might even know where Kyle went."

"OK," Art said. "So, we go south, down over the divide, then what?"

"We follow the gorge back up. If we're where I think, and we don't run into that lunatic, we'll find that big ditch at the head of the valley. Follow it down to where it goes."

"Like coming in the back door." Pasque smiled. "Might take him by surprise, after all."

Will smoothed his finger along the .45-70's receiver. "I'd like to surprise the bastard, all right," he said. "I don't care if he never even knows what hit him."

"OK," Art said. "Tomorrow we detour south. Then we'll look for this ditch. Right now I'm hungry. It's good to get away from those four walls for a while, but I gotta admit I miss Mary's cookin'."

Chapter Fourteen

"And the Need of a World of Men for Me"

It was hard to say which one of them most needed a hard run, The Guardian or the big horse. Cooped up in the corral for four days, the horse was plunging and dancing around even before the hostler got the saddle on him, acting snaky, like he was only half broke, whipping his head up and down and kicking out with his heels like a colt lashing out at shadows. This was fine with his rider. Fighting a bronc' was just what he needed to blow off some of the steam. If the horse hadn't been frisky that morning, he just might have gone and found himself a range bull to tussle with.

Tension ran up and down from his neck to his crotch. It had started the day before and gotten worse all night long. He had been heading into the dining room to have supper with Fontana and Luned and the hostler and one of the hired women as usual, but he had met up with Fontana right at the doorway to the dining room, and she had stopped him.

"Your scarf is twisted under itself," she had observed. "Let me fix it."

Without waiting his permission, she had reached up and straightened the silk bandanna. Her fingertips had brushed against his neck, had been cool and soft. She had stood so close that he had been able to smell her hair, and it had been like wild lavender and sweet clover. The hem of her skirt had swayed against his boots, and the curve of her bodice had been only an inch away from his chest.

Because of that moment he had been restless all night. He had spent the hours waking to any slight sound, unable to find a way to lie comfortably in his bed, and he hadn't gotten to sleep until he had given up and lay there on his back with his hands behind his head, staring at the ceiling and making up pictures of the woman who slept above. Then the sleep had come, and with it the dreaming.

In the morning he had washed with extra care and had shaved even more closely than usual. He had delayed going down to the kitchen for breakfast, telling himself he was free to set his own damned eating schedule, and, when he had finally gone downstairs, he had been told that Fontana and Luned had already eaten and were out riding together.

Now the hostler pointed out the way they had gone, figuring that he might want to go the same way. Toward the swimming pond. But Kyle only cursed and said why the hell would he care and swung the big horse in another direction. Not quite the opposite direction but enough to give the pond a wide berth.

The horse kicked, stopped, and planted all four hoofs, then kicked out and twisted his head to one side, probably sensing the impatience of the man in the saddle. The Guardian put up with the bucking and twisting until they were both breathing hard, then pounded with his heels and whipped with the rein ends to urge the horse into running at full speed out across the park, head held high and wild. Wind ripped at his bandanna and tore back his hat so it hung by its string at his back, and the saddle leather pounded his thighs and butt hard, and the blood that was pounding so hot in his body came up into his face. When he and the horse pulled up at last, both of them were red-eyed and panting.

He got down to stretch his muscles and breathe a minute, and, when he was back in the saddle again, man and horse were both calmer. He gave the horse its head to wander over toward the fringe of pines. His brain was in a kind of daze, not watching much of anything or seeing much of anything he did happen to look at, or thinking about anything except the sway of the saddle and the moving forward, and he didn't even pay attention to that. The horse moved on more or less where it wanted to, and he didn't realize they were getting close to the swimming pond until sounds of feminine laughter hit his ears.

He pulled up short and went to turn, but it was too late. At least they hadn't seen him, that much was good. Through the screening pines, he could just make out some glitters of blue mirror-shimmer off the pond here and there, and he could hear high, sweet laughter. He saw flashes of movement when the women moved about, but the trees were so thick that these were nothing more than teasing glimpses. He stared as though his mind still had not figured out where he was or what he was doing. Something behind him made a noise, and he whirled, his hand going for the Colt at his hip, only to find a stray old meat cow ripping grass among the fallen lodgepoles. He backed the horse gingerly, then turned, and rode quickly north. He was shaking and trembling more than he had from the race across the park. *Weakness,* he thought. *Women. Having my mind on those damn' women is going to get me killed, one of these days.*

He rode without stopping clear up to the main ditch, kicking the horse and cussing it up the hill until it was winded. At the ditch, he followed the flat path running along the embankment, riding upstream. He realized he hadn't patrolled up here in over a week. *Damned women can go around buck-naked in ponds and spend hours fixing their hair and stinking themselves up with perfume,* he thought, *but a man has work to do. Never find them up here looking after things!*

Coming around a corner in the ditch trail, he surprised the intruder. A real nosy one, looking everything over real close. Probably planting dynamite to blow the ditch clear down into the valley. The first thing The Guardian saw was a horse standing ground-reined on the ditch trail. It was wearing an Army saddle with a carefully wrapped picket rope dangling from it and a tightly rolled slicker strapped on the cantle. Then he saw the man in the flat-brimmed hat squatting down and studying gate Number Five. He had a pistol in a flap holster and was holding a Sharps carbine.

The Guardian pulled his bandanna up over his nose and his hat down low. His finger wiped the inside of his eye patch. *This son-of-a-bitch had picked the wrong damn' day to come sneakin' around Great North property,* Kyle said to himself. *Wrong damn' day. And it would be his last damn' mistake.*

The stranger saw him coming, and his reaction was simply to stand up. He held the Sharps by the barrel and courteously kept the butt grounded, raising one hand in greeting. The bandanna across the rider's face bothered him. By the time the rider got close enough so he could see the eye patch under the low shadow of the dark Stetson, his face lost color and the hand holding the rifle barrel was slippery with cold sweat. He was looking Death in the face. And he knew it.

"Nice day," he tried to begin. Words poured from him in a rush. "Just happened on your ditch here. Mind if I ask how these gates work? I've been an Army engineer for six years and never seen anything like these. They seem to pivot and lock somehow. Real interesting."

The Guardian rode on toward him. He rode past the man's horse and kept coming, not pulling a gun, not saying a word, just fixing the engineer with his one eye. Seeming as though he hoped the intruder would come up with the Sharps and start something.

But the engineer, too unsure of himself to do anything in the face of this apparition, stood there a moment too long. The rider did not charge, or threaten, or show any emotion at all. He merely urged the horse forward with invisible knee commands until the sweat-soaked chest of the big animal was against the engineer and was pushing him backward. With a yell and a splash he went into the ditch on his back, his carbine sinking to the bottom, himself being pulled along by the freezing water as he tried to stand, tried to fight his way to shore.

The water was armpit deep. His clothes became heavy with the water, but still floated him enough so that he couldn't get any footing. Finally he clawed his way to the side only to find that he could not climb the jagged, slimy rock. At times the current caught him and twisted him, at others it ducked him under the surface, making him turn and bob while it pulled him along down the ditch.

The Guardian rode up alongside the engineer's horse and unwrapped the picket rope, about fifty feet of lightweight manila. He tied a slip loop in one end and tied the other to the Army saddle, then trotted the horse down the ditch trail until they caught up with the half-drowned man, thrashing his arms against the water and trying to scream through the water pouring down his gaping throat. The Guardian swung the loop over the man's head and one arm, and tightened the slack. He used the ends of his reins to slap the engineer's horse into a run, then yelled and galloped beside it, both horses careening down the narrow trail. The drowning engineer at the end of the rope went bouncing off the rock sides of the ditch, being torn open by sharp granite, smothered in water. First his boots were torn off, then his wool shirt ballooned with water and ripped apart. He bashed into another rock while trying to defend himself with his one free arm.

By the time they got to the next gate, he was dead. The Guardian stopped the horse and looked at the floating body as it drifted past and came up short on the end of its tether, bobbing face down in the current. *Not much of a man,* he thought. *Lot of men would have lived through that little dunking.*

He led the horse down a path off the bank. The body came bouncing and halting up out of the water and down the side of the embankment. He let the horse drag it some distance from the ditch. There was a place where the workmen had quarried some fill dirt, and it was a good place for the engineer to lie a while. If anyone was with him, or came looking for him, it would serve as a warning. Later on, he'd get some of the construction crew to come out and bury him. Make a good lesson for those bastards, too.

He stripped the saddle, blanket, and bridle from the man's horse and threw them down next to the body. Not even worth lugging back to Crannog as trophies. Maybe he'd send somebody for the saddle some time. The horse could have its freedom. It would probably join the Crannog herd out there grazing somewhere.

He rode away, brushing the water off his pants and jacket and wiping his hands on his vest as if trying to dry them. He shouldn't have eaten that damned sausage for breakfast; his stomach was queasy, and the back of his throat had a bitter taste in it. He almost wished he had let the Army man take a shot at him or had let him put up some kind of a fight. But he was up here to protect the ditch, that's what his whole purpose in life was now; he couldn't go around taking chances. That's what Fontana expected him to do. What they didn't need was a bunch of government land developers snooping around.

He wanted to believe it, when he told himself that his job required him to be ruthless, but he felt a nagging doubt that irritated and infuriated him. Just as he felt that the two women, Fontana in particular, were the cause of his weakness. The cause of his failure to stay alert and sharp. He felt that they and their damned project had made him kill this man. And all the others. But he was indifferent to the others.

The Guardian resumed his ride upstream along the ditch. Spring weather took the cold edge off the air and there was some meager warmth in the sun, but the whole north-facing side of the mountain seemed cold nevertheless. Shadowy and lonely and quiet. Even the gurgling of the water running down the ditch seemed dismal. He wished he'd gone downstream to where the construction crew was opening a new feeder ditch above the reservoir. There, at least, he might have listened to some real men talking and watch them work, and it would take his mind off those damned women. Yep. Thinking about women was going to get him killed one of these days. He'd be off picking brain daisies about perfume and tight dresses someday, and some back shooter would get him. And no woman ever born was worth getting shot in the back.

As he approached the Number Six gate, the sounds of men talking brought him up short, and he drew out the rifle and cocked it quiet-like. He went on cautiously, rifle aimed ahead of him. He pulled the bandanna up over his face again. The inside of his eye patch felt clammy, and he wiped it dry with a forefinger. But it turned out the voices making conversation at Number Six gate were nothing to be afraid of. One was the fat man with one eye, squatting on the trail like a grotesque toad, wearing buckskins, drawing pictures in the dirt with a stick. The other man also looked familiar. He was short and stood bent over, a little man with elaborate whiskers and a sea captain's hat. The Norwegian. From down the valley. For some reason he couldn't figure out, the Guardian was surprised to see him.

It seemed like the toad was explaining the ditch gate mechanism to the Norwegian. They stopped talking but did not seem surprised when The Guardian came up to them. He did not dismount.

"What are y' doin'?" he demanded.

"This is my new friend," One-Eye said, pointing his drawing stick at the man in the cap. "He helps me. He knows about magic mechanisms!" His laugh was annoying and hoarse.

He said something to the Norwegian, pointed at The Guardian, then pointed down the valley where the deep gouge of the flood could still be seen plainly. The Norwegian replied, jabbering on and on in his foreign language until The Guardian got irritated.

"What the hell's he tellin' you?" he demanded.

"He was telling me a legend of Norway. You see."

"And what would that be?"

"In his country, the people believe that all water runs either north or south. The bad place is in the north. Hades. What you call Hell. Where evil lives, and demons and bad giants. All sorts of evil. Nothing good."

"I get the point. Where Satan's suppose to live, some kinda horse crap like that. Kinda like you. I notice you're always on the north side of the ditch." He almost smiled, but it was all on one side of his mouth, more like a sneer.

One-Eye laughed heartily at the joke. The Norwegian laughed with him, although he had no idea what had been said.

"No," said the toad, "but here's the thing they believe. They believe, you see, that streams flowing from the north carry evil in them, that no good comes of such streams. The water is cursed. Water flowing the other way, into their underworld hell, is good and beneficial. Hah hah!"

"That's funny?"

"Oh, young friend, you and I are more alike than you imagine! We one-eyed men can see more deeply into things. Haven't you learned that yet? All of the seeing . . . what goes on in the brain . . . is concentrated in the one eye. Hah! Think! Look at yourself! How many have you killed? How many have you beaten? And The Guardian before you, and before that? She has bewitched you. She has put you in a spell. Did she weep her big tears, with her two beautiful eyes, and tell you that only you, the killer of the old Guardian, could save the precious water for everyone? And now, now you find out that you are guarding water that is evil! That's the joke."

"Explain it to me."

"All this water. Look at it. The ditch cuts straight across the slope, does it not? All the water running into it runs out of the north, down the slope into the ditch? Never from the south! Hah hah! This man here . . . my new friend . . . blames your flood, blames his wife's death, blames everything on this evil water. He says my gate locks must be magic, to have held it back this long."

"And I think you're both damn' crazy." The Guardian scowled. "You deserve each other's company. Why the hell I don't shoot you is beyond me. Crazy freak! If you two want to stay alive up here, you just keep out of my way. Pay him part of your share, if you want to keep him around, but the two of you stay outta the way."

He wheeled the horse and rode back downstream again. Behind him, the toad and the foreigner went on talking in a language he did not understand, speaking of things he would not comprehend. He remembered Luned's matter-of-fact instructions to kill that creature, but. . . .

The Guardian stopped at the house, tied the horse to the porch railing, and stomped into the kitchen, demanding food. He took meat, a chunk of bread, and the pitcher of buttermilk, and sat on the edge of the porch steps, glowering at the mountains. Luned came around the corner, carrying her bow and arrow, glowing with self-satisfaction. The early summer days of sunshine had taken the pale white pallor from her skin.

She stood talking nonsense about how nice the day was and about what flowers were beginning to show themselves in the meadows and about the mare she saw with a fresh foal at its side, but Kyle's attention was focused on the slight suggestion of cleavage where her shirt gaped open below her throat.

Luned took his silence to mean he was in a sour and silent mood, as usual. As she went striding away, he watched her slender legs beneath the short skirt and thought how much he would like to see Fontana's long bare legs.

He clattered the plate to the porch, swallowed down the last of the buttermilk, and slammed down the pitcher. Let the cook come out and get it.

He grabbed the horse's reins with such abruptness that the horse startled and danced sideways; cussing, he took the ends of the leather and cut the animal's shoulder. Once in the saddle, he used his spurs on the horse's flanks. With his forefinger he wiped some grit from under his eye patch. He needed to find the construction crew and send a couple of them on a burial detail.

The next individuals unfortunate enough to be in The Guardian's path were four men and a boy working beside the road leading to the big house. He reined in angrily, scattering road dirt, and demanded to know what they were doing.

"Like you told us. Gettin' rid of this gatepost before it falls and hurts somebody."

"Takes four of you for one post?"

"Awful heavy. She might be rotted at the base, but she's still awful long and heavy."

"Why you wastin' time tryin' to chop it down?" he asked. "Unhitch that team and pull it outta the ground. You'll have to pull the butt end out anyway."

One of the men had been hacking away at the base of the tall pole with an axe. He straightened up and wiped his brow of sweat. "She's tough," he said. "Must go down four feet or better, and the core is pitch. Tough as hell."

"Well, you're wasting time," The Guardian growled. "Set fire to it. Blow it up with some blastin' powder. Just get it done."

The leader of this work party frowned and cleared his throat before venturing to look up. "Well, sir, fact is, we was hopin' to save the pole for firewood. That pitch pine, it makes awful good fires, even for bein' so smoky, an' we been workin' so much the last couple years we just don't have all that much time to go get proper firewood in for winter. We brought the wagon, and thought we'd cut 'er down and load it on back to the settlement for folks."

The Guardian's one eye frowned down, first at the workman and then at the miserable little notch he'd made in the base of the pole. "That the best you can do?" he said. "For a bunch of men that claim to be sawyers and builders, you sure as shit don't keep your tools sharp."

"Well, it's the pitch, y'see," one of the men replied. "Tried the cross-cut saw and got into it a ways, but she gummed up on us."

Kyle swung down abruptly and thrust the reins into the

hands of the boy, who was standing there open-mouthed and wide-eyed. The boy had heard of The Guardian and had seen him ride by, but he had never dreamed he would ever be standing so close to him. He stared speechless at the black clothes and the big gun.

"Gimme that dull axe," Kyle snarled, and the man gave it up.

He tested the edge with his thumb. It was not dull. He swung into the wood, hard, but the blow was flat to the grain and did nothing but bounce the axe back. He hunched his shoulder muscles and tried again, and again felt the shock of the wood springing back against the blade. He needed to make his cut at a steeper angle. He did, and the next blow brought out a chip the size of a plug of tobacco. His next blow, just a little steeper in the angle, glanced from the pitch pine and the axe buried itself in the ground next to the toe of his boot. "Son-of-a-bitch," he muttered.

The men and the boy said nothing. They didn't even breathe. He looked at the saw cut in the base of the pole and at the way the pole was leaning in its hole. "It's loose enough," he muttered, "might come right outta there." He turned to one of the men. "You. Climb up there with that rope and tie it on as high as you can. And you, what's-your-name, back that damn' wagon over here. I'll show you how to get your firewood down and loaded in one operation. Then maybe you four can get on to something more important."

"I'll unhitch the team," the man said, starting for the heavy hauling wagon.

"To hell with that," The Guardian said. "You want it loaded, don't you? I'll show you how, and we ain't gonna waste any time unhitching horses and buckin' this son-of-a-bitch into sections so we can lift 'em, either. You bastards would take the whole damn' day to do it. Back that wagon over here."

The driver did as he was told, backing the wagon to within a few feet of the pole. The Guardian jumped up into the wagon bed with the end of the rope and threaded the end under the seat so it hung down in front, alongside the tongue.

"Now one of you get under there. Pull 'er tight and tie it off to the runnin' gear."

The rope now ran taut from a point about fifteen feet up the leaning pole to the front of the wagon bed and down around the front axle. The two heavy horses stood ready. Kyle went back to the pole with the axe and gave it a few more strokes, as if he thought the wood had somehow softened. It was still dense as rock.

"Now!" he shouted. "Whip up your team and pull 'er outta there!"

The driver took hold of the bridle of the off horse and coaxed the team into an easy pull. The slack went out of the rope. The pole leaned farther. The wagon's running gear creaked ominously. The horses leaned into the leather collars as their big hoofs dug for traction. Their muscles bulged and rippled. There was a cracking sound from the gatepost. The Guardian swung the axe, laying into the base of the pole with it like a man gone mad. The same fever caught the driver so that he yelled his horses into even more effort, and the horses dropped their hind haunches down like huge men squatting to lift enormous weights, and together they rose again on the lunge. The doubletree groaned; the wagon's front wheels came up off the ground momentarily. Then came the sound of wood cracking, splitting the air like a rifle shot.

The boy's eyes were glued to the falling pole, but he had the presence of mind to scurry backward, holding the reins of The Guardian's horse, pulling the animal out of the way. He stared wide-eyed as the tall pole came down and down, faster and faster, and he saw that the pole was going to land right in the wagon bed, just like The Guardian had said it would.

And mostly he was right. Even a short section of a thick pitch log is heavy enough to make a man grunt to pick it up. Twenty feet of pitch log weighs like so much stone. This one came down into the wagon bed as planned. The trouble was, it did not stop there. As the draft horses reared and kicked at the doubletree in terror, the pole cut the wagon neatly in half, bending the angle irons and tearing them from the wagon sides, and went on splintering wood all the way to the front of the bed. It bashed through the driver's seat like it was a piece of crate wood.

When the dust cleared, the two quivering draft horses found themselves still hitched to singletrees, which were still hooked into the doubletree. From the doubletree hung the splintered remains of the long wagon tongue, which had completely busted off from the cracked axle. The wagon's wheels, front and rear, leaned at drunken angles toward each other. Most of the wagon bed was no more than big slivers of wood and bent metal.

The Guardian glowered at it. He wiped his eye patch. His gun hand twitched. The other men were frozen in place, too stunned, too afraid even to move. The boy, mouth dry as cotton and his face pale as cotton, too, could only clutch the reins with his sweating hands and stare at The Guardian, towering among the men, every muscle of his face raging.

The driver spoke calming words to the draft horses until they stood quietly, muscles still jerking and twitching under the hide. When he left them to see the damage, the corner of the Guardian's eye caught the movement, and he spun around. He froze the driver with his cold stare and went toward him, his one eye glaring. When his hand came up, the driver flinched from it, but it only dropped lightly on his shoulder. It was not a blow. The driver looked into his face.

"OK," The Guardian said with a smile that was crooked but was still a smile. "There's your winter firewood. Got you your kindling, too."

"Got our firewood now!" one of the workers chuckled. Another laughed: "*Really* got our firewood now!" And still another added—"And don't forget we got our kindling!"— while he tossed a chunk of floorboard at the first man. The boy, still holding the reins, was on his back in the grass, giggling uncontrollably.

The gunman in black smiled again and shook his head. After a while he took the reins from the boy and mounted the big horse and rode on across the sun-splashed field. He still needed to find that ditch crew and send a couple of men to bury the Army engineer that had gotten killed. He rode briskly, straight up in the saddle.

Chapter Fifteen
The Warning Comes

The shadows of the afternoon spruce were long and black on the meadow grass when The Guardian got back to Crannog. His young admirer jumped down from the top rail to open the corral gate when he rode up. The boy waited while Kyle dismounted and unbuckled the cinch, then he just couldn't wait a moment longer to go over and hold up a giant horseshoe for him to see.

"Look-it what one of the horses threwed this afternoon!" he said, proud. "And I found it! Martin says it ain't no good any more so I could have it."

The Guardian took it. "Worn pretty thin," he agreed. "Not worth nailing it on again."

"Look-it, though!" the boy said, when The Guardian gave it back to him. "I wanted to show y' I could bend it. See how strong I'm gettin'? I can bend it. With my bare hands!"

Sure enough, the metal in the curve of the horseshoe was worn so thin that the boy could manage to twist it when he put all his strength to it. The Guardian watched, but it was not the boy he was watching. The horseshoe brought back a memory, blurred and uncertain, of a blacksmith at a forge. And a message. It seemed important, and he had it in his brain somewhere, but couldn't put words with it.

Encouraged by The Guardian's seeming interest, the kid

went on straining until he had twisted the shoe's U shape into a backward S. He handed it to his hero. "See?" he said proudly. "Now it's like a letter or something. I bet I can even make it look like a big ol' double-U."

The Guardian gave it back, heaved his saddle to his shoulder, and started for the tack room. "Maybe you'll be makin' your own horseshoes, someday. But that one's seen the end of the trail. You can twist it any way you want," he said, "it's still just an ol' horseshoe. It done what it was made for, and nobody needs it any more."

It was another boy, an older one from the settlement shacks, out in the mountains, hunting, that came upon Art Pendragon, Will Jensen, Pasque, and the Pinto Kid. The boy was at least two days from the settlement and looking at another cold night with his one blanket and his poke of dried meat. He carried an old single shot .22, but hadn't gotten within range of any rabbits. He hoped to jump some spruce grouse, maybe, but he was pretty high toward the divide for them.

When the boy saw the campfire, he went careful at first until he made out that they looked like ordinary cowboys. He still hesitated; the settlement men had warned everyone not to talk about the valley or the ditches to anybody. But these cowboys were cooking meat, and he could smell coffee, too, and it got the better of him. He went on in, calling out as he went so that they wouldn't think he was sneaking up.

The older man turned out to be talkative. So was the one they called Kid, who wore a flashy vest and silver hatband. He fixed him a plate of hot venison, beans, and bread. Just about every time he got a good mouthful going, one of them would ask another question.

"So you live around here, I guess?" asked the Kid.

"Yueah," mumbled the boy, waving his hand off toward the east.

"Huntin'?"

"Yueah. Ain't seen nuthin.'"

"We were hoping to spot some bighorns," the older man said. "Maybe shoot a trophy."

"Hmm." His mouth was busy with the beans, which were some of the best he'd ever tasted. As soon as he swallowed he said: "Not bad eatin', bighorns."

The quiet resumed. Another man, the tanned one with the Mexican spurs, poured a cup of coffee for himself, and the boy wanted to ask for some but figured it wasn't polite. The older man fussed around with the grub sack, though, and came up with a stick of brown sugar which he broke, offering half to the boy.

"You seen any other men right around here?" the man asked.

"Nah," the boy replied. "You lookin' for somebody?"

"Might be. One of my riders. Came up this way a couple years back, and I just wondered where he got to, or if anybody'd seen him. Kind of dark character with one eye."

The boy chomped off a piece of the sugar stick and sucked on it noisily. He pointed the remainder north toward where the ditch was.

"Be a one-eyed man up yonder," he said. "I seen him. He's dark. I dunno but I guess he lives in a dugout, t'other side of the big ditch. You don't wanna mess with him."

Art looked over at Will, then back to the boy.

"Ever see his saddle?" the older man asked. "Maybe had a brand on it like that one over there?"

The boy looked at the Kid's saddle with the Keystone symbol stamped on the skirt.

"He don't have a horse, I don't guess," the boy said. "You

don't wanna mess with him."

In spite of efforts to bribe the boy into telling them more about the lay of the land to the north and about where he lived and with whom, Art and Will got nothing but short, vague answers in response to their questions. The boy volunteered nothing. Men at the settlement didn't like people talking, and no one wanted any strangers around. He'd been told *that* more than once, that's for sure.

Darkness fell, and the fire flickered to a small ruby glow deep in the ashes. The boy lay next to the fire and had his blanket and the horse blankets the fancy hatband had given him, and he was warm, but he couldn't sleep. These strangers worried him. He figured they were safe enough to be around, but he didn't want anyone from the settlement to catch him talking to them. He'd maybe stay for some breakfast, some more of those beans, maybe, and get him some coffee, and then be going.

He began to doze off, still aware of their breathing as they slept. But the full moon rose from behind the heavy clouds off to the east, and all of a sudden it hit him full in the face. His eyes flew open, startled by the glare. He threw a hand across his eyes, but not before his mind flashed on a memory of another night of white and stunning moonlight, back at Crannog. That time he was sleeping outside and the moon rose and showed him that woman, the small one with the bow and arrow, all in a white gown like a ghost in the moonlight, standing out in the open field, staring up at the moon. Her arms were down at her sides, and her hands turned palms up like she was praying or making a sacrifice like that Indian in the picture book or something.

He'd heard stories about this one, not just from other kids, but from some of the women. She sometimes floated through the moonlight, and sometimes showed up miles away from where they'd seen her. She almost never talked to children. More than once he'd felt she was somewhere watching him do stuff.

The boy slid silently out of the blankets and tugged on his old boots. He quietly rolled his blanket and his grub sack together and gathered up his gun. He gave one longing look in the direction of the pot of beans, sitting next to the dying embers, but crouched low and hustled himself out of there. He figured he'd hightail himself back over the ridge. His heart was pounding right out of his shirt. But he thought if he kept going, he could come to Crannog by dark the next day, or maybe the next. He'd find The Guardian, or else the strange lady with the bow and arrows, and warn them that there were strangers prowling around. Maybe they'd give him something for telling them. But he'd better tell somebody, before they found out he had eaten with them.

A fair amount of time later, the boy was miles away, walking hard, trying to stick to the high places along the ridges where the trees and underbrush didn't grow so thick. Once he stopped to take a shot at a good, fat-looking rabbit, big for a cottontail, but he only wounded it. Following the damned thing, he got himself turned around a little and lost so much time he knew he'd end up spending a night out again. He gutted out the rabbit and stuffed it with what he hoped was sweet grass—at least, it was long and green—and put it in his poke.

He sat against a tree, moody, cold, and sad, munching more of the jerky meat, his blanket wrapped around him, waiting for nightfall. A few hours after dark that huge moon rose again, and again he could almost see the strange pale woman floating out there at the edge of the wood. He tried to sleep, but couldn't. So he rolled the blanket and tied it to the poke, slung the rope over his shoulders, picked up his rifle, and went on, sneaking through the eerie moonlit forest like a boy running from something, but staying away from the darkest of the shadows.

When he came to water, he drank. When his stomach trembled, he chewed jerky meat. And so he went on, through the early hours of dew and the rising heat of the late morning. In the afternoon he smelled wood smoke and soon found himself at the edge of the settlement meadow. And, eerily, he saw her, the pale woman, crossing the open grass toward him.

"You are Martha's boy," she said as she approached. She looked at the gun and the bulging poke sack.

"I been huntin'," he said. "Wanted a nice young buck, maybe, but I went two days and got nuthin' but this here cottontail. Least he's fat."

He trembled in her steady gaze. She seemed already to know his secret.

"Martha will be glad for it," Luned said. He wished she wouldn't look at him that way, like she saw into his head. She knew what he'd seen already, without him saying anything.

"I seen some men," he blurted. "Four riders. 'Way up on that ridge over Divide Cañon. Had big rifles with 'em . . . lookin' for bighorns or elk, way I figure it."

"And what else?"

"What?"

"What else did you learn? What did you say to them?" The pale woman turned to walk with him toward the houses, putting her hand on his shoulder and then letting it slide down to cup his shoulder blade. It calmed him and got him stirred up all at the same time. His eyes strayed to the way her white dress swirled around her ankles; his nose took in the cool perfume of her body against the smell of the sun-warm grass.

His mouth opened before he knew it, and he began to

chatter, pouring out details he didn't even think to re-member, details like the brands on the saddle fenders and the one man's silver hatband and the kinds of rifles they carried. He told how he'd had coffee with them and venison and the best beans he'd ever eaten, and that they asked about a one-eyed man, and he said it was the ugly-looking black man who had a hut above the big ditch probably.

Her hand caressed his back, and her voice made his mind sleepy. He started to forget he was in a hurry to get home with this cottontail for his mother.

"Have you told anyone else?" she asked. "Have you seen The Guardian since seeing these four men?"

"Aw, I never do see him. Don't want to, neither! Mean sonuvabitch, 'scuse me."

"That's all right, then," Luned said. "I'll tell him to watch for strangers."

"Better tell 'im about them rifles," the boy added.

"I shall," she replied. "I certainly shall. And should you see him, don't speak to him. Let me. Now, you hurry and show your rabbit to your mother."

The boy went on alone, his legs scurrying him toward the shack in which he lived with his mother—and his father, when he was around—but his mind dawdled along behind him, thinking how nice the meadow smelled and how the sun was so warm and all and felt even more warm on that shoulder where her hand had lingered, and that he hadn't known a fellow could hear so many bird calls out here, if he listened.

Luned strode across the grass toward the big house, Crannog. She knew who the riders were. She knew why they had come.

The Guardian was relaxing in the parlor that afternoon,

sitting back in a big chair with his feet up on an oversize ottoman, idly looking at stereopticon pictures. Most of them were scenes of New York City and Niagara Falls. And there was a whole box of pictures showing other places in the world.

When Luned entered, it was like a breeze had snatched a white dress off the clothesline and blown it down the hall and into the parlor. She came straight to his chair, sat down on the ottoman, and rested her hand on the top of his boot.

"Some men are coming," she said, sending apprehension out of her eyes and straight into his head.

"Anybody special?" he said, controlling the tight pounding already starting to hammer at his heart. He thought of shifting his leg out of her reach, but didn't do it.

"Dangerous men," she said. "Dangerous to all of us. You must take no chances with them."

"Who are they?" he said. "You know, don't you? You know."

"They seem to be hunters," she said. Her eyes shifted from his when she said it, and, by that, he knew she was keeping something back. "But I think they may be from the Army, looking for the Army man you killed."

"How'd you know he was Army? Or killed, come to that? I never told you."

She breathed deeply once, twice, a third time. She sat very stiffly erect and looked into his eyes again. Her hand remained on his boot.

"I know much. More than you know. You think you are always alone out there and act alone, but if it were not for my vigilance. . . ."

The Guardian's good eye widened, and his brow lifted curiously. Now he shifted his leg away from her hand. She had said too much, had nearly gone too far.

Silence filled the parlor. It flowed from the walls, drifted down the drapes like dust, and came along the bare, wood floor to pool itself around the two people sitting there like porcelain figures. He gazed into her eyes steadily and without blinking, and his mind went back trailing along the path that had led to this day. It did not seem now, looking back on it, like it was he who killed those men, any of them, except maybe the ones drowned in some flood. Somebody else was the will and the reason, not him.

He stood up, and she rose from the ottoman, and he wondered at the smallness of the woman and of the strength of her will. He looked down into her face, his eye calm and cold.

" 'Bout suppertime," he said. "I'll be out early in the mornin', see about those four strangers. An' you don't know anything else to help, that right?"

Luned crossed to the window that faced west, so that she was silhouetted in the low late light of afternoon. Her shape was distinctly that of a woman, and a small woman at that, but there was no sign of weakness anywhere in her. She did not look at him when she spoke, but went on looking out the window.

"Two things," she said.

"What's that?"

"Two things you must know."

"Oh?"

"They are looking for a one-eyed man."

"How do you know?"

"I know. A boy from the shacks spoke with them, two days ago. He thought they meant the hermit up on the ditch. But it's you. It's you they mean."

"And they're goin' to find me, too," he said. "I'm gonna see to that."

"There's a second thing. The boy said they are carrying ri-

232

fles, big rifles. For hunting. At long range, you cannot match them."

"I'll take the Henry, then," he said. "The heavy one."

"But you are still only one man, and they are four. When they see you . . . perhaps they have spyglasses."

"Field glasses, most likely," he said, "if they're hunting. Or if they're Army."

"When they see you, they will have all the advantage. They may shoot from ambush with their hunting rifles and kill you before you see who they are. If they learn how dangerous you are . . . if they talk to anyone, learn anything that might put them on their guard . . . they will shoot first and at long range." She turned and came to him and gently put a finger upon his eye patch.

"Take this off, tomorrow," she said. "You will not need it. Wear your hat low. And pull your kerchief up over your face. Take off the eye patch and keep your bad eye in shadow. Then they will not know you are The Guardian, and you'll be able to get close enough to use your rifle. Or take one of the shotguns."

"You seem to have made quite a study of how to kill men with guns," he said.

"You must get close before they suspect you. Think this way . . . if you walk up to them, without them seeing who you are, they will be holding their rifles at their sides, with one hand. You know the way. Then you can surprise them with your revolver. If you suddenly draw your gun, they will either drop the rifles to draw their pistols, or they will bring the rifles up so as to shoot, and both will take too much time. Your only chance is to get close before you shoot."

There was a long silence in the cold, echoing room.

"You must kill them," she said simply.

"That's my job," he said. "Though I dunno know why

you're worryin'. I thought the rule was that if one of them drills me, he gets to take over guardin' this place. Isn't that the way it works? That's the way you had it work with me."

"You must kill them," she said. "You must."

"Then I will," The Guardian said. "Now supper's on."

Chapter Sixteen

Four Men, One Grave

After supper, the wind began to rise. The Guardian was having his smoke and coffee on the leeward leg of the long porch. All the western sky was dark, like the bottom of a well, with no stars and without the familiar silhouette of the mountain range to the west. The wind felt strange, coming out of the south, as if it were blowing over the mountains but, when it saw Crannog, changed direction to strike it. The few lone-standing pines near the big house bent and bobbed, twisting and struggling to get back upright. Cottonwood trees and chokecherry thickets showed the silver sides of their leaves and whipped their limbs against each other.

The wind poured around the corner of the house, and miniature dust devils whirled on the porch behind it. It purred low and shrieked high, looking for something. A grain bucket left standing against the stables suddenly went clanking and rolling away, and the horses in the stable nickered and whinnied.

He took a last deep draw on his smoke before grinding it out under his foot, and his eye narrowed as he tilted the coffee cup to drain off the dregs. He was thinking of the four riders. Whoever those boys were up there, if they were still up there on the divide, they weren't going to get much sleep tonight. It'd give him a good advantage, tomorrow.

He rose earlier than the cook, so he built a fire in the range and set the coffee pot to boil while he fried eggs and bacon. It wasn't bad, this—he liked having the morning to himself. The place could be a cozy home for a man, if he could always do things his own way, like this. Get some rest from the women. A man could sit at the window, watch daylight coming onto the land, nice and slow, have his coffee strong and his eggs just right, and nobody hanging over him to see what else he wanted. A man could listen to the crackle of the fire in the stove and the birds outside chirping up the sun and sort of plan his day, peaceful-like.

It was light enough, when he finished, so he went back upstairs for his coat and gun and came down again, and went to the stable. He got his horse ready and strapped the long scabbard under the fender, but it had to face backward because the big Henry rifle was too long to let it stick out forward. Harder to get it out that way, from the saddle, but he figured that if he got into a fix where he needed to shoot at long range, he'd have time to get it out. Thinking of that, working there in the early morning among the smells and sounds of the stabled horses, he tried to remember what it had been like in earlier times, before he was forever figuring how to kill and not be killed. What kind of morning did he get ready for every day, back in that time before all this killing? He couldn't remember. He didn't even remember whom he had been with. His memory was without faces.

He took all four boxes of shells for the rifle and an extra box of shells for the Colt. He stuffed his food bag into the bedroll, tied it and his slicker behind the cantle, and headed out.

Every once in a while, ever since killing Fontana's guardian, he thought about Luned warning him about riding downstream. He didn't want to believe it, and didn't think he did, but all the same he headed for a place where the horse could cross the ditch. From there, the game trails would bring him out onto the ditch up above gate Number Six. If those four riders went north from where Luned had said they were, they had found the ditch. Or soon would. They would follow it downstream, not knowing he was behind them. Upstream.

He rode all the way without stopping except once to get off and stretch the cramp out of his back. He came out high on the ditch in mid-afternoon. Farther on, the mountain turned steep and was covered in loose rock; he was high enough, probably four, five miles above the Number Six gate. He crossed over and rode downstream along the ditch path, finding no sign of horse tracks or man tracks. No sign of the fat black toad, either. A way past the Number Six, it hit him that he hadn't noticed the hole or the flat rock. Probably he had just overlooked it.

Something in the breeze, or some instinct, made The Guardian suddenly wary. He rode the horse down into the ditch, then up the other side so he could stay in the trees. Soon after, he looked down through the trees and saw them, four specks moving 'way down in the valley. They were just getting to the bottom of the long slope below the ditch. Not coming fast, but coming. When they hit the steep part of the mountain, they'd have to get off their horses and lead them, making long switchbacks back and forth to traverse it. From where they were, they could see the ditch far up the mountain, and they would make for it.

The Guardian sneered. He wiped his hand on his shirt and put his finger to his bad eye. It felt a little strange not to have the patch on. He wiped the eye and watched the four specks struggling up the mountain. They should have kept on following the creekbed, he thought. Longer way to get to the ditch, but you can ride all the way.

He knew this place well. He knew where they would end up, coming the way they did. They would get to the dike of loose dirt and rock dumped from the ditch construction and be tired and aching in the legs. They couldn't climb it right there, not with horses, so they'd figure to go downstream, and they'd come to where that Army engineer was buried. They'd make camp there; it was the only flat place on the mountain.

He had plenty of time and all the advantages. He'd go up to the high crossing and camp for the night; at first light he'd ride down the ditch path. He'd be there when the sun hit their camp. He'd watch them fool around with breakfast, and, afterward, they'd ride on along the base of the ditch. When they found a way up to the ditch path, he'd be behind them. Most places on that path, two men could ride abreast since it was built for teams of horses pulling rock sleds and scrapers, but not every place. Some places had eroded, and the path was narrow. He'd wait for one of those narrow places. That way, when he opened fire on them, at least one of them would be in the way of the others, and all of them would try to jerk their horses around to face him, and on the narrow track they'd get in each other's way again. The long rifles would be of no use.

He imagined the sudden roar of his shots, the four men wheeling their horses around on the narrow path with rushing ditch water on one side and the long drop on the other, horses rearing at the shots, men trying to grab the rifles from the scabbards at the same time they were trying to stay in the saddle. And he'd be calm and quiet, and probably get all of them before even one of them got out a rifle.

Down the slope, Art was the first to dismount because of

the incline, then Pasque. The Pinto Kid and Will urged their horses a few hundred feet farther up the hill, then they got off and climbed. The four were spread out, each one looking for his own way up, tugging his horse along behind him. The sweat poured off the men and foamed on the horses; the pack horse on its long lead rope sulked and balked at climbing the loose rocks.

"Hold it!" Art said suddenly, tipping his hat back to wipe his brow with a sleeve and then leaning forward, with an elbow on a knee, to catch his breath.

The others stopped, digging their heels in where they stood so as not to go rolling back down the mountain. "What's up?" the Pinto Kid said.

"That's the question," Art said. "Workin' away at this climbin', nobody's watchin' that ditch up there. Man with a rifle could pick us off easy as pie. Will, see if you can get over here to where I am and give me your horse. You take a Forty-Five Seventy and work your way up ahead of us to watch that ditch."

"You sure that's a ditch?" the Kid said. "Damn' dumb place for it."

"What else could it be?" Art asked. "Look how that line of dirt runs clear around this mountain and over to that next one. Gotta be either a ditch or a road. Let's get movin'. And stay spaced out . . . if anybody slips, I don't want him takin' the others with him."

"Nice of you t' care," Pasque panted as he picked his way upward.

Will went on ahead, taking a zigzag route so his feet could find their own footing while he watched the ditch. He was thinking about his shoot-out with the dark rifleman up here. It seemed a long time ago, but now that he was looking for the man again, it all came back to him as clear as anything. He felt some of the fear again. Not the fear of dying in some meadow where no one would even find his bones, but a remnant of that fear, a memory of it that quickened his reflexes. If he saw that big horse and rider up there on the ditch, he'd know him. And he'd shoot first this time. He'll have to shoot downhill, Will reasoned, shifting his Winchester to the other hand to grab a rock for balance. Uphill like this, he could hit him easily. Still, Will couldn't deny his fear, being out in the open just like the last time. He scrabbled ahead a few feet, looked all around for signs of movement, then scrambled a few more feet up the steep slope.

He made it to the base of the dike, where there wasn't any grass. Nothing but loose dirt and rock rubble. He looked up and wiped his sleeve across his brow. A man might be able to climb up here, but not a horse. The four of them were going to have to follow the wall until they got to a place to climb it. He waved the Winchester and his hat to get Art's attention, then signaled that he and the other two should begin working their way eastward.

Once they'd topped the shoulder of the mountain, the going got easy enough so that the four could ride again, Will scouting ahead. The others joined him, sitting his horse in a flat open meadow, where spring water came up in a bunch of aspen and where the grass was good.

"It's a ditch all right. And there's a way up onto it," he told them. "I went up there. Found fresh horse tracks, goin' downstream. Reckon if that bastard patrols the water, he's been by here in the last day or two, probably won't be back for a week."

Art looked around, took a squint at the angle of sun over the western ridgeline, stretched his arms, and wiggled his neck around to take the kink out. "It's early, but maybe we oughta camp right here. Pasque, Kid, why don't you unpack the horses and get a fire goin' for supper, and Will and me'll go on down this ditch a ways. Just take a look, then come back in an hour or so."

Will and Art found nothing but horse tracks going both ways. Both men caught a sense of something, something that wasn't quite right. When they returned, they found a cooking fire going and the coffee pot steaming on it. At first they couldn't see Pasque and the Pinto Kid, but then, off in a corner of the clearing, they saw them kneeling over a pile of dirt. Pasque held the camp spade.

"What is it?" Art said, dropping his reins and walking over to them.

"A grave," the Kid said. "I was collectin' some wood and found it. Real fresh. Me and Pasque thought we oughta dig in there. You know."

Art looked down at the grave. The first thing he thought was that it was Kyle's. "Yeah. Probably the thing to do."

Pasque felt the spade strike something that wasn't dirt and wasn't rock. It gave a little when he pushed at it. He put the spade aside and started scooping dirt out with his hands.

"Saddle blanket buried here," he said. "Feels like there's a man under it. Or rolled in it, maybe. No, here's an edge. It's just laid over him."

The group stood around the shallow hole looking like figures in a painting of a funeral. Pasque, on his knees, was looking up at Art. Art, thumbs hooked in his gun belt, stared down at the blanket-covered figure. The Pinto Kid was to one side, hands on his knees, leaning in to get a better look, and Will stood slightly behind, holding his reins. The horse, oblivious to the human drama, lowered its head and cropped grass.

"Better check and see if we know 'im," Art said at last.

"Yeah," Pasque said. "Guess so." He brushed and

scooped more dirt away so that the outline of the head and chest under the gray saddle blanket was visible. Then he gingerly peeled back the blanket a little at a time. All four men seemed to exhale at once when they saw the eyes. One was puffy, bruised, blood caked under it. The other was wide open, staring into the late afternoon sky. It wasn't Kyle.

They studied the body with respectful concern, commenting on the torn, brown shirt ripped to shreds, the tan line on the forehead, the bruises on the arms and face. Pasque used the spade to move the scrap of shirt to one side, and they saw the rope marks around the chest.

"Poor bastard took a beatin'," the Kid said.

"Skull looks busted there, too," Pasque added.

Art looked close. "That's an Army buckle he's wearing. But he don't look right somehow. No blood. It's like he was washed off before they put the blanket over him."

"I'll take care of your horse," the Kid said to Art, breaking off from the group. He had seen enough.

Pasque pulled his kerchief up around his nose against the smell of the corpse and checked the pockets. Nothing there.

Will saw the dead man had no gun belt or knife sheath, and he remembered being up here without his guns after the rifleman had stripped him of his. "Just like he done to me," Will said. "I'm thinkin' he got Kyle, too. Same way. He takes everything. Don't know why he didn't kill me, too. Somewhere up here we're gonna find Kyle."

"Might as well fill that hole up again," Art said.

"Still want to camp here tonight?" Pasque asked, gently drawing the gray blanket over the face. "Down in New Mexico you couldn't get a *vaquero* to sleep within a mile of this."

"If you boys don't want to, we won't," Art said. Pasque began shoveling dirt back into the hole. Will walked his horse back toward the supper fire and began to undo the cinches. The Kid had Art's saddle off and was giving the horse a rub with the blanket.

"Guess so," Art said.

That night, each time Art stirred and came awake, he saw at least one of the other men sitting up, wrapped in a blanket, rifle across his knees, unable to sleep. He smiled, but it was a grim smile. It was one of those times he was thankful that he had always given Keystone riders plenty of time and ammunition for target practice. Anything moving out there in the faint light of the half moon, be it a bear or coyote or man, would get drilled dead center by a Keystone bullet. No question about it.

A couple of miles west, on the higher side of the ditch, The Guardian made his camp, a big boulder to his back and a screen of high fir trees on one side. He picketed his horse close and made his fire with aspen twigs—less smoke, less smell for others to pick up—and kept it going just long enough to heat coffee water. That and bread would be his supper. Come dawn, he'd drink the leftover coffee, cold, and chew on some of the meat and bread while he rode.

There was a third camp, a mile east of the meadow campsite and the grave. Facing the open ridge, still sheltered by trees on three sides, the boy shivered in his blanket next to a ragged little fire. He had built it with pitch pine, because it was easy to light, and cedar twigs he had broken off a tree. He huddled his .22 single-shot against his chest and sometimes patted the pocket of his old jacket in which were all the cartridges he owned. He, too, was waiting for dawn.

He knew what The Guardian was out to do.

The man his mother said was his father wasn't home

much, but last time he was, he had told about burying a stranger up here. The boy knew the place. He had described a big Army buckle with **US** on it, and how they had left it on the body to rot in the ground. The boy meant to have it. He'd help The Guardian get rid of the strangers, too, and get himself a reward. A new gun, maybe. He knew about the room full of guns and saddles. But even with his old rabbit rifle, he could kill a man. Cartridges for the .22 were hard to come by, so he had learned to be a good shot.

He wanted the beans, too. Stories had it that The Guardian always took the guns and stuff, but the boy didn't figure him to take the men's food. He knew they had a big sack of those beans, and flour and fixings, too.

He hunkered down into his blanket and felt his shins roasting at the fire while his back was shivering cold. Finally he drifted into sleep and dreamed of carrying home trophies and food and being more than just "Martha's kid."

At pre-dawn in timberline country the sky goes from star-plastered black to dark starless blue. Stands of twisted pines and Alpine firs and spruce trees all clump together as dark blotches; the crumbly gravel soil gets the color of tarnished gold. With some moonlight, even a half moon, the sharp clear air takes on a bluish cast; other colors lose meaning in that pale moon, so that Will's red shirt looked brown and Art's tan shirt looked more dirty yellow. It's the coldest time of the night, when faint wisps of air start moving from the warmer valleys, up the slopes toward the Divide.

Art woke up again, and found Will sitting there at the fire pit, stirring around for hot coals. "Went to bed too early," he whispered.

"Is that it?" Art said in a half voice. He didn't know the time, but it couldn't have been later than four a.m.

"Nah. Not really. You remember when we were up on the ditch yesterday . . . found that gate with the wood bridge across it?"

"Yeah."

"Down below the ditch there was that open ridge. No trees on top, just down both sides. And lots of rock outcroppin's for cover? Somethin' tells me we oughta go there."

"Instead of ridin' down the ditch tomorrow, you mean," Art said.

"I mean right now. Right away. I don't know why, Art, but this place feels like a trap to me. Gives me the willies. I think somebody knows we're here and is waitin' for first light."

"Yeah? How so?"

"Don't you smell it?"

"What?"

"You know. Pine smoke. Pine with lots of pitch in it. Somebody's got a fire goin' somewhere. And it ain't this one. Y' just catch a whiff once in a while."

Art sniffed, puzzled. "Seems to be downslope of us."

"Come to think of it, we never scouted that direction," Will said. "Heavy timber, steep. I think we oughta get to that open ridge and find us some cover. Come dawn, I'll bet he heads for here. Might be right here where he caught *that* Army fella." Will nodded in the direction of the grave. "It's prime for ambush, us in the open and heavy trees all around. Nowhere to go except up the ditchbank, and he could pick us off there, one by one."

"I'll start wakin' the boys," Art said.

"I'm gonna get those rifles unpacked," Will said, "and I'll start gettin' the horses ready. You want t' take all the bedrolls and gear with us?"

"We'll leave it. Travel light. If your ol' pal shows up and

takes it all, even with the pack horse, he won't travel very fast. And I don't see anywhere he could go that we couldn't follow."

So in the eerie light well before dawn, four ghost figures in chaps and Stetsons saddled and bridled their horses, whispering to the animals all the while, sloshing the canteens to be sure they were full before hanging them on the saddle horns, feeling in the saddlebags for spare ammunition and field glasses. They left the pack horse on a long picket rope and swung to the saddles with no more noise than the squeaking of leather, and silently followed single file as Will led them east into the trees on the faint game trail he knew would bring them to the open ridge beyond.

The mountains on the eastern horizon had a light blue halo by the time they reached the place, and the stars had faded out. They tied the horses to scrub timber behind the highest rocks and spread out toward the high point of the ridge, rifles in hand, checking the skyline ahead and then the dark fringe of forest below. The odor of a pitch pine smudge was stronger now.

"Art!" Pasque whispered loudly, signaling at something over the hill. Will and the Pinto Kid froze in place.

Art crouched and hurried to Pasque's side. "What?"

"There." He pointed his rifle at the tree line below. There was a niche in the forest, a three-sided little opening facing the bare ground of the mountain shoulder, and in it a lone figure was curled up almost on top of a smoldering heap of ash.

Art used the field glasses. "Get Will," he said.

Pasque waved his rifle and made a come on gesture to Will.

Art handed Will the field glasses. "That your man?" he asked.

246

Will looked. "Not likely," he said softly. He took another careful survey of the boy's campsite. "No sign of a horse. And whoever's scrunched up into that blanket, he ain't very big. Some kinda gun there next to 'im, but I can't make it out. Not a lever action."

Art took the glasses and made his own study, and agreed with Will.

"Art?" Will said.

"Yeah?"

"I think it's that kid."

"I think so, too," Art agreed. "Pasque, take a look."

Pasque also found the little mound of blanket somehow familiar. The pathetic fire, the absence of any sort of food cache or pack, the small rifle, reminded the three of the boy who had walked into their camp back on the Divide.

"Jesús," Pasque said, pronouncing it the New Mexico way, "you don't suppose he came to help us? Warn us, maybe? What would bring that *muchacho* clear up here, anyway? I got a hunch, Art, that we're lookin' at one pretty *muy* little *caballero*."

"Want me to go down there an' wake him up?" Will asked.

"No," Art said. "He ain't the big dark one-eyed bastard, so we'd better leave him and watch our backs. He'll be up directly and maybe come find us. We got a bigger problem to worry about. Pasque, why don't you get yourself settled here where you can glance at the kid from time to time. And keep your eye on those trees down off the other side. That rider could sneak way down the slope and come up that way, if he figured us to be at the ditch.

"Will, you Injun your way up to that high point there and cover the ditch path. Me, I'll get down in the rocks where the Kid is, and we'll watch the way we came. If that shooter is comin', we'll give him till about noon to do it."

247

"Y' really figure he's around?"

"Dunno. Maybe not. I guess maybe smellin' that kid's campfire made me spooky. Then seein' that kid down there . . . let's just see. Come about noon, let's one of us scout on down this ditch for another place to camp. We're gonna take this thing real slow."

Art had good reason to be spooky, even though he didn't know what was causing it.

The Guardian was coming. At his cold camp above the ditch, he had awakened with first light and taken care to bring in his horse and saddle before doing anything else. He had hunkered down next to the dead ashes of the fire and eaten his hard bread washed down with cold coffee. Then, before mounting up, he had pulled the long Henry rifle from the scabbard. The magazine was full. He had taken a cartridge from the pocket of his chaps and slid it into the chamber.

Now he rode cautiously through the thick timber and avoided riding across openings in the forest. He considered going up to the ditch path, but decided he was just imagining that something about the running water would somehow help him, and that he'd be better off down where the trees gave cover.

The horse was snaky and restless. It whinnied when it smelled the Keystone pack horse tethered at the edge of the clearing. The Guardian worked his horse into a position behind an old ponderosa and peered around. There was nothing else moving, just a horse on a long lead, cropping grass. There were packs on the ground, and bedrolls left near a fire pit. He spotted the food bag hung high from a limb.

He dismounted and went ahead, Colt in hand. They hadn't stayed here for long. Their horses had been picketed together and were eating the grass, but only the one place.

They had not been here long, judging by the single piles of horse shit. Four bedrolls, four men.

The grave had been dug up. And then covered up again. If they were looking for that Army guy, they had found him. He stopped and listened for a long time, checking every tree and shadow around the clearing. Nobody there. Army? He went back to the pack horse, took it by the lead, and spoke quietly to it, asking it to tell him where it came from. The horse rolled its eyes, but didn't rear away from him. The brand was a sort of box, tapered, with a curved top, and he felt that it was a brand he should know, or had known, but it made no sense to him now. Bent Box? He rubbed it to see if there was anything in the box, but, if there was, it hadn't been burned in deep enough. Just a . . . window brand?

He found the same brand on the packsaddle that had been hung up in a scrub cedar, and on the canvas bedroll covers. Seeing it on the bedrolls sent a shiver wiggling up along his spine, and, when he closed his eye, he seemed to see an image of a house and a woman, and he shuddered it away with the image of the other house and the other woman. At least there was no sign of the four being Army. So who they were didn't matter. Wouldn't matter even if they were Army. What mattered was how many and what their guns were. He found saddle carbines in among the other gear, and a long box with nothing in it. They might be out there somewhere with just their holster guns. But, unless they were lugging an empty box around with them for some reason, they more likely were carrying some heavy artillery.

He found the tracks leading out to the east. He mounted up and followed through the trees. The sun wasn't up yet, but the early slant of the light made some of the tracks of the four horses show up as deep shadowy depressions. When the tracks got to the edge of the timber, The Guardian knew the lay of the open ridge ahead. He holstered the Colt, dismounted, and tied the horse back inside the trees. He pulled out the Henry.

He reached up with a finger to wipe his eye patch and remembered again that it was in a saddlebag. Fontana's idea, he recalled. He wiped his bad eye with his finger, pulled the black hat further down against the rising glare ahead.

The first man he spotted was Will, up on the high point, watching the ditch, a long way off. The Guardian dropped to his belly and wiggled into a little dip in the ground, made sure he hadn't been seen, then searched the skyline for the others. Art stood up to take a look around, and The Guardian spotted him. Nearby he thought he saw a hat. Then the sun glinted off something shiny, some kind of decoration. Where was the fourth man? Farther along the ridge, farther down? Probably. So there was one watching the ditch path, two watching their back trail, one covering the downslope.

A smart man would ride around this, not mess with it.

That's not the way the women want it, he thought grimly. *They need to be protected, even if men get killed. Even if I get killed. And if one of them kills me, those women'll get him to wear these clothes and ride the ditch and keep on protectin' their precious water. Maybe it's gotta be that way. Like a bunch of cow elk standing there all calm as hell while they watch the bull elks tryin' to kill each other. Don't matter which bull wins, 'cause one always will, and the cows'll keep on makin' more calves 'cause that's what they do.*

The Guardian narrowed his good eye and studied the man-specks up on the boulder-strewn ridge. He planned his attack, figuring how it would go if he did one thing, how it would go if he did another. He could probably crawl around and pick off the man highest on the hill, but there'd be three left to catch him in the open. Those middle two, he could try some long shots here from where he was. Except that then the high one would have an easy shot at him.

He turned his attention toward Pasque's location, farther down the ridge. Finally he saw a movement, just a quick one, like a flick of a shadow, and he was certain that someone was there just over the rise and out of sight. It would be best, probably, to get on the horse and work down through the timber and then ride up on that lowest man on the ridge, the one he couldn't see. Just charge him like before and get him. Then he'd have the other three between himself and the ditch. It'd be a stand-off, probably, but with that lowest man taken care of he'd at least be able to work his way along from rock to rock up the ridge. The other three would have nowhere to go without making a run across the open.

The Guardian moved in a crouch, snaking his way back into the trees, and untied his horse.

Down below the other side of the ridge, at the edge of the timber, the boy stirred and moaned. He sat up in his blanket and looked around. Pasque saw the movement and took up the field glasses for a better look, turning his back on the trees down the slope in the other direction where the Guardian was tightening his cinch and checking his Henry rifle and his Colt.

Pasque saw that it was the same boy, the same one who had come into their camp back on the Divide. Hungry-looking little shaver. Pasque watched him through the glasses and hoped he would stay put and out of the way of any flying lead. He figured the kid probably had sense enough to take cover when the shooting started.

When prairies catch fire, the flames send a beacon of gray smoke a mile into the sky. It attracts hawks, and eagles, and prairie falcons, and soaring turkey vultures. Even owls, large and small, rise in the noonday light. The raptors know what the smoke means: rodents are running for their lives, just ahead of the line where the smoldering grass flashes into flames. There are voles and mice, rats and gophers, prairie dogs. Along with larger game, like rabbits and woodchucks and badgers, they dash into the unburned grass, only to be picked off by the circling hunters.

Like a mountain vulture drawn by campfire smoke, another figure came along through the trees on the mountain above the ditch. The deep shadows hid his blackness and his leather clothes were of a color with the tree trunks. For all his huge, jostling mass, he moved like mist through the trees. Finally he came to where the trees were not so thick. There he paused and leaned on his iron staff and looked down past the pines and across the wide ditch. There, on the open ridgeline, he saw Will sitting against a rock, gazing down the mountain. Farther on, he saw Art and the Pinto Kid sitting in a surround of boulders, a kind of natural fort.

Four horses grazed near the edge of the woods. So he knew that a fourth rider was farther along the ridge. After studying on the scene a while, he also knew where the Guardian might be. It is not certain, but he may also have known about the small boy with the small rifle at the edge of the timber down below the ridge.

The fat, dark-faced creature grunted in satisfaction before lowering his bulk onto a fallen log and leaning back against a tree to watch.

Chapter Seventeen

Four Against the Guardian

Through field glasses, Pasque watched the boy stick his hand into a greasy sack and put something in his mouth. Probably cold jerky for breakfast, poor kid. Pasque should have been paying less attention to the urchin's morning meal and more attention in the opposite direction.

Down the other side of the ridge, the Guardian began to move, urging his horse through the trees with little whispers, until he got to the clearing's edge. Ahead of him was nothing but bare open ground, sloping up toward the first of the four riders. He could see Pasque up above, with his back to him, field glasses to his eyes, watching something on the other side of the hill. The Guardian looked around for the other three, but couldn't see them. Which meant they couldn't see him, either, at least not right away.

The thing to do was to ride quietly up the hill as far as he could. He might even make it to the flat stretch, and that would leave him only about fifty yards to cover up the slope. If he got to the flat, that's where he'd put the horse into a hard run. Between surprise and speed, there was a good chance he'd get that rider before he got him. He didn't see any other way to do it.

Low clouds were gathering in the early morning sky, but, for the moment, shining under them, the rising sun made a blinding glare behind the man on the ridge. For a few minutes it gave the Guardian an advantage—the man had the sun in his eyes, so the guardian would get farther up the slope before being spotted. But soon the sun would rise enough to blind him as well, before it slipped up behind the overcast. His brow furrowed under the dark Stetson. Sun rising on that man, then on him. Sunrise first for one of them, then for the other. Likely be the last sunrise for one of them, too. The thought was tugging a memory into his mind. Something somebody had told him somewhere. He scowled, trying to re-member, the scowl making his face ugly. Abruptly he gave up on it with a curse and cocked his rifle and put the heels to the horse.

The horse shied at the kick and started dancing sidewise at the next one. He still had some morning ornery in him. The Guardian straightened him out with the reins and gave him knee pressure, keeping his eye on the man on the ridge. If he had been looking at his horse instead of the other man, he would have seen that the horse's ears were twitching. It meant the snake wasn't ready to settle down yet, but trotted unevenly instead, dancing on the uphill side. Maybe it was spooked by the sun flash, or maybe by the silence. Or maybe whatever passes for imagination in horses was just acting up this morning. No matter the reason, The Guardian hadn't yet covered half the distance, when the horse tried to kick around on him and at the same time let out a whinny that would wake the dead.

Pasque turned at the sound and saw the rider coming. He let the field glasses fall and brought his rifle up at almost the same time he saw The Guardian's rifle come to bear on him, at least as well as it could with the horse doing its waltz and stumbling on the loose rock and slick grass of the upslope. The Guardian got off the first shot, but the horse stumbled at that moment and spoiled the aim. The Guardian heard the *wham!* of his big-caliber Henry rifle and felt the kick, but didn't see where his shot went. Pasque hesitated, wanting to make sure this was their man. Then he saw the Guardian jump down from his saddle to his feet and lever a second shell into the rifle. Pasque brought up his own gun. There was another *wham!* from the Henry. Pasque heard the whine of the ricochet off rocks close to him.

Out the corner of his eye, he saw Art running toward him, crouching low and yelling, but he couldn't tell what. Pasque raised up and squeezed off a round from the .44 Rimfire, and through the smoke he saw the dark figure of The Guardian drop and flatten out.

"Behind you!" Art was yelling, pointing down to where the boy was camped. Art checked the other side of the hill to make sure The Guardian was taking cover, then he stood up and took careful aim, like a hunter taking a shot at an elk or deer—elbows out wide for balance, one foot ahead of the other, head cocked over the stock.

Pasque watched wide-eyed as Art's .45-70 roared and the smoke went rolling down toward the boy.

The boy went dodging into the trees.

"Little son-of-a-bitch shot at you!" Art panted, running up.

Pasque looked over the rock toward where he had last seen The Guardian, and ducked down again. "Art, stay low!" he said. "Our friend in black is down there, somewhere. And I don't know what his rifle is, but it's no rabbit gun. What do you suppose that kid's thinking? Is he helping that Guardian or ditch rider or whatever he calls himself?"

"Looks like it," Art said. "Look, you don't have much of a position here. Now that we know where he's at, we oughta. . . ."

There was another *pop!* as the boy fired again from down in the trees, followed in a couple of seconds by another shot. *Pop!* This one kicked up the dirt near them.

"That little bastard," Art said, pulling his Colt and sending a shot toward boy's position. "We need to move back."

What the two men didn't know, as they scrambled along in the shelter of the ridge, watching the trees for signs of the kid with the .22, was that The Guardian was also on the move, running downhill, then across the slope and up again, darting from boulder to tree stump. He was making for the ditch, or as close as he could get before the others spotted him. At one point, he looked up to see two men with rifles momentarily outlined on the ridgeline, and he stopped and steadied himself for a shot at them. He was still panting from the run, and, before he could settle the Henry down for a good shot, the sun played one last trick on him, glinting full in his face just before sliding up into the gray haze. The Guardian wiped his eye with his finger and swore to himself.

Nearby, the Pinto Kid caught that glimpse of movement and laid the Sharps .45 across a rock, careful to put his gloved hand under the forestock to keep it from getting scratched. But by the time he had adjusted the peep sight and set the trigger, The Guardian moved behind a drop-off. The Kid swung the barrel to where he figured The Guardian would reappear, squeezing off his shot a half second too soon and succeeding only in making The Guardian drop to his knees and crawl into the shadow of an overhang, where he stayed put.

Art and Pasque were heading toward him. The Pinto Kid turned his head to follow their progress. He heard a *pop!* far-away in the trees and saw a puff of dirt flying up well behind Pasque. Somebody else was taking potshots at them, but he didn't change the position of the Sharps. Whoever was down there with that little gun was no threat compared to this *hombre* under the hill below him.

"Who was that?" he called when Art and Pasque were closer.

"Aw," Art said as they ran up, "Pasque says it's that damn' kid that came into camp, back a few nights ago. We figure he's helpin' that other lunatic defend the damn' ditch or somethin'." Art thumbed back his Colt and let another shot fly in the boy's general direction, then holstered the revolver and got down in the protection of the natural rock fortress. "Damn' kid," he repeated.

The world went quiet again, and the smoke from the rifles drifted off into nothingness and no longer rang in the men's ears. There was nothing moving anywhere on the mountain save for the water flowing full and noiselessly through the ditch and the clouds overhead curling their enormous billows around each other and folding and boiling up again into ever darker and darker masses. Noon came, and the three Keystone men scrounged in their chaps pockets for bits of jerky and leftover biscuit and hoped that Will was OK up by the ditch.

The day grew ever darker. They kept their voices down, and while the Kid kept watch on the drop-off down one side of the hill, Art and Pasque took turns watching the line of trees. Nothing moved. At least the Keystone men did not *see* anything moving.

Down below, The Guardian realized that the overhanging ledge would give him a good twenty or thirty feet of cover, and at the highest part he could stand up without being seen from the ridge. He studied the terrain below and calculated a route that would take him back to the trees—he could belly downhill, feet first, backward, keeping his rifle trained on the ridge, sort of squirm along protected by the overhang until he got to the big split boulder down below. From there he could snake along, hidden by a low ledge that he could see, and he'd come to a dry gulch leading down to the trees. By then he'd almost be out of range and could make a run up the hill. His mind was on the water, and the ditch.

It had been stupid to attack like that and leave them closer to the ditch than he was. What he had to do was get to it before they did. They could break it open. That was what they had come to do, like all the others. He had to protect it. The only important thing was the water.

The crawl down the hill went slowly, lying on his belly and squirming along feet first, unable to avoid the sharp rocks and mountain cactus and trying to keep the sand and dust out of his eye while watching up the ridge for any sign of men or rifle barrels. The swollen black clouds came farther down and flattened out against the divide and came down still farther into the valleys. A wind smelling of rain came up and wafted over the ridge and the slope, but The Guardian kept wriggling and snaking his way. He made it to the split boulder where he rested. There he braced the Henry rifle in a good solid branch of the bush and waited in case one of the interlopers might show himself.

The day grew late under a sky that was solid black with heavy clouds. He gave up the vigil and squirmed along to the low ledge, sneaked along in the cover of it, and then down the dry watercourse to the trees. There he would stay huddled under the shelter of a spruce whose branches made a tent clear to the ground as the thunder echoed off the far mountains and the lightning split the horizon sky and big drops of ice-water rain pelted down.

Up on the ridge, the four found what little shelter they could under overhanging lips of the boulders. The Pinto Kid got to figuring it was a while since they had seen anything of the kid with the .22 and that it might mean he was sneaking over to their horses, either to steal them or what was on them. So he traded rifles with Art and had Art cover him while he made a run down the long open slope to where the horses were. There was no shot from the .22, no movement in the trees other than the wind whipping the branches. The Kid got saddlebags and slickers off the horses and carried Will's up to him. He filled Will in on what was happening, and his fear that the boy was going for the horses. Then he and Will trotted back to the stone fort, both keeping a wary eye on the forest below.

With their slickers and cold food from the saddlebags, the four men figured they'd make it through the night pretty good. Better, anyway, than hunkering down trying to stay dry under nothing but a Stetson.

Above the ditch, a black lumpy figure with one eye squeezed his fat body back into a cave in the dirtbank where low fir branches made a curtain. There he squatted like a swollen toad in its hole. He gobbled handfuls of parch and pemmican from a leather bag and pulled his elk-skin cape around to cover his belly and legs. His distorted face wore a grin, as if he were vastly amused at some cosmic joke. Hunkered back in his hole on the cloud-shrouded mountain beside the silently flowing water, he went on chewing and grinning, listening to the forest for sounds that he alone could hear.

The Pinto Kid had been right. The boy, Martha's child, had been near the horses. Late in the afternoon he had thought of the men's horses, guessing that they had be tied out of the way somewhere, since they weren't up there with the men, and that where the horses were was where the food would be.

He had moved like a wary squirrel, rising up to look around him and then dropping into a crouch to move again, peering out from behind each tree, straining his ears for the slightest sound. He had heard a couple of shots from the other side of the ridge and froze. He had forced himself to stay still and wait out the silence for a long time before moving again. He had heard a horse whinny somewhere ahead of him. He froze again.

When he was close to where he had thought the whinny had come from, the boy saw a man coming down the open slope above him, a lone man wearing chaps that flapped when he walked and carrying a heavy rifle. This was better than he had hoped for. He'd help The Guardian even the odds and get himself a big rifle to boot. Silently he had slid back deeper into the trees and edged along, keeping one eye out for the cowboy and one for the horses. The horses were picketed in an open patch of grass. They had their heads up, listening to the man approaching. The boy scrunched down on his stomach behind a log and rested the forestock of his .22 on it. The range was just right; he'd often shot a rabbit in the head from this distance. A man's head was bigger.

The Pinto Kid moved among the horses, talking to them, taking slickers and saddlebags, unaware of the boy waiting just inside the edge of the woods. Martha's boy got ready. But before he got a good bead on the man, he heard a whizzing sound and felt and heard a thud on the log. He turned to see an arrow, quivering and humming, with its point half buried in the old wood.

His mouth moved, but no noise came out. He couldn't blink, and he thought he had peed his pants. He rolled to his side, forgetting the .22 resting on the log, and she was standing there—Luned from the house—standing there with another arrow fitted to her bowstring and aimed right at him. She said nothing, but he knew that, if he made a noise or a move, he was as good as dead.

At the horses, the Pinto Kid untangled one of the picket ropes and re-tied the others farther away. He spoke quietly to each horse, assuring them that they would get water soon. He picked up his stack of slickers and saddlebags and went back up the slope. After he was well gone, Luned gestured to the boy's rifle.

"Unload that," she said. "Come with me."

He obeyed. He did not speak until he was on her horse, sitting on the saddle in front of her and holding to the horn. The jogging of the horse made it hard for him to stay on. They were headed in the direction of Crannog.

"I was helping," he finally said. "They was four of them."

"You would have been killed," Luned said. "Why were you there?"

"They got bags full of food. I seen it."

"When you need food, you come to the house. I will give it to you."

"But I was helpin' out," he argued weakly.

"It is not for you to do," she said. "Not yet."

"Coulda got me a bigger rifle off'n that man, too," he said. "Someday maybe I'll be the one guardin' that ol' ditch and get t' keep everythin'."

"Perhaps you might at that," she said, guiding her horse through the gathering darkness. "Perhaps, after all, you might."

The fat dark figure in the cave knew that Luned and the boy were gone, even though no one else had heard them go. White queen's knight and white queen's pawn had been removed from the play. Now it would be king and king's knights against the remaining white knight. Now the creature would sleep, eager for the next day's moves.

The Keystone men slept very little that night. Art kept thinking about their positions: where each man was, where The Guardian was, what the terrain was like, how they should move when it came daylight again. He worried about each of his men in turn, worried that the Kid might catch a bullet because he was sort of new to all this, worried that Will might . . . well, might do something.

In his sleep, Will twisted this way and that on the cold ground. Every time he drifted off, he dreamed about the day The Guardian had robbed him of his gear and horse and his pride, and he woke shivering and knew it was fear and not the cold.

Pasque thought of Elena and of home, and admitted to himself that he was not sorry he had come here to be with these men. It was good to be with them, even if the outcome was uncertain. Still, he thought of his wife and their warm room in the adobe house, far away to the south.

The Pinto Kid shivered in his slicker and saddle blanket, and what little sleep he got didn't seem so much like sleep as like some kind of scene he was watching from a distance. He saw himself lying there, knees drawn up against the cold, and, looking down at himself and the other sleeping figures, he did not know why he was there. Not at all.

The first gray streaks of sky finally came. Among the rocks, the four shapes were black blurs, and the horizon blended sky and trees into one shadow. Will sat up, rubbing his legs to get the blood moving. He couldn't stop worrying about the horses for some reason, and, when he saw Pasque open one eye to look up at him from the blankets, he whispered—"Goin' down and check those horses."—and hunched away as quietly as he could, feeling his way over the ground.

An hour passed, and another, and now the sun was just behind the eastern ridge about to come up. Art scanned the woods below them with his field glasses, but there was no sign of Will. He made a plan, putting Pasque and the Kid in the best places he could find where they could scan the slope below them and protect their backs at the same time. He was about to set out down the hill when they saw Will coming up. But he was coming slow, sort of wandering back and forth, weaving like a man who wasn't watching where he was going. He was carrying something, but it wasn't his rifle.

When he got near, they could see that it was an arrow. His face was the color of ash. His eyes had the same look as before when he had wandered away from the Keystone.

"Your rifle?" Art said.

"Huh?" Will turned and looked back. "Yeah. Had one. Down leanin' against a log there." He waved in the general direction of the trees.

"What have you got there?" Pasque asked.

Will looked at the arrow in his hand. "Same arrow. See?" Will said. "It's the same again. Like before. See it? I thought I seen somethin' white last evenin', when the Kid was down there. Told y' about the arrows, last time I was up here, and everybody looked at me like I was outta my mind, but now look at this. Same thing. Real nice . . . steel point . . . same thing."

Art put an arm around Will's shoulders and helped him to sit down behind the boulders. Will's head slumped over his knees.

"Can't be here, Art," he said. "Just can't be here. We're

gonna get killed this time. There's that spook with the bow and arrows . . . there's that damn' kid . . . there's. . . . We just can't be here, Art."

"Art!" It was the Pinto Kid, pointing up at the ditch. "He's up there!"

Art and Pasque wheeled to see where the Kid was pointing just in time to get a glimpse of a dark movement on the ditch path.

"I thought he was down below us," Pasque said.

"Must have worked his way up there again," Art said. "Get down until we see what he does. Get Will down behind those rocks. Damn but I wish he hadn't lost that rifle."

"There!" The Kid swung his Sharps toward the spot. It looked like somebody—had to be The Guardian—with just his head and his rifle showing above the edge of the ditch path. The Kid hesitated to shoot, but the man on the ditch path didn't. His first shot exploded a rock at the Kid's feet and sent splatters of lead and slivers of granite flying. Will caught one in the leg.

"Jesus Christ!" the Kid cried, triggering off a wild shot in the general direction of the ditch and slamming himself down behind the boulders.

Art winced, thinking that the Kid should have gotten off an accurate shot before getting down. *Dammit.* He methodically checked his supply of shells and then got comfortable behind his rock and put the big .45-70 into action, using two shots to get the range of the rim of the ditch and then watching for the slightest sign of movement. When The Guardian's rifle barrel showed over the edge, Art squeezed off a shot at it, and The Guardian's rifle went off at the same instant, sending lead whizzing right over their heads. Another shot plowed into the stones just in front of them.

When Art's eyes got strained from staring, it was the Kid's

turn. But the Kid always had to line up his peep sight just right, and cushion his forestock and barrel from bouncing on the granite from the recoil, so each of his shots would come way too late after The Guardian's.

Pasque didn't have all that many shells for the .44 Rimfire, so he held back. When he peeked out from around the rocks, it was to look for some way to circle around the rifleman on the ditch. But he just couldn't see how to do it.

All morning long it went on. The Guardian crawling from one spot to another, always staying next to the running water on the far side of the ditch path, out of sight of the Keystone men below, moving upstream and downstream, lying down again, bellying up to the edge, spotting a man's leg or arm or hat showing and taking a shot at it. He was making two shots to their one, keeping them cramped down behind their little pile of boulders while his slugs, hitting the ground, showered them with dirt.

At one point, Will jumped to his feet, after two shots nearly hit him, and yelled at The Guardian as he thumbed the hammer on his Colt until he had emptied the cylinder toward the ditch. Art and Pasque pulled him down just as one of The Guardian's bullets came whining past him.

"Stay the hell down!" Art ordered. "What are you tryin' to prove?"

Pasque lay back against one of the bigger rocks.

"OK?" Art asked.

"Yeah."

Dammit, Art thought. Just dammit.

They had a little to drink, and a little to eat. The shooting kept up and the day got warm and there seemed to be no end possible for this. Stalemate.

Around noon, clouds began to form over the western range of mountains, but they were the high kind, the kind that would just float away. Will seemed in a kind of daze, like a man who had too much to drink. Pasque made jokes and grinned, but with his teeth clenched. The Pinto Kid was getting nervous. He kept whipping his head around to make sure The Guardian wasn't looking down his sights from another part of the ditch. The way he was jumping around, the Kid would never get a good bead on the bastard.

Art had been in his share of shoot-outs, but never one that dragged on like this. One gun against four. The four should have been able to decide it a long time ago. He didn't say anything to the others, but Art was thinking of pulling out. Even if they managed to put this damned ditch rider out of action, they wouldn't know what to expect farther down the line. He came from a settlement, or a ranch, or something, and there'd be more men with rifles. Art was thinking it was about time to get to the horses and hightail it toward home. To hell with this Guardian and his irrigation ditch. Wasn't worth getting killed over.

Still, it wouldn't be settled until they found Kyle. Or found his grave, like they had found the other one. Kyle was probably dead, but they couldn't go back without knowing.

Chapter Eighteen

The Final Gambit

Along toward mid-afternoon, without warning, The Guardian began shooting again, snapping off shots as fast as he could, peppering the ground all around the Keystone men, his bullets kicking up storms of dust and pebbles and slivers of granite while they cowered behind the boulders. When it stopped, Art risked taking a look.

"I'll be dammed," he said.

Pasque twisted around and looked. "That's asking for it," he said.

The Guardian was standing in full view on the edge of the ditch path, holding up a revolver with a white cloth tied to it. He yelled something, but Art's ears were still numb from the all the rifle shots and he couldn't make out the words.

"What?"

"Parley!" came the voice.

Art stood up. "What's your proposition?"

"Colts," the Guardian said, waving the revolver. "Enough of this rifle play. We go to Colts. One of you, one at a time, up here."

"What's he talking about?" the Kid asked.

"Seems he wants one of us to climb up there and shoot it out with Colts," Art said. "He's probably as tired of this deal

267

as we are. I think we'll take him up on it."

"Who's gonna go?"

Who, indeed?

The Guardian stood on the ditch and took deliberate aim. His shot plowed a furrow in the ground, ten yards east of the Keystone riders' rock pile.

"When the shadow reaches that mark!" he yelled, voice hoarse. "Be up here!"

Art looked at the furrow and the angle of the sun. Half an hour, no more. He leaned back against the rock, glad to be able to stretch his legs and let his head drop toward his chest. Who was going to go up there? Or who was going *first*? It was pretty clear that it had to be he.

Pasque stood, stretched, and went over to Art, where he knelt down while checking the loads in his Colt. "Figure I'll go up there and deal with this badman, this misbegotten son-of-a-bitch. That OK with you, Art?"

Art's face was sad when he looked up. "No, it ain't."

"Well, I know Will sure as hell can't do it," Pasque said. "Look at 'im. Shakin' all over. He'd jump at his own shadow." Pasque lowered his voice. "And I hate t' say it, but the Kid would get butchered. No chance at all."

"That's why I'm goin'," Art said.

"When was the last time you tried your fast draw?" Pasque asked. "At least I'm in practice. And I'm younger'n you."

Will came to them, crawling on his knees and staying in the safety of the rocks in spite of The Guardian's assurance of a temporary truce. He put a hand on Art's knee and looked into his face. In his eyes was the sadness of a man condemned to death.

"Art?" he said. "Look, Art, we can't break up. Don't you see it's the same?" His voice trembled and shook. "His game is to pick us off one by one. He didn't take me on until he knew I was alone. See? You know the kind. A loner. Mean as hell. Man alone like that, figurin' he's protectin' something, he gets strange. Cold in the heart, see. We can't go up there one at a time, he'll knock us off like crippled coyotes."

"So we go together, you're sayin'," Art said. "You without a rifle and your hands shakin' like a drunk. Sorry, but that's what it looks like. You think he can't take us in a bunch? You think I want to use you three as targets while I get a bullet into him?"

Pasque pointed down the ditch. "I say we go down that way, uphill of the horses. Climb up onto the ditch downstream of him."

"And then what?" the Pinto Kid asked. "Just walk up on him, just like that?"

"Damn right," Will said. "All together. He's like a damn' droolin' stray dog, and you don't give him a chance to jump you. You just don't do it."

"I agree," Pasque said. "We walk up on him together, and, by God, he'll either back down or we cut him down!"

The Kid looked at the ground, then looked up again. "Well, I know I'm tired of messin' around this way," he said. "Let's go up there and get 'im."

Art stood up. "Wait a minute. Anybody seen that little piece of turd with the rabbit rifle lately?"

There had been no sign of the skinny boy all day.

Art stood there, tall in the sunlight, rifle in hand, looking around. The other three felt twinges of shame at having cowered in the rocks.

Each man checked his Colt. Each one straightened his clothing and dusted the dirt from his Levi's. Each man set his Stetson straight on his head. They were ready. Together, and ready.

The Guardian was also preparing himself. He took off his

chaps and laid them carefully beside the ditch and put the rifle on top of them. As he straightened up, he heard a noise, a clanking sound as of metal hitting rock. It came from downstream and across the ditch.

"I know you're there!" he called out. "Enjoyin' yourself? Might be gettin' yourself another recruit today to take my place. Where are you?" He scanned the ditchbank, careful to watch for the other four men as well. He could not see the black figure in the old buckskins, but knew he was there all the same. He sensed his presence.

"You just stay hid," he continued. " 'Cause you know, you crazy toad, I'm goin' to get you one of these days. Luned said I should, first chance I get, and I'm thinkin' I've already passed up too many chances. These here water gates will get along just fine without you keepin' your one eye on them."

Pasque, Art, the Pinto Kid, and Will scrambled to the top of the ditchbank, and the four of them stood there, together. Except for Will, they still had their rifles. Their revolvers were loose in the holsters and ready for use. Their hat brims were pulled low to shade their eyes. Upstream, standing at the edge of the water, they saw the lone figure in black clothes leaning out over the ditch as if talking to somebody. They heard the sound of his voice.

The Guardian heard their boots on the gravel and turned to see the Keystone men, shoulder to shoulder, blocking the ditch path. They moved forward slowly, deliberately, never blinking.

"Art!" Will suddenly said.

They stopped. Hands hovered over revolver butts. The Guardian stood like a post planted there, his hand ready for the draw. He knew he had to wait for them to get closer.

"Art!" Will said. "It's not the same one!"

"What are you talkin' about?" Art said in a hush.

"It ain't him. That's not the one that got me."

"Well, it's sure as hell the one that killed the poor bastard you found buried down there. Probably the one that got Kyle. Same one that's been shootin' at us all morning."

"What if there's more than one?" Pasque asked. "He looked to be talking to somebody a minute ago."

"Just keep on your toes," Art said. "We deal with this one first. But keep on your toes."

The Guardian saw them move forward again. They were coming into pistol range, together. "One at a time!" he taunted.

They kept walking.

"My men ride together, and they fight together!" Art shouted back. "You can take us all on, or back down! Your choice!"

"Your partner down there came alone!" The Guardian called back. He meant the Army man. But Art thought he meant Kyle.

"There's four of us now!" Art yelled. "One brand! You can walk away or try to take us on! It's your call!"

The Keystone men stopped and waited.

This is crazy, Art was thinking. *Like something a bunch of town drunks would do! I haven't tried to draw and shoot fast in two years. And any second now, somebody's going to do something that would light off this fireworks show, and somebody's gonna get bad hurt. Maybe die.*

The Guardian waited, standing by the flowing water. His muscles toned themselves, relaxed themselves, all down his back, all the ligaments and sinews. He waited; he imagined how the next moments would go. He wondered if he would die, and which one would kill him. One of these four probably would kill him, or maybe he'd get killed by some back shooter he hadn't counted on. These four could have gotten somebody else to throw in with them for an ambush. Maybe that Norwegian, getting even for his wife getting killed. Maybe the fat one-eyed toad. They'd come from behind, from upstream. He had no way to know. Right now the enemy was in front of him, coming upstream.

To The Guardian, it felt as if the sun had stopped moving and the ditch water had stopped running, and in the timelessness he was seeing how it would happen, how it would be. His hand would go down quickly for his Colt, and he'd slick it up out of the holster so smooth, like he was just wiping his hand up along the leather, and the gun was coming with it like it was part of him, and then he'd be pointing it without even thinking about it. The sounds of gunfire would roll away across the valley and smash the stillness and the timelessness. The recoil would feel good and strong and real.

In his mind he saw how he would flick the hammer back and how he would tighten down on the trigger even before he had the hammer on full cock. And these latest challengers, they'd go down. He'd shoot the one with the silver hatband first. He looked the most dangerous. Then the older one who did the talking. Then he'd swing the Colt real quick to the short one and drop the hammer, and that one would go down, too, and then last he'd shoot the one standing next to the edge. The .45 slug would knock him right off the ditch, and he'd go rolling down over the rocks.

The Guardian's right hand hovered over his holster, calm and solid. Ready. His bad eye felt sweaty and gritty, so he brought up his left hand, real slow and easy, and with one finger he wiped it. As he did, he remembered he wasn't wearing his eye patch.

It was Will who recognized the gesture. "Art," he said in a hushed voice, sounding like a man about to whisper his last wishes on earth. "Art! Look!"

"Yeah, Will."

"Art, it's Kyle!"

"What?"

"It's Kyle. Look at 'im!"

Art stared hard at the man in black, and the one good eye looked back.

"Kyle?" Art shouted across the killing ground between them. "Kyle? That you?"

The Guardian's hand lowered a fraction of an inch toward the gun butt. He stared at the other man, the one doing the talking. Now his palm was so close to the gun he could sense it through his skin, like an itch, and he was trying to focus himself away from the one who talked. Tried to swing his mind toward the other men—the one with the silver hatband, the skinny one next to the edge. One of them had said something. He didn't know what. But the one who talked started to look like somebody. Maybe he ought to aim for him first, instead of the one with the silver hatband.

"Kyle! Kyle! It's Art! And Pasque? You know Will. And the Pinto Kid?"

The Guardian's hand was touching cold metal. The killing was about to begin. Except that his eye flickered. It blinked once, twice, flicked back and forth across the four faces in front of him. He didn't know which one to aim at. Then the faces blurred. The Guardian's hand rested on the Colt, but he turned his head and looked at the water running in the ditch. He looked up toward the mountain. Water and evil, and north-running creeks. The sound of water became a roar to his ears. That older man's mouth kept moving, but he couldn't hear the words, yet, somehow, he knew him. The Guardian felt like he was dying already, giving in to darkness, a man swaying and spinning in a crowd of strangers who were speaking and he couldn't hear them. He knew he had to say something, but what? The blood was pounding. Red haze was blinding his eye.

That one man. That skinny one on the edge of the ditch. Didn't I kill him? His name is Will. Will. But Will is all beat up and drunk now. Will's a drunk. I have to find the man who did it to him, too, 'cause Art expects it and the Keystone. . . . Art. Pendragon. Keystone. Who was going to kill Art? Where was The Guardian?

Kyle's hand went limp and flopped across his holster because it had no muscles left in it. One leg buckled beneath him, and he went down in a slow, red-spinning spiral with the four faces swirling past and the roar of ditch water. Finally the coolness of gravel ground against his cheek before all went black and quiet.

Art and Pasque stayed with the unconscious man, shading his face from the sun and putting wet kerchiefs on his forehead while Will and the Pinto Kid scouted the ditch in each direction to determine if the Guardian had helpers. They found his horse, put the chaps over the saddle and the rifle in the scabbard, and led it down to where their own horses were picketed.

Kyle came to himself slowly, and, even when he got his speech back, he felt weak and dizzy, like a man with the sickness. Four pairs of arms were there to help him down the ditchbank and over to the horses. They sat him down against a log. Art stayed beside him, and neither one had anything useful to say. He and Art just sat there together, looking off over the mountains. Pasque, Will, and the Kid looked after getting the horses to water and went back to the other camp for the pack animal and their gear. When they got back, they re-packed everything except what they needed for the night.

They ate without talking. Kyle ate with them, although the look on his face told them he was still far away, somewhere. He heard their voices when they spoke, but couldn't sort out what they said. He could taste the food and feel the air getting colder, so he knew he was alive. He shivered when the sun dropped down and the evening breeze swept up from the valley. He was alive, and his senses were feeling things there at the camp, but his mind was wandering around, numb and blank as it recalled scenes from the two years that had gone by since he had left the Keystone. He saw himself in one scene, like a picture in the stereopticon, where he was standing in front of Fontana on the stairway of Crannog. In another one, he was dragging the Army engineer through the ditch, and in still another scene he was riding an endless meadow when somebody shot at him. Kyle stared straight ahead and wondered if he had killed other men. It seemed like he had done something very wrong, and it seemed like he should feel guilty about it, but he just felt blank. He couldn't get his mind interested in the questions.

His drugged thoughts took him upstream along the ditch, moving against the water but kind of floating along above it, seeing the creeks and springs coming down the mountain to pour into it, and the gates, and always the movement of the water.

Art, Pasque, Will, and the Kid finished with their meal, drank up the last of the coffee, and one by one wandered out among the dark trees to do a little personal business. While Art was doing his, he heard the sound. The sound of metal on rock, like somebody banging away with a crowbar. The sound went on and on, ringing sharply down the slope to them and past them and down into the valley to echo back again. It kept up for half an hour.

The Pinto Kid was all for going out there to see what it

was, but Art didn't like that idea. He'd spent the morning pinned down by a man on that ditch path, and didn't take to the notion of shooting it out all night.

"What is it, do you suppose?" Pasque said.

"Dunno," Art said. "Doesn't sound like a machine of any kind, or a hammer. Sounds like a metal bar, like somebody whacking a length of drill rod on rock."

Then there was a noise behind them in the dusk. They turned to see Kyle standing up. "The gate," he said, "that toad figgers to break open the gate, drown us down here. You break down those gates and all hell breaks loose. People get killed."

And before anyone could do anything to stop him, Kyle grabbed up Art's Winchester and was running upslope toward the sound. He was yelling.

"STOP IT! STOP! NO MORE! NO MORE!"

When he saw the ditchbank, little more than a strip of light-colored earth running along through the dark, Kyle stopped. He cocked the Winchester. He fired, then fired again and again, shooting blindly through his own gunsmoke, the Winchester flashing in the dark, bullets caroming off rocks somewhere up the mountain, gunsmoke rising in the starlight. Kyle fired the last round from the magazine and still cocked the rifle and pulled the trigger, the hammer making a dull click in the dark. He finally slumped to his knees with his head bowed.

"No more," he said. "Stop."

The sound of the metal bar on stone had stopped, and did not resume. The Pinto Kid and Art helped Kyle back down to camp.

"You reckon he killed 'im?" the Kid asked.

"I doubt it," Art said.

"Don't know as anyone can," Kyle mumbled, stumbling along between them.

The first hours of dim morning light found all five in the saddle, riding back along the way that had brought the Keystone men to this place. Off across the valley, on the other side of the divide, the shining peaks became brilliant in the rising sun. They glistened there, silver-red, the reflected light looking as if the sun itself were coming up in the west. Art and Pasque rode in the lead, picking out landmarks. Kyle rode straight in his saddle, wearing his eye patch, looking around as if seeing the country for the first time. The Pinto Kid rode beside him, humming to himself and idly braiding and unbraiding the ends of his reins. Will Jensen brought up the rear, leading the pack horse. The animal carried ample food and gear for five men, and the four long rifles.

Epilogue

Luned followed their tracks for two days before knowing for certain the five riders would never turn back. She returned to Crannog with the news.

Hearing of her protector's betrayal, Lady Fontana kept to her room for two days, considering how to explain in the settlement that her "husband" and Guardian had gone without leaving a successor. Finally she realized that no explaining was needed. She was, after all, not only beautiful and powerful and soon to be wealthy when the project came to culmination; she also controlled all the water, the source of life itself.

She might have gone after him with tears and promises, holding out the remains of her pride to him like a ruined woman holding out her stillborn infant. She could have pursued him with rage and indignation, saying that all the shame and weakness were his, and that decency demanded that he undo the damage and put everything right again.

However, in any pursuit there would be a measure of surrender. She considered sending some men, all the men if necessary, to force him to return both for their benefit and for hers, and for the good of the Great North project. This, too, would be to surrender some part of herself. More correctly, it would demean her. Money, land, irrigating below the mountains, these were only secondary to the single essential thing, which was the source of the water. The source of life. All else can change hands, can prosper and fail, can fall and rise again in other hands, in later days, but there must always be the water.

Her duty was to stay at the source of life.

Three more years were to pass. Then, one day in late summer, not yet autumn, a strangely pale young woman dressed in pale yellow would ride up to the front steps of the Keystone. There she would point to Kyle Owen, in front of all assembled, and would accuse him of desertion, cowardice, and unfaithfulness.

And Kyle Owen's odyssey would begin again.

THE WESTERNERS
ZANE GREY

The very essence of the American West is in the stories of Zane Grey, an author whose popularity has not flagged since his first Western novel was published in 1910. He wrote more than sixty novels, including the classic *Riders of the Purple Sage*, and the stories collected here for the first time in paperback are shining examples of his best. Included in this volume is "The Ranger," first published in 1929 but never before in the form Grey himself intended. Here is a rare opportunity to experience the short stories of Zane Grey, restored and corrected to the author's original vision, a vision that has remained unmatched for nearly a century!

- -

JANE CANDIA COLEMAN

BORDERLANDS

In this thrilling collection of brilliant short stories, award-winning author Jane Candia Coleman takes us on an exciting tour of the different borderlands of the Old West, some real, some emotional, borderlands that mark endings . . . but also beginnings. From settlers on the Montana-Canada border to Pancho Villa's bold attack on New Mexico, these tales tell of daring and courage, adventure and danger. They feature journeys made by people looking for a better life, to escape an old life—or simply to stay alive.

DOUBLE
EAGLES
ANDREW J. FENADY

Captain Thomas Gunnison has been entrusted with an extremely vital cargo. His commerce ship, the *Phantom Hope*, is laden with two thousand Henry rifles, weapons that could turn the tide of victory for the Union. Even more important, though, is fifteen million dollars in newly minted double eagles, money the Union needs to finance the war effort. So when the *Phantom Hope* is attacked and crippled, Gunnison makes the only possible decision—he and his men will transport the gold across the rugged landscape of Mexico, to Vera Cruz. Gunnison's caravan could change the course of history . . . if bloodthirsty Mexican guerrillas and Rebel soldiers don't stop it first!

MEN BEYOND THE LAW

These three short novels showcase Max Brand doing what he does best: exploring the wild, often dangerous life beyond the constraints of cities, beyond the reach of civilization . . . beyond the law. Whether he's a desperate man fleeing the tragic results of a gunfight, an innocent young man who stumbles onto the loot from a bank robbery, or the gentle giant named Bull Hunter—one of Brand's most famous characters—each protagonist is out on his own, facing two unknown frontiers: the Wild West . .. and his own future.

___4873-6 $4.50 US/$5.50 CAN

River Walk

Rita Cleary

Many accounts have been written of the historic expedition led by Meriwether Lewis and William Clark across North America, but author Rita Cleary offers the story from a very different point of view—through the eyes of John Collins, who is persuaded to join the expedition by his friend, a hunter who will supply meat for the voyagers. Of all the risks of the journey, both natural and man-made, perhaps none will prove as dangerous for Collins as his love for Laughing Water, a young Mandan widow with a child. Lewis and Clark's pact with the members of the expedition strictly forbids desertion for any reason. For Collins, his sworn oath becomes not only a question of honor, but a matter of life and death.

___4922-8 $4.50 US/$5.50 CAN

DOUBLE VENGEANCE
John Duncklee

Joe Holly has his assignment. The army is sending him to Fort Huachuca, deep in the heart of Apache territory. It's no easy post. Apache raiding parties are a fact of life there, and the area is known for its thieves and hardcases. But they're the least of Joe's worries. His real mission at Fort Huachuca is a secret. He's working undercover to find out who at the fort is supplying information to the gunmen who have been robbing the army's payroll deliveries. He knows he can trust no one. He knows his life is on the line if he's discovered. What he doesn't know is just how many layers of lies and betrayal are waiting for him. He doesn't know yet—but he'll find out.

___4929-5 $4.99 US/$5.99 CAN

Graciela of the Border

John Duncklee

Jeff Collins knows horses. He works as a horse trainer on the Sierra Diablo ranch in Arizona, and he is mighty good at it. But he wants more. He's dreamed for years of having his own ranch. He sees his chance when he wins a blue roan in a high-stakes poker game. This isn't just any roan; it is carrying the foal of a great racehorse, and that foal is Jeff's ticket to his dreams. When that roan is stolen and herded along with other horses toward the Mexican border, Jeff knows where he has to go. But he doesn't know what will be waiting for him when he gets there. The border is a dangerous place, a harsh land filled with bandits and outlaws—and the woman who will change his life . . . Graciela of the border.

_4809-4 $4.99 US/$5.99 CAN

Dorchester Publishing Co., Inc.
P.O. Box 6640
Wayne, PA 19087-8640

MAN ON A RED HORSE

FRED GROVE

Jesse Wilder is a man who has seen more than his share of violence. A former captain in the Army of Tennessee, he is inducted into the Union army as a "galvanized Yankee" after the Battle of Shiloh. After the war he heads to Mexico to fight with the Juaristas against Emperor Maximilian. That costs him the life of his wife and his unborn child. All he wants then is peace. But instead he is offered a position as a scout on a highly secret mission into Mexico, where bandits are holding the Sonora governor's daughter for ransom. The rescue attempt is virtually a suicide mission; the small group is vastly outnumbered and is made up of men serving time in the garrison jail. Jesse has every reason to walk away from the offer—but he can't. Not when one of his wife's murderers is second in command to the Sonoran bandit chief.

__4771-3 $4.50 US/$5.50 CAN